"Clever and sharp. . . . A well-timed story reminiscent of *Gone Girl* and Caroline Kepnes's *You*. Learning the complicated and 'grass isn't always greener' details of the influence lifestyle is another fascinating aspect of this book and will have readers thinking twice before daydreaming about those 'perfect' lives on Instagram." —*Booklist* (starred review)

"Lloyd dramatically highlights the artificiality of influencer culture and the toxicity of society's social media obsession." —*Publishers Weekly*

"Smart, gobble-at-a-sitting thriller about life as a yummy mummy influencer and the dark side of Instagram." —*The Guardian*

"Dramatic and suspenseful, with a touch of humor to lighten the tension. I'll never look at social media the same way again." —*BuzzFeed*

"That Ellery Lloyd is the pen name for married literary couple Collette Lyons and Paul Vlitos makes this cynical take on marriage and motherhood in the age of the influencer all the more delightful. . . . Lloyd's sharp take skewers fake celebrity, mompetition, and the allure of the curated online persona." —*Reader's Digest* (50 Best Fiction Books to Read This Year)

"Not since reading *Gone Girl* have I found such a satisfyingly furious speech tucked in the midst of a thriller." —*CrimeReads*

"A thriller to the end, *People Like Her* is a timely study on the consequences of allowing complete strangers to influence us IRL, especially as it relates to the vulnerable, private work of mothering." —*Romper*

"Beyond being a brilliant skewering of social media and influencer culture, *People Like Her* is, quite simply, a damn good thriller. . . . With three unreliable narrators, the novel reads like *Gone Girl* on steroids in all the best ways and is sure to keep you distracted from Instagram for a good long while." —*Bookreporter*

"The world of social media becomes the stage for a story of obsession." —*PopSugar*, Best New Mystery and Thriller

"*Gone Girl*-esque . . . [a] slick, sharp debut thriller." —*Sunday Times* (London)

"Tight thriller. . . . It's a great contemporary subject, examining Instagram culture and the consequences of sharing too much of yourself on social media." —Press Association

"A cautionary tale about the perils of being a social influencer, and might just be the first example of Instagram noir." —*Evening Standard* (London)

"A gripping and timely exploration of the darker side of internet fame, *People Like Her* is a tense page-turner sure to keep you up past your bedtime!"
—Katherine St. John, author of *The Lion's Den*

"Social media has never been so dark or so compelling. A disturbing peek into the world of influencers and how it affects their families, *People Like Her* had me hooked right up to the jaw-dropping end."
—Samantha Downing, *USA Today* bestselling author of
My Lovely Wife and *He Started It*

"Suspenseful, thought-provoking, clever, and I suspected everyone. The insights into human nature were spot-on, the characters felt true to life, and I was genuinely gripped. . . . A truly brilliant and a refreshingly original read."
—Karen Hamilton, author of *The Last Wife* and *The Perfect Girlfriend*

"Don't read this book on the train—I missed my stop. . . . On one level, *People Like Her* is a thrilling, witty page-turner that makes you laugh out loud. But on another, it is a sharp dissection of a very modern way of life [and] will make you look at twenty-first century life in a different way."
—Holly Watt, author of *To the Lions*

"I loved it! I was actually holding my breath towards the end. Such a chillingly dark examination of what can happen if you filter the reality . . . through Instagram and pretend to be someone you're not."
—Nikki Smith, author of *All in Her Head*

"Just inhaled *People Like Her* in a single sitting. A cautionary tale for instafluencers everywhere. Breathlessly fast, brilliantly original. Bravo, Ellery Lloyd!"
—Clare Mackintosh, *New York Times* bestselling author of *After the End*

"I was immediately hooked by *People Like Her* and the intoxicating, dangerous world of the mummy influencer. It's a twisty, eye-opening exposure on how much attention is *too* much attention—I would tap the like button on this book again and again!"
—Sara Shepard, *New York Times* bestselling author of
Pretty Little Liars and *Influence*

People Like Her

People Like Her

A Novel **Ellery Lloyd**

♡ ◯ ◁

HARPER

NEW YORK • LONDON • TORONTO • SYDNEY

This book contains references to self-harm and baby loss.

HARPER

Published in a slightly different form in the United Kingdom in 2021 by Macmillan.

A hardcover edition of this book was published in 2021 by HarperCollins Publishers.

FIRST HARPER PAPERBACKS EDITION PUBLISHED 2022.

Library of Congress Cataloging-in-Publication Data has been applied for.

ISBN 978-0-06-299740-1

22 23 24 25 26   LSC   10 9 8 7 6 5 4 3 2 1

For Zu

I think it is possible that I am dying.

For quite some time now, in any case, it has felt like I have been watching as my life scrolls past in front of my eyes.

My earliest memory: It is winter, sometime in the early 1980s. I am wearing mittens, a badly knitted hat, and an enormous red coat. My mother is pulling me across our back lawn on a blue plastic sled. Her smile is fixed. I look completely frozen. I can remember how cold my hands were in those mittens, the way every dip and bump of the ground felt through the sled, the creak of the snow beneath her boots.

My first day at school. I am swinging a brown leather satchel with my name written on a card peeking out from a small plastic window. EMMELINE. One navy knee sock is bunched around my ankle; my hair is in pigtails of slightly unequal length.

Me and Polly at twelve years old. We are having a sleepover at her house, already in our tartan pajamas, wearing mudpacks and waiting for our corn to pop in the microwave. The two of us in her hallway, slightly older, ready to go to the Halloween party where I had my first kiss. Polly was a pumpkin. I was a sexy cat. Us again, on a summer's day, sitting cross-legged in our jeans and Doc Martens in a field of stubble. In spaghetti-strap dresses and chokers, ready for our end-of-school leavers' ball. Memory after memory, one after another, until I find myself starting to wonder whether I can call to mind a single emotionally significant scene from my teenage years in which Polly does not feature, with her lopsided smile and her awkward posing.

Only as I am thinking this do I realize what a sad thought it is now.

My early twenties are something of a blur. Work. Parties. Pubs. Picnics. Holidays. To be honest, my late twenties and early thirties are a bit fuzzy around the edges as well.

There are some things I'll never forget.

Me and Dan in a photo booth, on our third or fourth date. I have my arm around his shoulders. Dan looks incredibly handsome. I look absolutely smitten. We are both grinning like fools.

Our wedding day. The little wink I'm giving to a friend behind the camera as we are saying our vows, Dan's face solemn as he places the ring on my finger.

Our honeymoon, the pair of us blissed out and sunburned in a bar on a Bali beach at sunset.

Sometimes it is hard to believe we were ever that young, that happy, that innocent.

The moment that Coco was born, furious and screaming, whitish and snotty with vernix. Scored into my memory forever, that first glimpse of her little squished face. That moment they passed her to me. The weight of our feelings.

Coco, covered in confetti from a piñata, laughing, at her fourth birthday party.

My son, Bear, a fortnight old, too small even for the tiny sleep suit he is wearing, cradled in the arms of his beaming sister.

Only now does it dawn on me that what I am seeing are not actual memories but memories of photographs. Whole days boiled down to a single static image. Whole relationships. Whole eras.

And still they keep on coming. These fragments. These snapshots.

One after another after another. Tumbling faster and faster through my brain.

Bear screaming in his carrier.

Broken glass on our kitchen floor.

My daughter on a hospital bed, curled up in a ball.

The front page of a newspaper.

I want this to stop now. Something is wrong. I keep trying to wake up, to open my eyes, but I can't—my eyelids are too heavy.

It is not so much the idea of dying that upsets me as the thought I might never see any of these people again; all the things I might never have the chance to tell them. Dan—I love you. Mum—I forgive you. Polly—I hope you can forgive me. Bear . . . Coco . . .

I have an awful feeling something terrible is about to happen.

I have an awful feeling it is all my fault.

Six Weeks Earlier

CHAPTER ONE

Emmy

I never planned to be an Instamum. For a long time, I wasn't sure I'd be a mum at all. But then who among us can truthfully say that their life has turned out exactly the way they thought it would?

These days I might be all leaky nipples and little nippers, professional bottom wiper for two cheeky ankle biters, but rewind five years and I guess I was what you'd call a fashionista. Ignore my knackered eye twitch and imagine this frizzy, pink-hued mum bun is a sleek blow-dry. Swap today's hastily daubed MAC Ruby Woo for clever contouring, liquid liner, and statement earrings—the sort that my three-year-old daughter would now use for impromptu pull-ups. Then dress it all in skinny jeans and an Equipment silk blouse.

As a fashion editor, I had the job I'd dreamed of since I was a problem-haired, bucktoothed, puppy-fat-padded teen, and I truly, truly loved it. It was all I'd ever wanted to do, as my best friend, Polly, would tell you—sweet, long-suffering Polly; I'm lucky she still speaks to me after the hours I spent forcing her to play photographer in my pretend shoots, or strut with me down garden path catwalks in my mum's high heels, all those afternoons making our own magazines with yellowing copies of the *Daily Mail* and a glue stick (I was always the editor, of course).

So how *did* I get from there to here? There have been times—when I'm mopping up newborn poo, or making endless pots of puréed goo— when I've asked myself the same question. It feels like it all happened in an instant. One minute I was wearing Fendi in the front row at Milan Fashion Week, the next I was in joggers, trying to restrain a toddler from reorganizing the cereal aisle in Sainsbury's.

The career change from fashion maven to flustered mama was just a happy accident, to be totally honest with you. The world started to lose interest in shiny magazines full of beautiful people, so, thanks to shrinking budgets and declining readership, just as I was scaling the career ladder, it was kicked out from under me—and then on top of everything else, I found out I was pregnant.

Damn you, the internet, I thought. *You owe me a new career—and it is going to need to be one I can build around having a baby.*

And so I started blogging and vlogging—I called myself Barefoot, because my stilettos came with a side order of soul-baring. And you know what? Although it took me a while to find my stride, I got a real buzz out of connecting with like-minded ladies in real time.

Fast-forward to those first few months after giving birth, and in the 937 hours I spent with my bum welded to the couch, my darling Coco attached to my milky boobs and the iPhone in my hand my only connection to the outside world, the community of women I met on the internet became a literal lifeline. And while blogging and vlogging were my first online loves, it was Instagram that stopped me from slipping too far into the postnatal fog. It felt like a little life-affirming arm squeeze every time I logged on and saw a comment from another mother going through the same things I was. I had found my people.

So, slowly, it was out with the Louboutins and in with the little human. Barefoot morphed into Mamabare, because I'm a mama who is willing to grin and *bare* it, warts and all. And take it from me, this journey has got even crazier since my second little bundle of burps, Bear, came along five weeks ago. Whether it's a breast pad fashioned from rogue Happy Meal wrappers or a sneaky gin in a tin by the swings, you'll always get the unvarnished truth from me—although it may come lightly dappled with Cheeto dust.

The haters like to say that Instagram is all about the perfect life, polished, filtered, and posted in these little squares—but who has time for all that nonsense when they've got a ketchup-covered curtain climber in tow? And when things get hard, both online and off, when wires get crossed, when food gets tossed, when I just feel a little lost, I remember that it's my family I'm doing all of this for. And, of course, the incredible crew of other social media mamas who've always got my back, no matter how many days in a row I've been wearing the same nursing bra.

You are the reason I started #greydays, a campaign sharing our real stories and organizing meetups IRL for us to talk about our battles with the blue-hued moments of motherhood. Not to mention that a portion of the profits from all #greydays merchandise we sell goes toward helping open up the conversation around maternal mental health.

If I were to describe what I do now, would you hate me if I said "multi-hyphen mama"? It's definitely a job title that confuses poor old Joyce from next door. She understands what Papabare does—he writes novels. But me? *Influencer* is such an awful word, isn't it? Cheerleader? Encourager? Impacter? Who knows? And really, who cares? I just go about my business, sharing my unfiltered family life and hopefully starting a more authentic discussion about parenting.

I built this brand on honesty, and I'll always tell it like it is.

Dan

Bullshit.

Bullshit bullshit bullshit bullshit bullshit.

Because I have heard Emmy give this same little talk so many times now, I usually don't even notice anymore what a weird farrago of inventions and elisions and fabrications and half-truths it is. What a seamless mixture of things that could have happened (but didn't) and things that did happen (but not like that) and events that she and I remember very differently (to say the least). For some reason, tonight is different. For some reason, tonight, as she is talking, as she is telling the room her story, a story that is also to a considerable extent our story, I find myself trying to keep count of how many of the things Emmy is saying are exaggerated or distorted or completely blown out of proportion.

I give up about three minutes in.

I should probably make one thing clear. I am not calling my wife a liar.

The American philosopher Harry G. Frankfurt famously differentiates between lies and bullshit. Lies, he claims, are untruths deliberately intended to deceive. Bullshit, on the other hand, comes about when someone has no real interest in whether or not something they are saying is true or false at all. Example: My wife has never *fashioned* a breast pad from a Happy Meal wrapper. I doubt she has ever been anywhere near a Happy Meal. We don't live next door to a Joyce. Emmy was, if the photographs at her mum's house are to be believed, a slim, strikingly attractive teenager.

Perhaps there comes a time in every marriage when you start fact-checking each other's anecdotes in public.

Perhaps I am just in a funny mood tonight.

There is certainly no denying that my wife is good at what she does. Amazing, actually. Even after all the times I have seen her get up and do her thing—at events like this all over the country, in village halls, in bookshops, in coffee shops and coworking spaces from Wakefield to Westfield—even knowing what I know about the relationship of most of what she is saying to anything that ever actually happened, there is no denying her ability to connect with people. To raise a laugh of recognition. When she gets to the part about the gin in the tin, there is a woman in the back row *howling*. She is a very relatable individual, my wife. People like her.

Her agent will be glad she got the bit about grey days in. Excuse me. *Hashtag* grey days. I noticed at least three people wearing the sweatshirt as we were coming in earlier, the blue one with #greydays and a Mamabare logo on the back and the slogan GRIN AND BARE IT on the front. The Mamabare logo, by the way, is a drawing of two breasts with a baby's head in between them. Personally I would have gone for the other logo, the one of the maternal teddy bear and cub. I was overruled. This is one of the reasons why I have always resisted Emmy's suggestions that I should wear one of those things myself when I come along to this kind of event, why mine always turns out to have been accidentally left back at the house—in another bag, say, or in the dryer, or on the stairs, where I had put it out so I would definitely not forget it this time. You have to draw the line somewhere. Some fan, some follower, would inevitably ask for a photo with both of us and post it immediately on their Instagram feed, and I have no interest in being captured online forever in a sweatshirt with breasts on it.

I like to believe I still have some dignity.

I'm here tonight, as always, in a strictly supporting capacity. I'm the one who helps lug the boxes of mama merch in from the cab and helps unpack them and tries not to visibly cringe when people use expressions like "mama merch." I'm here to lend a hand pouring glasses of fizz and passing around the cupcakes at the start of the evening, and I'm the person who steps in and rescues Emmy when she gets stuck talking to anyone for too long or who is too obviously a weirdo at the end of it. If the baby starts crying, I am primed to step up onstage and lift him carefully out of Emmy's arms and take charge—although so far this evening he has been as good as gold, little Bear, our baby boy, five weeks old, suckling away quietly, completely oblivious to his surroundings or the fact that he is up onstage or pretty much anything apart from the breast in front of him. Occasionally, in the general Q&A section at the end of the evening, when someone asks Emmy about how having a second child has affected the family dynamic or how we keep the spark in our marriage, Emmy will laughingly point me out in the audience and invite me to help answer that question. Often when someone asks about online safety, I'm the person to whom Emmy defers to explain the three golden rules we always stick to when posting pictures of our kids online. One: we never show anything that could give away where we live. Two: we never show either of the kids in the bath, or naked, or on the potty, and we never, ever show Coco in a swimsuit or any outfit that could be considered sexy on an adult. Three: we keep a close eye on who is following the account and block anyone we're not sure about. This was the advice we were given, early on, when we consulted with the experts.

I do still have my reservations about all this.

The version of events that Emmy always recounts, the one about starting to blog about motherhood as a way of reaching out and seeing if there was anyone out there who was going through the same stuff as her? *Complete* bullshit, I'm afraid. If you really think my wife fell into doing this by accident, it just goes to show that you have never met my wife. I sometimes wonder if Emmy ever does anything by accident. I can vividly remember the day she first brought it up, the blogging thing. I knew she was meeting someone for lunch, but it was not until afterward she told me the person she'd met with was an agent. She was three months pregnant. It was only a couple of weeks since we'd broken the news to my mum. "An agent?" I said. I genuinely don't think it had occurred to me until then that online people had agents. It probably should have done. On a regular basis, back when she was working in magazines, Emmy would come home and tell me how much they were paying some idiot influencer to crap out a hundred words and pose for a picture, or host some event, or burble on their blog. She used to show me the copy they would send in. The kind of prose that makes you wonder if you've had a stroke or the person writing it has. Short sentences. Metaphors that don't make sense. Random weirdly specific details scattered around to lend everything an air of verisimilitude. Oddly precise numbers (482 cups of cold tea, 2,342 hours of lost sleep, 27 misplaced baby socks) shoehorned in for the same purpose. Words that are just not the word they were groping for. *You* should write this stuff, she used to joke; I don't know why you bother writing novels. We used to laugh about it. When she got back from lunch that day and told me who she had been talking to, I thought she was still joking. It took me a long time to get my head around what she was suggesting. I thought the end goal was some free footwear. Little did I suspect that Emmy had already paid for the domain name and bagged both the Barefoot and Mamabare Instagram handles before she had even written her first sentence about stilettos. Let alone that within three years she would have a million followers.

The very first piece of advice her agent gave her was that the whole thing should feel organic, as if she'd just fallen into it through sheer chance. I don't think either of us knew quite how good at that Emmy would be.

Inasmuch as it is based on a complete rejection of the significance of the truth and the moral duty we owe to it, Harry G. Frankfurt suggests that bullshit is actually more corrosive, a more destructive social force, than good old-fashioned lying. Harry G. Frankfurt has considerably fewer followers on Instagram than my wife does.

"I built this brand on honesty," Emmy is saying, just as she always ends by saying, "and I'll always tell it like it is."

She pauses for the applause to die down. She locates the glass of water by her chair and takes a sip.

"Any questions?" she asks.

I have a question.

Was that the night I finally decided how I would hurt you?

I think it was.

Obviously I had thought about it many times before then. I think anyone in my position would. But those were just silly little daydreams, really. TV stuff. Completely unrealistic and impractical.

It works in funny ways, the human mind.

I thought somehow if I saw you, it would help. Help me hate you less. Help me let go of the anger.

It did not help at all.

I have never been a violent person. I am not an angry person, naturally. When somebody stands on my foot in a queue, I am always the one who apologizes.

All I really wanted was to ask you a question. Just one. That's why I was there. I had my hand up, at the end, for ages. You saw me. You took a question from the woman in front of me instead, the one whose hair you complimented. You took a question from the woman on my right, who you knew by name, the one whose "question" turned out to be more of an aimless anecdote about herself.

Then someone said that was all the time there was for questions.

I did try to talk to you, afterward, but everyone else was trying to talk to you as well. So I just stood around, holding the same glass of lukewarm white wine I had been nursing all evening, and tried to catch your eye—but didn't.

There was no reason for you to recognize me, of course. There was no reason why my face ought to have stood out from the crowd. Even if we had talked, even if I had introduced myself, there is no reason for my name—or hers—to have rung any bells at all.

And seeing you there, seeing you going about your life as normal, seeing you surrounded by all those people, seeing you laughing and smiling and happy, that was when I knew. When I knew that I had been lying to myself. That I had not moved on, had not come to terms with anything. That I had not forgiven you, could never forgive you.

That was when I knew what I was going to do.

All I had to work out was how and where and when.

CHAPTER TWO

Dan

People often remark that it must be lovely for me, being a writer, getting to spend so much time at home and see so much of Emmy and the kids. I suppose one thing this illustrates is how little work most people think being a writer involves.

Six in the morning—that was when I used to get up. By six fifteen I'd be at the kitchen table with a pot of coffee and my laptop, looking over the last paragraph or two from the day before. By seven thirty, I would aim to have done at least five hundred words. By eight thirty, I'd be ready for my second pot of coffee. By lunchtime, ideally, I would be getting near my word-count target for the day, meaning I could devote the afternoon to plotting out the next bit and answering emails and chasing payment for the bits of literary journalism I used to knock out with a glass of wine in the evenings or over the weekends.

That was then.

A few minutes after six o'clock this morning, I was creeping downstairs in the dark to try to avoid waking anyone up in the hope that I might get a little work done before the rest of the household woke (and in about 66 percent of cases immediately started yowling or screaming or demanding things). On the very lowest step, I stumbled on some kind of talking unicorn, which skittered across the floorboards and started singing a song about rainbows. In the darkness, ears pricked, I held my breath and waited. I didn't have to wait very long. For such a small creature, he has quite the pair of lungs on him, my son. "Sorry," I said to Emmy, as she handed him over. "You might want to check his nappy," she told me. As I was passing Coco's room, a little voice asked sleepily through the door what time it was. "Time to go back to sleep," I said.

Bear, on the other hand, was up for good. I took him down to the kitchen and changed his nappy and stuck him in a new outfit and deposited the old one in a bag on top of the washing machine, which I noted would need emptying later, and then we sat on the couch in the corner by the fridge. For the next half an hour, he screamed as I jiggled him on my knee and tried to get him to drink from his bottle. Then I burped him and put him in a carrier and walked him up and down the garden for another half an hour while he screamed some more. Then it was seven o'clock and time to hand him back to Emmy and wake Coco up for her breakfast.

"My God, was that an hour?" Emmy asked me.

To the minute.

Christ, it takes a lot of energy, having two kids. I don't know how people whose children don't sleep as well as ours manage it. We were extremely lucky, Emmy and I, in that right from early on, three or four months old, Coco was sleeping a solid twelve hours a night. Down, out, sparko. If we took her to a party in a car seat, we could just put her down in a corner or in the room next door, and she would snooze the whole evening away—and from the looks of things, Bear is going to be the same. Not that you'd know any of this from Emmy's Instagram account, of course, with all its talk of twitching eyelids and dark bags and frayed, knackered nerves. It was obvious from the start that as brands went, "the mum whose baby sleeps like a dream" was a nonstarter. No content there. To be honest, we don't make a big thing of it with other parents of young children either.

A little after eight—8:07, to be precise—with Bear down for his first nap, with Coco and Emmy upstairs discussing my daughter's outfit for the day, with two hours of solid parenting behind me, it's time to microwave the cold cup of coffee I made myself ninety minutes ago, fire up the laptop, and attempt to will myself into an appropriate state of mind to begin the day's creative labors.

By eight forty-five I have reread what I wrote yesterday and tweaked it, and I am ready to begin getting some new words down on the page.

At nine thirty the front doorbell goes.

"Should I get that?" I call up the stairs.

In the past three-quarters of an hour I've written a grand total of twenty-six new words and am currently debating whether or not I should delete twenty-four of them.

I am in no mood for interruptions.

"*I'll* get it, shall I?"

There is no answer from upstairs.

The doorbell rings again.

I let out a pointed sigh for the benefit of the empty room and push my chair back from the table.

It's at the back of the house, on the ground floor, our kitchen. When I first bought this place back in 2008, with some money that came to me when my father died, it was for me and a bunch of mates to live in and we hardly used this room at all, except to hang up the washing. It had a threadbare couch in it, a clock that didn't work, a sticky linoleum floor, and a washing machine that leaked every time you used it. The back window looked out onto a little concrete area with a corrugated plastic roof. One of the very first things Emmy suggested when she moved in was that we get rid of all that and extend into the garden and turn this into a proper living-cooking-dining area. Which is exactly what we did.

The house itself is at the end of a terrace of identical Georgian houses about half a mile from the Tube, opposite a very gentrified pub. When I was first looking to buy in this area, it was pitched to me as up-and-coming. Now it has very much up-and-come. There used to be fights outside the pub opposite on a fairly regular basis come chucking-out time on a Friday night, proper rolling-on-a-car-hood, torn-shirt, smashed-pint-glass dustups. Now you can't get a table for brunch at the weekend unless you've booked one, and the menu features cod cheeks, lentils, and chorizo.

One of the reasons I try to get as much writing as I can done in the morning is that after about midday the doorbell never stops. Every time Emmy asks a question on Instagram like, "Coco has decided she doesn't like her multivitamin—which new one should we try?" or "Does anyone know a serum that can get rid of these eye bags?" or even "Our blender has broken—which one do you mamas recommend?" she immediately gets a flood of messages from PRs asking if they can courier something round. Which is precisely why she does it, of course—it's quicker and cheaper than an Amazon order. All this week Emmy has been moaning about her hair, and all this week companies have been sending us free hair straighteners, free styling products, free shampoos and conditioners in ribbon-tied bags stuffed with tissue paper.

I don't mean to sound ungrateful, but I'm pretty sure that when Tolstoy was writing *War and Peace* he didn't have to get up and sign for another box of free stuff every five minutes.

To get to the front door, you go past the end of the stairs up to the first floor (three bedrooms, one bathroom) and past the living room, where the sofa and TV and toys are. Squeezing past a pram, a balance bike, a micro scooter, and the overloaded coat rack, I step for the second time on the same dropped unicorn and swear. You would hardly believe the cleaner came yesterday. There are Lego bricks everywhere. Shoes everywhere. I have turned my back for five minutes, and the place is a total fucking mess. The novelist and man of letters Cyril Connolly once rather sneeringly wrote that the pram in the hallway is the enemy of art. In our house the pram in the hallway is also the enemy of being able to get down the bloody hallway. I inch my way around it, check my hair in the mirror, and open the door.

Standing on the doorstep are two people, a man and a woman. The woman is youngish, in her late twenties perhaps, not unattractive, vaguely familiar-looking, with ash-blond hair tied back in a messy ponytail. She is wearing a denim jacket and from the looks of things had been just about to try the doorbell for a fourth time. The man is slightly older, thirtysomething, balding, bearded. At their feet there is a large bag. The man has another bag over his shoulder and a camera around his neck.

"You must be Papabare," says the woman with the ponytail. "I'm Jess Watts."

The name is vaguely familiar too, but only as we are shaking hands does it come to me from where.

Jesus Christ.

The *Sunday Times*.

It's only the journalist and photographer from the *Sunday* bloody *Times*, here to interview and photograph Emmy and me.

Jess Watts asks me if I would mind giving them a hand with the bags. Of course not, I say. Then I pick up the large bag with a slight grunt and gesture them into the house.

"Do come in, do come in."

Apologizing about us all having to squeeze around the pram and everything else, I lead them through to the living room. The mess is even worse in here. Someone appears to have shredded the leftover weekend papers and thrown them about the place. The TV remotes are on the floor. There are crayons everywhere. As I turn to tell the cameraman where to dump his bag, I catch Jess making a note of something with a pen in a little notebook.

I am about to say something about how I thought they were coming on Wednesday—that's certainly what the note on our fridge calendar says, the day I remember Emmy and myself discussing—when I realize this *is* Wednesday. It is unbelievable how easy it is as the parent of a new baby to lose track of the days. I can remember Sunday. I can remember Monday. What on earth happened on Tuesday? My mind is a blank. I suspect when I opened the door my face was a bit of a blank too.

"Can I get you a cup of tea?" I offer. "A coffee?"

They order one white coffee with two sugars, one herbal tea with a little honey if we have it.

"Emmy!" I call up the stairs.

I really think my wife might have reminded me that today was the day the *Sunday Times* were coming. Just mentioned it, you know. Perhaps when I came to bed last night or handed over the baby this morning. I have not shaved for a day or two. My hair is unwashed. One of my socks is inside out. I would have had time to scatter some interesting books around, as opposed to a sun-wrinkled two-day-old copy of the *Evening Standard*. It's hard to look like a serious person when you are standing there in an old denim shirt with two buttons missing and a smear of porridge on the lapel.

The *Sunday Times*. A five-page spread. At home with the Instaparents. I make a mental note to email my agent about the article and let her know when it is coming out. No publicity, as they say. It would be good to email her anyway, to be honest, just to remind her I'm still alive.

The man with the camera and the interviewer are now discussing whether to do the shoot or the interview first. He starts wandering around the room taking light readings, looking thoughtful. "This end of the house is where people usually take photos," I say helpfully, pointing through to the conservatory. "On this armchair, with the garden behind." Not that I'm usually in the photo shoots, of course.

Sometimes, occasionally, I am just out of shot, pulling faces at Coco or observing. More often, when the house gets invaded like this, I retreat to the studio at the end of the garden with my laptop. I say *studio*. It's more of a shed. But it does have a light bulb and a heater.

The woman has taken down from one of the bookshelves a photograph from our wedding day—Emmy and me and her childhood friend and maid of honor, Polly, the three of us arm in arm and smiling. Poor old Polly; she obviously hated that dress. Emmy took our wedding day as an opportunity to give her best friend—a pretty enough girl, even if she does dress a bit like my mum—the makeover she had always politely but firmly refused. It was a public service for her single friend, Emmy said, before looking over the guest list and asking if I had invited anyone without a girlfriend, wife, or partner. Personally, I thought Polly's dress looked great, but every time the camera was pointed in the other direction or Emmy wasn't looking, I would catch her covering up her bare arms and shoulders with a bobbly cardigan or taking off a high-heeled shoe to rub the ball of one of her feet. To her credit, no matter how uncomfortable she felt, Polly kept a smile on her face the whole day long. Even if the eligible friend we sat next to her at dinner did spend the whole meal chatting up the girl on the other side of him.

"So I understand you write novels, Dan," the woman from the *Sunday Times* says, with a faint smile, putting the picture back. She says it in the manner of someone who's not even going to pretend that my name is familiar or that they might once have read something I'd written.

I sort of laugh and say something like, "I guess so," and then I point out the hardback and paperback copies of my book on the shelf and the spine of the Hungarian edition next to that. She angles the hardback copy out a bit, examines the cover, and lets the book fall back into place on the shelf with a slight clunk.

"Hmm," she says. "When did it come out?"

I tell her seven years ago, and as I'm saying it realize it was actually eight. Eight years. It's hard to believe that. It certainly came as a shock to me when Emmy gently suggested that it was time for me to stop using the author's photo from the back cover as my profile picture on Facebook. "It's a nice photograph," she told me reassuringly. "It just doesn't really look like you." *Anymore* being the unspoken word hanging in the air.

The photographer asks me what the book was about—that question authors always hate, with *was* providing the final twist of the scalpel. At one time I probably would have told him that if I could boil down what it's about to a single sentence or two I would not have needed to write the thing. In another mood I might have joked that it was about two hundred and fifty pages, or £7.99. I am no longer quite that much of a twat, I hope. I tell him it is about a guy who marries a lobster. He laughs. I find myself warming to him.

It was pretty well received at the time, my novel. Generous cover blurb from Louis de Bernières. Book of the week in the *Guardian*. Reviewed with only mild condescension in the *London Review of Books* and with approval in the *Times Literary Supplement*. Film rights optioned. On the back flap, in my leather jacket, leaning against a brick wall in black and white, I smoke with the air of a man with a bright future in front of him.

It was a fortnight after the book came out that I met Emmy.

Seeing her for the first time across the room will always remain one of the defining moments of my life.

It was a Thursday night, the opening of a mutual friend's bar on Kingsland Road, the height of the summer, an evening so hot that most people were standing outside on the pavement. There'd been free drinks at one point, but by the time I arrived there were just a load of buckets of melted ice with empty wine bottles in them. The crush at the bar was three deep. It had been a long day. I had things to do in the morning. I was just looking around for the mate whose bar it was to say hello and goodbye and apologize for not staying longer when I spotted her. She was standing at one of the tables by the window. She was wearing a low-cut jumpsuit. Back then, before it went an Instagram-friendly shade of cerise, Emmy's hair—a little longer than it is now—was more or less its natural shade of blond. She was eating a chicken wing with her fingers. She was literally the most beautiful person I have ever seen. Emmy looked up. Our eyes met. She smiled at me, faintly quizzically, slightly frowning. I smiled back. I could not see a drink on the table. I made my way over and asked if she wanted one. The rest is history. That night she came back to my place. Three weeks later I asked her to move in with me. I asked her to marry me within the year.

It was only much later that I realized how little Emmy can see without her glasses when she doesn't have her contact lenses in. Not for ages did she confess that they had been bothering her earlier—something to do with the high pollen count, perhaps—and she had taken them out, and her smile across the room that night had been at a vague pink shape she could just about sense was staring in her direction and assumed was a fashion PR. It was only later I found out she already had a boyfriend, called Giles, who was on a work secondment to Zurich, and was as surprised to learn they were no longer in an exclusive relationship as I was to learn of his existence. There was an awkward moment a fortnight into things when he called and I answered and told him to stop pestering Emmy, and he told me they'd been going out for three years.

She has always had a fairly complicated relationship with the truth, my wife.

I guess that business with Giles might have bothered some people. I guess some couples, starting out, might have felt it cast a bit of a pall over things. I genuinely can't remember it troubling either of us very much at all. As I recall, by that weekend we were already telling it as a funny story, and very quickly after that it became the centerpiece of our repertoire of dinner party anecdotes, both of us with our agreed part to play in the telling of it, our allotted lines.

"The fact of the matter is," Emmy would always say, "I knew from the moment I met Dan he was the man I was going to marry, so the fact I was seeing someone else seemed irrelevant. I had already broken up with Giles in my head; he was history. I just hadn't got around to telling *him* that yet." She would shrug sheepishly as she said this, offer a rueful smile, glance across at me.

I used to think it was all quite romantic, to be honest.

The truth is, we were probably both pretty insufferable in those days. I imagine most young lovers are.

I can vividly recall announcing to my mother over the phone (I was wandering around the flat in a towel at the time, wet-haired, holding a cigarette, looking for a lighter) that I had met my soulmate.

Emmy was like no one else I had ever met. She is still unlike anyone else I've ever met. Not just the most beautiful woman I have ever laid eyes on but the funniest, the cleverest, the sharpest, the most ambitious. One of those people you know you need to be on your best form to keep up with. One of those people you want to impress. One of those people who get every reference before you have even finished making it, who have that magic that makes everyone else in a room recede into the distance. Who have you saying things you've never told anyone within two hours of meeting them. Who change the way you look at life. Half the weekend we used to spend in bed, the other half in the pub. We would eat out at least three nights a week, at pop-up restaurants serving Middle Eastern small plates or at modern barbecue joints that don't take reservations. We went out dancing on Wednesday nights and did karaoke on Sunday afternoons. We went on city breaks—to Amsterdam, to Venice, to Bruges. We dragged our hangovers out for 5K runs, laughing and shoving each other along when one of us started to flag. When we weren't out in the evening, we used to spend ages together in the bath, with our books and a bottle of red wine, occasionally topping up our glasses or the hot water.

"Things can only go downhill from here," we used to joke.

It all seems a very long time ago now.

Emmy

You know that thing that middle-class women do the day before their cleaner arrives? Running around the house, picking up the most embarrassing bits off the floor, giving the bathroom a wipe, putting stuff in piles, so the place isn't quite such a mortifying mess?

I don't do that. Never have. I mean, obviously, we have a cleaner who comes twice a week, but our house is usually *tidy*. It was tidy before we had children, and it is tidy now. Toys go away before bedtime. Storybooks are back on the shelf. Piles on the stairs are not allowed. No mugs on the countertop. Socks left on the floor get thrown away.

Which means the hours before a camera crew arrives for a shoot are always spent *untidying*. Don't get me wrong, we're not talking empty pizza boxes and unwashed pants—just a light dusting of knitted dinosaurs, Lego bricks and talking unicorns, a two-day-old newspaper lying here, a collapsed cushion fort there, and some single shoes in awkward places. It takes effort to calibrate just the right level of chaos, but dirty isn't aspirational and perfect isn't relatable. And Mamabare is nothing if not relatable.

I can only tackle the mess making, of course, after I've seen to my social media feeds. It's not a routine Dan's especially keen on, but Bear is his responsibility for the first hour of each day because I need both hands and my whole brain to catch up on what has happened overnight.

Prime posting time is after the kids go to bed, when my million followers have poured their first glass of wine and dived headfirst into a scroll hole instead of summoning the energy to talk to their husbands. So that's when I schedule my seemingly off-the-cuff, in-the-moment, but actually prephotographed, already-written posts. Last night's was a photo of me with a sheepish grin, standing against a yellow wall, pointing at my feet in trainers that were clearly two halves of separate pairs, with a screaming Bear strapped to my front in the sling that, for some reason, he hates with a passion. It was accompanied by a description of being so sleep-deprived I'd left the house that morning with my sweatshirt on backward and one pink Nike and one green New Balance on my feet, and a cool east London kid on the number thirty-eight bus telling me approvingly that I looked fresh.

It certainly *could* have happened. I write in the style of honesty, so it's useful if there's a small grain of truth in my posts. My husband is the novelist, not me—I just can't seem to manage total fiction. I need a little spark from real life to fire up my imagination to craft an anecdote that sounds plausibly authentic. I also find it's easier to keep track of my maternal misadventures that way, to avoid contradicting myself, which is important when I need to wheel the same stories out in interviews, panel talks, and personal appearances.

In this case, there was no cool kid, no mismatched trainers, and no public transport. I had just nearly nipped to Tesco with my cardigan on inside out.

I ended the post by asking my followers what their own most sleep-deprived mum moment is—it's a classic engagement trick, pushing them to post a response. And of course, the higher the engagement, the more brands are prepared to pay you to flog their wares.

Overnight, I've got 687 comments and 442 DMs, all of which I need to acknowledge or reply to. Some days this takes longer than others—if there's a depressed mother who seems dangerously unhappy, or one at her wits' end with a colicky baby who screams nonstop, I take care to send something personal, something kind. It's tough to know what to say in a situation like that, having never been through it, but I can't bring myself to leave these women hanging when it seems like every-one else in their lives has.

Hi, Tanya, I type. *I know it's so hard when they just cry, cry, cry. Is little Kai teething? Coco really suffered when her front two came through. Gnaw-ing on a frozen banana seemed to help, or have you tried those powders? Promise me you'll look after you too, mama—can you nap when he naps? You will get through it and I'm with you all the way.*

My reply is seen instantly, almost like tinytanya_1991 has been star-ing at her phone ever since she hit send, and I can see that she is already typing her reply as I move on to the next message.

You are NOT a terrible mother, Carly, and you must never doubt that your little one loves you. You really should talk to someone, though: a doctor? Your mum? Maybe take a walk to a café and have a chat with the waitress. I'm sending you a link to a help line too.

The message sends, but is unread. On to the next.

Oh, Elly, you are too kind, and of course I recognize you from last week's event. My sweatshirt is from Boden—amazing to hear it even looks great the wrong way around.

I'm not quite sure how I manage it, but today I'm done and showered within my allotted hour and can hear Dan loitering at the bedroom door, no doubt counting down the seconds, from 6:58 a.m.

In addition to all the usual things I need to get up and deal with, today I also have to think about what to wear for the shoot. The Mama-bare look is one that my husband once described as "children's TV presenter minus puppet badger." A lot of printed dresses, bright slogan T-shirts, jumpsuits. The wardrobe selection process is a bit painful due to the extra weight I put on when I was pregnant with Coco and could never lose because snapping back to a size eight would be so off-brand.

So a jaunty skirt it is; this one is green and covered in tiny lightning bolts. My yellow T-shirt says MY SUPERPOWER IS PARENTING. I know, I know. But what can I do? So many brands send me their matching slogan tees, Coco and I *have* to wear them occasionally.

I've been desperate to get my roots done, but I knew this shoot was coming up, and there was also last night's talk. Too sleek, and it won't sit well with my followers, so an inky part and a two-day-old blow-dry it is. I give it a quick brush then tease a lock so it stands out at almost ninety degrees from the side of my head. That rogue strand has been featuring heavily on my Instastories this week ("Argh! I can't do a thing with it! Anyone else have one stubborn piece of hair with a mind of its own?!"). I now have a spare room full of lotions and potions to help plaster it down—as well as ten thousand pounds from Pantene, whose new product will prove to be the solution to my hair woes.

When you make such a big deal out of only ever flogging products you actually use, you have to create ever more elaborate scenarios in which they're necessary.

Coco has been sitting quietly in her bedroom throughout, propped up in front of her iPad watching something involving flowers, castles, and glitter. I pull the T-shirt that matches mine (MY MAMA HAS SPECIAL POWERS!) out of her chest of drawers and hold it up.

"What do you think about wearing this today, Cocopop? It's the same as Mummy's one," I say, tucking a soft blond curl behind her ear and giving her a peck on the forehead as I breathe in her powdery scent.

She takes off her pink headphones, pops the iPad on the bed beside her, and tilts her head.

"What do all the words say, Mummy?"

"Do you want to try reading it, pickle?" I smile.

"M-y . . . m-a-m-a . . . h-a-s . . . ," she says slowly. "I can't do the rest, Mama."

"Well done! So, so clever. It says, 'My Mama Has a Beautiful Crown.'" I smile, helping her down from the bed. "And you know what that means, Coco? If Mama is a queen with a crown, that makes you . . ."

"A PRINCESS!" she squeals.

To tell the truth, Coco's princess obsession is a bit inconvenient, content-wise. Obviously, the modern mama party line is that pink stinks. They're all meant to be rebel girls and little feminists-in-training, but my daughter is firmly in the fairy queen camp—so unless I want a screaming meltdown on my hands, that's what she gets. Or at least that's what she thinks she's got. Luckily, she can't read that well yet.

"Now, would you like to help me with a very important, secret job?" I ask her, giving her a handful of blueberries, which she absent-mindedly starts popping into her mouth.

"What is it, Mama?"

"We are going to make some *mess*!" I whoop, scooping her up off the bed and carrying her downstairs.

I supervise as she makes, and then kicks down, a tower of velvet scatter cushions. We fling a few teddies at the radiator, send some storybooks skidding across the parquet, and scatter pieces of wooden jigsaw puzzle on the floor. I am laughing so hard at her utter delight in destroying the living room that I only notice just in time that she has my three-wick Diptyque candle in both hands and is about to chuck it at the fireplace.

"Okay, pickle, let's put that one down, shall we? Job done in here, I think," I say, putting the candle on a high shelf. "Shall we go and find your tiara upstairs to finish that outfit off?"

Gold plastic tiara located under her bed, I kneel down to Coco's height, look her in the eyes, and hold both her hands. "Some people are coming to talk to Mummy now, and take some photos. You're going to be a good girl and smile for them, aren't you? You can do some magic princess twirls for the camera!"

Coco nods. I hear the doorbell go.

"Coming!" I shout, as Coco bounds down the stairs ahead of me.

When my agent agreed to this interview, I was slightly nervous they'd go for the-perils-of-selling-your-family-online angle, as serious newspapers tend to. But the editor agreed to a list of topics they wouldn't touch on, so here we are, with the staff photographer and a freelance journalist, asking me jolly questions I've answered a million times before. She ends with a flourish.

"Why do you think people like you so much?"

"Oh, goodness, do you think that's true? Well, if it is, I guess they connect with me because I'm just like them, because I allow myself to be vulnerable—I ask for their help, I make it a two-way conversation. You can't mama alone—it really does take a village. All of us are in it together, all plugging away in our sleep-deprived, peanut butter–smeared, sugar-fueled fogs."

Actually, do you know why they love me? Because this is my *job*—a job I happen to be very, very good at. Do you think you get a million followers by accident?

It took a while to get Mamabare just right. To be honest, I thought I'd come up with a killer concept the first time around in Barefoot. That if I was prepared to put in the work, I could eventually earn enough from a shoe blog and social media to replace my magazine salary. I was as obsessed with the big fashion influencers as anyone else, even though I knew rationally that none of it was real. I had wasted plenty of evenings comparing their perfect Prada lives to my own, my bedtime creeping ever later as my eyes glazed over at shots of them crossing roads in Manhattan and posing outside pastel-colored houses in Notting Hill—and now at least I could justify that to Dan as research.

My now-agent, Irene, had just made the shift from representing the actresses we put on the magazine's pages to the influencers my snobbish editor was doing her best to keep off them, so I approached her with my genius idea. She told me bluntly that I'd missed the boat. Liking shoes was not enough of a *thing*, apparently, and wouldn't stand out in an already crowded market. I might have only just got wise to the influencer game, but the big fashion players were already untouchable.

Irene was happy to represent me, but mental health and motherhood were the next big untapped markets. "By all means, start your little shoe blog to understand the mechanics of it," she said, "plus it's a good backstory to make the whole thing feel more organic, more authentic. Then, once you've chosen whether to have a breakdown or a baby, come back to me, and we'll pivot."

Four months later, I was in her office, waving my scan.

When my daughter was born, I started off sharing photos of me beaming with new-mum pride and a face full of no-makeup makeup, of sun-dappled afternoons in the park and sprinkle-topped cakes I'd just baked. I talked about how happy I was, my amazing husband, how Coco never cried. Naively, I thought that would instantly win me followers.

I quickly realized, though, that for a British influencer, it really doesn't work like that. It turns out that each country has its own quirks when it comes to Instagram parenting. I'd been taking my cues from the American moms I admired, who all waft about in cashmere, keep their Carrara marble worktops pristine, dress their kids in plaid shirts and designer denim, and run everything through the Gingham filter to give their photos a subtle vintage effect. A little more googling uncovered that Australia's lithe, free-spirited mamas all pose against surfboards in crochet bikinis, with their salt-scrunched hair and their tanned blond toddlers. Swedish Instamums wear flower crowns while they coo at babies lying around in grey felt bonnets on pastel washed-linen sheets.

You see, with a bit of research, social media makes understanding what people all over the world connect with very simple indeed. Follower numbers and engagement figures rise and fall depending on how good or bad your hair looks, how funny or heartfelt you are in this caption, how cute or not your kid is in that shot, how consistent and contrived your color palette is. So you can adjust your lipstick, your living room, your family life, your filter accordingly.

And what did my foray into Instagram anthropology uncover? That here in the UK, nobody likes a show-off. We want naturally pretty women, goofy grins, rainbow colors, honest captions, and photogenic disarray. We may wear expensive T-shirts with slogans about being superheroes and bang on about empowerment, but as any UK Inst-amum worth her six-figure campaign knows, if you admit to so much as being able to boil an egg competently, you'll lose a thousand fol-lowers overnight. You have to be unable to leave the house without at least a splotch of Bolognese or a splatter of baby puke on your shirt. You have to arrive late for nursery at least once a week—just a couple of minutes, mind you; nobody likes a one-pound-per-minute fine—and forget World Book Day annually.

I found that the more "authentic" I was, the more followers I won, and the more those followers "liked" me. If that sounds patronizing, I honestly don't mean it that way. Sorry, the Sisterhood, but when it comes to online life, women just don't respond well to other women's success—if comparison is the thief of joy, Instagram is the cat burglar of contentment.

The last thing I want to do is make a woman feel like she's not living up to some impossible maternal standard, so I invented the perfectly imperfect mama for my followers. Because only when you become a mother do you realize just how much judgment there is lurking around every corner—a bit like betting shops are invisible unless you're a gambler or you don't see playgrounds when you're child-free. What-ever it is you're doing, there's someone—husband, mother-in-law, judgy health visitor, unhelpful waitress—who thinks you're doing it wrong. I never do, though. My whole *thing* is that I'm just muddling through too. The world is full of people who want to tell mums off, so when they DM me their questions, or put their hands up at my events, I smile and nod and legitimize their life choices. I tell them that's just what I did, or how I felt too. Cosleeping? They've been doing it since caveman times, Mama—just enjoy the snuggles! A beige-food-only diet? Little Noah will grow out of it eventually.

I still find it astonishing how upset some people get about social media and the picture-perfect unattainability they think it promotes; how smugly people point out, as if they've cracked the Rosetta stone, that influencers' lives probably aren't all that great beneath the filter. Novels are written about it, endless broadsheet opinion pieces, bad movies dedicated to perfect online lives that are actually crumbling behind the scenes, appearances kept up only for the lucrative ads. It doesn't seem to have occurred to anyone that it might happen the other way around.

Even prettier in the flesh than on Instagram, Emmy Jackson hurtles down the stairs of her Georgian town house in an increasingly fashionable area of east London with a flurry of apologies: "Ignore these awful roots; I just haven't had the time to sort them out since baby Bear arrived. I'm so sorry for the mess—finding a cleaner is on my to-do list! I hope you've brought the camera that drops a dress size as I'm ninety-eight percent cake at the minute!"

She curls her bare feet up under her on the mustard velvet sofa as we chat. Her daughter, Coco, a cute three-year-old with a mop of blond curls and a face familiar to aficionados of Emmy's social media feeds (on which she has been appearing since the day she was born), is happily bouncing on the seat next to her. The new baby, Bear—"We made a list of characteristics we wanted him to have, and then listed animals we associated with those characteristics"—is in Emmy's arms. She tells me that in the first five weeks of his life, his pictures have already been liked over two million times. Beneath a layer of toys, scattered craft materials, and discarded crayons, the living room is elegantly appointed. Her broodingly handsome husband, Dan, a writer, stands at the floor-to-ceiling bookshelf, idly turning the pages of his own novel and occasionally chuckling to himself.

Emmy—known as Mamabare to her million-plus Instagram followers, the first of the British Instamums to hit seven figures—reaches for her Mamabare-branded mug and takes a sip. She loves nothing more than a nice cuppa, she says, although like most of her fans she rarely has time to sit down and enjoy one. "Drinking this while it's still hot is like a week in a spa for a mum," she jokes. "If sharing my little life with a million other mothers on Instagram has taught me anything, it's that really, we're all the same—doing our best, taking it one day at a time. You just gotta make it through the night, Mama!"

I had to stop reading at that point. I could feel something rising in my throat.

It took me a while to come back to it. To make it to the end. There was nothing in the piece I did not know already, of course. No claim I had not seen her make before, no anecdote unrecycled.

I had been hoping for a hatchet job, but instead it was a cover story and, inside, a five-page feature with photos of the four of them—mummy, daddy, son, and daughter—in their beautiful house, sitting on their expensive sofa, sun streaming through the window from their beautiful street. Four people without a care in the world. Four people whose idea of a tragedy is someone putting one of baby's red socks through the wash with all of Dad's white shirts. Who in their whole lives have never lost anything worse than their house keys. I swallow.

Despite the stresses that must come with being one of the UK's most followed families, Emmy and Dan are clearly still deeply in love—you can just tell from the way they look at each other. Emmy points to their wedding photo, jostling for space on the shelf with framed pictures of their children, where they are both beaming. "It's revolting, I know"—she laughs—"but I honestly still feel like that, every day. I knew the instant I met Dan that he was The One.

"I married my best friend—the funniest, kindest, cleverest man I've ever met. We may drive each other up the wall sometimes, but there's nobody I would rather be on this journey with," she says, resting a hand on his shoulder.

And that's when I spotted it. Right there, staring at me, in the big photo, the one of them all together in their living room. Three letters— the top of an r, the tip of a d, then a space, then the upper half of what looked like a capital N. There in the mirror behind their heads, the one next to the window, the big, slightly foxed mirror, peeking in reflection over the shutters. A glimpse of the name of the pub opposite their house: ___rd N____.

It was all I needed.

CHAPTER THREE

Emmy

It's an odd thing, social media celebrity. When I see someone do a double-take or nudge a friend and gesture in my direction, it takes me a second to remember that there are a million people who know exactly who I am. I have a moment of wondering if I have my skirt tucked into my knickers before I realize that they are staring at Mamabare, not my bare arse. Half the time they want to chat too—which is actually better than just staring, as that can get a bit awkward. I shouldn't complain really—being approached is simply what happens when you're so very approachable.

It happens three times between my front door and my agent's office. It was just staring from one guy who got on at the same station as me. The creep didn't even help me down the stairs with the pram. He *could* have been just your standard perv, but there was something in his eyes that suggested he'd seen me in my underwear. Whoever started #bodypositivemama deserves a thump—our feeds have been a sea of rippling #mumbods recently, all of us Instamums posting pics with handfuls of paunch to prove we love our stretch marks and spare tires because we "grew a person in there," nobody daring to say that actually they *might* like to lose a few kilos.

The next one is Ally, an aspiring Instamum from Devon, who asks for a photo in front of the Oxford Circus sign. She spots me from a distance and literally runs down the platform to demand a photo—one of the perils of being permanently dressed in on-brand primary colors is that I'm so easy to spot—then enlists her embarrassed husband to take it, barking orders and checking the angles every few attempts ("Higher! Can't you get the sign in? My shoes aren't in the shot!").

"This is the first weekend away that Chris and I have had since Hadrian was born. He's two now. I literally cannot believe we've bumped into you. You are my idol. You made me believe in myself as a mother. Like I can still be *me*, even though I have a baby," she gushes as she checks the photos.

"You're the reason I started out on my own influencer journey after I got sacked when I was six months pregnant. I just thought, *Here is a mama building her own business on her own terms. Being a strong woman with a baby and something important to say.* The Mamabare feed is like my bible." She clasps her hands in front of her and shakes her head.

By this point, Bear has started to cry. Ally actually looks like she might too.

"That's incredible to hear, Ally, thank you, but I'm certainly no saint! I'm so sorry, I'm going to have to run—little Bear needs a feed, and I draw the line at getting my boobs out on the Bakerloo line! Tag me and I'll make sure I follow you back," I say as I march off with a smile.

The third person, who introduces herself as Caroline, stops me by the ticket barriers to share her battles with postnatal depression. I have, she says, been such an inspiration. Just knowing that there was someone out there who got where she was coming from, who had been through the dark nights too, stopped her from feeling so alone. Stopped her from doing something silly, from really losing it. She pulls her #greydays reusable coffee cup out of her handbag, and waves her Mamabare phone cover at me.

"Always remember, you are the best mama you can be, Caroline. Your little human thinks you're a superhero," I say, wrapping my arms around her.

I lumber up from the station with the pram under my arm and get three steps from the top before anyone offers to help. I flash them a quick smile and say I am fine, thanks. I'm dreading getting this baby up the five flights to Irene's office. You would really think, as Britain's leading agent for online parenting stars, she would have an office that was a little more accessible. Then again, Irene has never shown any sign of being interested in babies. It's entirely possible she chose an office at the top of the tallest, narrowest staircase she could find in this hellishly busy part of London as a deliberate ploy to discourage her clients from bringing their offspring along when they come to see her.

I put the pram down and fish my hand sanitizer and phone out of my bag. I have seven missed calls, all from Dan. *Christ*, I think to myself, picturing Dan trying repeatedly and with increasing irritation opening and closing the same three kitchen cupboards in search of a jar of pesto while Coco whines for her lunch. *What's the crisis this time, Dan? Oh, you can't find the fucking colander.*

Then, a microsecond later, it occurs to me that something really *might* have happened, and for every second that Dan does not answer his phone, my panic escalates.

It keeps ringing. I tell myself it is fine and I am being ridiculous.

It still keeps ringing. I tell myself that he has probably just locked them both out or is checking whether he needs to pick up anything for dinner.

Still ringing. Probably, I tell myself, it was just a pocket call and that is why he is not picking up now. I'm sure they are at the playground and having a lovely time.

His phone keeps ringing.
His phone keeps ringing.

The name of a pub. Three letters. An r, a d, and a capital N. It's lucky I've always been good at crossword puzzles. Come to think of it, Grace used to enjoy them too. The funny thing with crosswords and that sort of business is that even when you think you are stumped, even when you have put the paper aside and gone off to do something else, your brain is still working on the answers you didn't get, ticking away, making the connections that had your conscious brain perplexed. Then when you pick the paper up and sit down with your pencil again a few hours later, there they are, the answers, just waiting for you to write them down.

I strode off confidently down a blind alley at first. As far as the r and the d were concerned, they surely—in a pub name—had to be the second half of Lord. Lord N____?, I thought. Why, it must be Lord Nelson, of course.

My mouth was dry. My heart was thumping.

From reading Mamabare's posts, from reading Emmy's interviews, from listening to her talk to other people like her on podcasts, I have accumulated over time a little treasure trove of information about where she and her family live. I know, for instance, that they live east. I know they are only ten minutes from the Westfield shopping center. I know they are close enough to a big park to walk there with a buggy, and that when Emmy worked in magazines she sometimes used to cycle to work along the canal. I know there is a Tube station and a Tesco Metro and where they live is equidistant between two schools (the good school and the other place, as Emmy always calls them). I know they do not live in any of the places I have seen or heard Emmy complain about being priced out of. I have heard her say at least twice how much she wished they lived closer to a Waitrose. I know there is a petrol station just around the corner where she sometimes used to go for nappies and/or magazines and/or emergency chocolate when Coco was first born.

Not much to go on, until now.

According to Google, there are eight pubs called the Lord Nelson in London. Three are too far west. One is too far south. One is way, way out, practically in Middlesex.

That left three. The first looked promising, when I typed the post-code into Street View. The road looked like the kind of place I could imagine someone like Emmy living. It was just around the corner from the Tube. There was a petrol station in walking distance and a Tesco Metro. It was the house itself that was all wrong. There was no way Emmy Jackson lived behind those greying net curtains, in a house with a front door painted with red gloss paint. Neither of the places on either side of it were any good either. One had a load of posters in the window for an animal welfare charity; the other had a load of weeds growing out of the cracked concrete of the front garden and a car on bricks on the driveway.

The second Lord Nelson was next door to a high-rise.

The third Lord Nelson had metal shutters up on all the windows and appeared to have been out of business for some time.

I was genuinely stumped. I actually retrieved the magazine from the recycling pile to look at it again and check I hadn't made some kind of mistake, that I had not missed some crucial detail. There it was: definitely a pub, definitely directly opposite their house, and those were definitely the letters visible through their front window. It did not make any sense. Unless everything Mamabare had ever said and written about her neighborhood was an elaborate act of misdi-rection? Unless they actually lived in a completely different part of London to the one they claimed?

But none of the other five Lord Nelsons in London fitted the bill *either. One was opposite a park. One faced onto a dual carriageway. None of the frontages of any of the pubs matched with what was visible through the photographed window of Emmy and her husband's house.*

I turned off the computer in frustration and went through to the kitchen to make myself a cup of tea. It was almost ten o'clock. What had started as an evening of great excitement had gradually turned flat, then curdled. I went through to the living room and turned on the news. It was all bad. After about five minutes I turned it off and went to bed.

I had switched the bedside light off and checked my alarm and was thinking about something else entirely, about a couple of things I needed to do in the morning, when it hit me.

Lord Napier.

There was a pub opposite the railway station in the town where I grew up called the Lord Napier.

I switched the light back on. I went through to the computer. As it warmed up and turned on, I drummed my fingers impatiently on the edge of the keyboard.

There are three pubs called the Lord Napier in London. There is only one in east London. I looked it up on Google Maps.

It is five minutes from a Tube station. It is around the corner from a petrol station. It is a quick stroll from a Tesco Metro. It is nearish to the canal.

I checked how long it would take to get from the pub (or opposite it) to Westfield. The answer: exactly ten minutes, on the Central line.

I clicked on Street View. I entered the postcode. I reached across for the paper. I looked from screen to photograph and from photograph to screen again. We had a match. I scrolled the screen around until I was looking at the house opposite. It had new curtains, a freshly painted dark grey front door, shutters.

Hello, Emmy.

Dan

Answer your phone. Answer your phone. Answer your fucking phone.

It's definitely ringing. Ringing and ringing and then going to voice-mail. Emmy must be above ground by now. Why is it still going to voicemail?

Jesus Christ.

I suspect every parent has experienced this at some point. That feeling, that gut-twisting, pore-prickling feeling, your throat tightening and your pulse pounding in your temples and your breath catching in your throat and your eyes frantically scanning the crowd at waist height, at child height—and the child who was holding your hand literally two seconds ago nowhere to be seen. And even as half of your brain is telling yourself not to be so silly, that she's just slipped off to have another look at something in the window of the toy shop you passed a few minutes ago, has just seen something that caught her eye (a poster, a snack stand, something shiny) and wandered over to investigate, the other half of your brain has already leapt to the worst possible conclusions.

We are in Westfield, the mall, the one near the former Olympic Park. Coco and I have already been to two shoe shops and are now in a third. Having finally found a pair of proper, sensible shoes that fit and which she does not entirely hate, I let go of her hand just for a second to pay and to take charge of the bag, and when I turn back to ask if she fancies an ice cream she's gone.

I don't panic immediately. She's probably just behind one of the displays. Perhaps she's gone back over to look at those glittery trainers with the lights in the heel, the ones she was so taken with earlier.

It's not a large shop. This being a quiet Thursday afternoon, there aren't a lot of other people in here. It doesn't take more than a minute or two to establish that Coco is no longer on the premises. In those few brief minutes I have gone from apologetic to anxious to outright panic mode. There are at least two people in the shop, people who work there, who do not appear to be serving anybody. What I cannot understand is why they are just standing around.

"A little girl. The one who was with me." I hold my hand out to indicate Coco's height. "You didn't see where she went?"

They both shake their heads. As I am leaving, I hear someone calling after me that I've forgotten my bag. I don't go back.

There's no sign of my daughter outside the shop either.

We're on the second floor, down at the John Lewis end, just by the escalators. I run to the top of them, trying not to picture Coco using the escalator on her own, telling myself that surely someone would have stopped her.

The nearest set of escalators is empty.

That is when I first try to call Emmy. Is there anywhere, I want to ask her, that Coco especially likes to go in Westfield? Since I hate the place and everything it stands for, it's usually the girls who come here on their own while I push Bear in his pram around the park. I try to rack my brain for anything either Emmy or Coco might have said about their trips together. Is there a particular shop she always wants to look in, that she talks about? A particular playground? Somewhere they enjoy going? Nothing springs to mind. Again Emmy's mobile goes to voicemail.

I'm obviously looking pretty frantic by now. Passing people are giving me sidelong looks, glances of concern.

"A little girl," I say to them. I do the thing with my hand again. "Have you seen a little girl?"

Apologetic shakes of the head, shrugs, gestures of commiseration. Every time I spot a child, my heart gives a lurch, then sinks as I realize it's wearing the wrong coat, or it's the wrong size, or the wrong gender.

I am painfully aware that every decision I make now, every incorrect

decision, is costing me time. Do I run down this way, to see if she's
around this corner? In exactly the same amount of time Coco could be
disappearing around a different corner in the opposite direction. And
every second I spend hesitating, that's another second wasted too. Is
Coco already on one of the lower floors? Has she gone back to the
elevators? Has she wandered off to try to find the play area I know she
and Emmy sometimes visit? There's somewhere called Soft Play, isn't
there? Is that in the same building? Or is that somewhere different?
I'm picturing a bouncy castle, but inside.

I try Emmy's phone again.

All around me on the concourse, people are going about their everyday business, drifting along with what seems to me infuriating
slowness. I decide to try the elevators first. I squeeze around a couple
holding hands, jump right over someone's wheely bag. In the window
of one of the shops, I catch a glimpse of myself as I run past: pale, wild-
eyed, on the verge of a meltdown.

What I can't understand is why no one has stopped her. Would you
not stop a lone three-year-old and ask them where they were going, if
one passed you in a mall? I mean, somebody must have clocked her.
Surely someone, you would think, would have the gumption to stop
a little kid like that and ask them where they're going, where their
mummy or daddy—or whoever—is. You would imagine. You would
hope.

Apparently you would be mistaken.

I move to overtake someone shuffling along with their head bowed
and their eyes fixed on their iPhone, and nearly collide with someone
else doing exactly the same thing coming in the other direction.

There is no sign of Coco by the elevators. The display tells me one
elevator is on the ground floor, and the other is making its way up to
the top—the third floor—where I am. I run back to the balustrade
and look over. I can't see my daughter anywhere. By this time, I'm increasingly convinced that something awful has happened, something

really awful. The kind of thing you read about and shudder. The kind of thing you hear about on the news.

That's when I see her. Coco. Standing outside a bookshop on the ground floor.

"Coco," I shout. She doesn't look up. "Coco!"

I take the stairs of the escalator three or four at a time, gripping the sides, practically throwing myself down it, pushing roughly between a young couple standing two abreast, not caring when one of them clucks their tongue after me.

"Coco!" I shout again, leaning over the side of the balustrade on the first floor. This time she does look up, but only to try to work out where the voice calling her name is coming from. I shout it again. Finally, she glances in my direction, smiles vaguely and waves with one arm, then returns her attention to the display in the window, which is advertising the latest in that series of books about a family of wizards and witches.

Thank God. Thank God. Thank God. Thank God. Thank God.

Not only have I located my daughter, but she has got someone with her, a grown-up. Thank God for that too. That one person in this mall, at least, at last, has shown enough common sense and enough community spirit to intervene when they see an unaccompanied three-year-old wandering about. They are standing next to each other, the two of them, apparently checking out the shop display together.

I feel a great surge of relief.

From this angle and distance, I can't make out much about the person Coco is standing with—I can see them only from behind and as a vague reflection in the shop window—but I assume, I suppose because of the anorak they are wearing, that they are an older person, someone's granny perhaps. I suppose it is the colors of the anorak—pink and purple—that give me the impression the person wearing it is female. I can already feel the apologetic words, the effusive thanks, forming in my throat.

A pillar passes between us.

A second or two elapses.

My daughter is standing outside the bookshop on her own.

For a moment, my brain flatly refuses to process this.

All the way down the final escalator, I keep my eyes fixed on Coco, as if some very basic part of my brain believes if I take my eyes off her for a second, even to blink, she will vanish too. Thankfully, there is no one on this escalator between me and the bottom. I quick-shuffle down the steps as fast as I can, one hand hovering over the rubber banister in case I stumble.

The last three or four steps I jump.

I land with a grunt.

It is about twenty feet from the end of the escalator to the entrance to the bookshop. I skid it in three long, sliding strides.

"Ooof, Daddy," says Coco.

I'm aware that I am squeezing her too hard, but I can't stop myself, just as I can't stop myself lifting her up and swinging her around in my arms.

"Daddy," she says.

I put her down. She straightens her dress.

My heart is still thumping.

"Coco. What have we told you, what do Mummy and I always say, about wandering off like that?"

My aim is to sound calm but firm. Stern but not angry.

It is that age-old dilemma: the simultaneous urge to tell them off for scaring you versus the overwhelming desire to let them know how much they are loved.

I do my best to catch my daughter's eye, have attempted to squat down to her level, the way the advice manuals all tell you to do when you are trying to have a serious conversation with someone Coco's age.

"Do you hear me?" I ask her. "You must never, never, never, never do that again, darling. Do you understand?"

Coco nods, very slightly, half her attention still on the window display.

She is safe—that is the main thing. My daughter is okay. As for what I thought I saw from the escalator . . .

It must be raining again outside, because people with anoraks are everywhere. Some are old. Some are young. Some of them still have their hoods up. I look around, but no one seems to be paying us any special attention. None of the anoraks looks familiar. They are black, blue, green, yellow.

Perhaps I was mistaken, I think. *Perhaps Coco was not standing with anyone. Perhaps someone just happened to be looking at the window display at the same time as her, happened to be passing. Perhaps—perhaps—what I thought I saw was just a trick of the light, a glitch of the brain, the reflection of a reflection.*

I think it is fair to say I am not doing very much sophisticated joined-up thinking at this precise point in time.

I give Coco another hug, a longer one this time. After a while I can feel her starting to lose patience, to squirm a little in my arms. It takes a few seconds for me to work up the will to let her go.

And that's when I finally notice what my daughter is holding.

CHAPTER FOUR

It is astonishing how much you can find out about someone, once you know their address.

14 Chandos Road.

Once you know someone's address you can easily go online and find one of those property websites, see how much the house last sold for and have a look at some photos, even check out the floor plan if you are lucky. The last time 14 Chandos Road was on the market, back in the late noughties, it went for five hundred fifty thousand pounds. Emmy has written quite a bit on her blog about the changes they made to the place after she moved in—in addition to the conservatory and extension they added to the back, they knocked a wall through in the living room, got rid of the three-bar fire with fake plastic coal, the carpet in the bathroom, and the turquoise tiles in the downstairs loo, and set up the back room on the first floor as a children's bedroom. Which means that room in the front upstairs must still be the master bedroom, the one with the en suite. It's all so easy. It's all just there in the public domain. Two clicks, three, and as you trace your finger on the screen it feels as if you're walking through their house, invisible, a digital ghost. Emmy always talks about wanting a larger garden. I can see why. Goodness knows where they had room to fit a writing shed.

Once you know someone's postcode, you can easily figure out where their local coffee shop is, the one they talk about stopping by on their morning walk every day, the one their husband sometimes goes to to sit in and write. You can click on Street View and you can follow the route they would walk on their way to the Tube in the morning, on their way to the park. You can make a reasonable guess where their daughter goes to nursery, the quickest route for them to take to get there in the morning. You can work out pretty quickly which is the little playground Emmy talks about passing on the way and the shop where Coco always wants to buy sweets.

It is a very strange feeling. A little dizzying, even.

There are times when it feels like you are looking down into a pond—a fish pond, I guess, like the one we used to have at school, in front of the entrance to the science block—and all the fishes are swimming around it blithely, obliviously. You can see them going about their business, doing their thing, and a part of you knows that at any moment you could drop a stone or start poking around with a stick and see them all scatter and panic. Or you could bend down and pluck one out of the water and into the choking air, just like that, if you wanted to, and all the others would be nosing urgently around the weeds, tails flicking, turning this way, turning that. And there are times when you know that you would not be able to do that sort of thing to another living being, not really, not you.

And then there are times when you are not so sure.

I used to be such a nice girl, back in those days, back at school, all those years ago. Such a polite girl. Such a kind girl. Those were the words that always got used to describe me.

There have been times recently when the thoughts I have found myself thinking, the things I have imagined myself doing, the kind of human being into which I seem to be turning, have genuinely terrified me.

Dan

It is absolutely hideous. That's the first thing that strikes me about the object that Coco is holding. I don't think I'm exaggerating when I say it is the ugliest, dirtiest stuffed toy I have ever seen. Its eye buttons are chipped. Its ears are grimy and sucked-looking. One of its overall straps is broken. Its mouth looks like a surgical scar. My immediate instinct is to snatch it out of Coco's hands and chuck it as far as I can, slam-dunk it into the nearest bin, then see if there are any wipes or hand sanitizer in my backpack.

The second thing that strikes me is that Coco was definitely not carrying it when she wandered off.

We've had several conversations about not swearing in front of the kids, Emmy and I. Usually, I'd like to point out, it's Emmy who slips up in this regard. Who drops an F-bomb when she opens a cupboard and a bag of flour leaps out and bursts on the counter. Who calls someone a wanker under her breath (not quite quietly enough to escape little ears) as they cut in front of us in a queue at an airport. Who has to wriggle out of explaining what a dickhead is at the dinner table. On this occasion—blame the adrenaline still coursing around my body, my still-jangling nerves—it's me whose temper gets the better of them.

"Jesus Christ, Coco, where the fuck did you get that?"

There's always that horrible moment after you snap at a child when you see their eyes widen, moisten, can see the child retreating into themselves. That moment when you feel yourself desperately wanting to recall the words, stop them reverberating in the air. She tries belatedly to tuck the toy behind her back.

"Nowhere," she says.

"Show me."

Eventually, reluctantly, somewhat unexpectedly, she complies.

"Thank you," I say.

I kneel down to inspect the thing. Is it meant to be a dog? A bear? A monkey? It's impossible to tell. If it ever had a tail, it doesn't have one any longer. I really hope it's not my daughter who has been sucking on its ears.

"Where did it come from, Coco?" I ask her again, a little more calmly, in a tone of voice intended to sound coaxing rather than upset.

"Mine," she replies.

"I'm sorry, darling," I tell her. "But I don't think it is yours, is it?"

I'm literally holding the thing between pinched forefingers.

"Do you want to tell me where you got it, Coco? Do you remember?"

She avoids eye contact.

"Did you find it somewhere?"

She shrugs one shoulder noncommittally.

If she can remember where she found it, I tell her, we could go and put it back there again. It must belong to someone, this teddy, I point out. Another little girl or boy. And whoever it belongs to must have dropped it or lost it or maybe it fell out of the bottom of their pram, and how did she think they would feel when they got home and realized?

"Mine," she says again.

"What do you mean, yours?" I ask her.

She does not answer me.

"If you don't tell me where you got this thing, Coco," I tell her in my firmest, most imposingly parental voice, "it's going straight in the trash."

Coco pulls a face and shakes her head.

"I'm serious," I tell her.

No response.

"Final chance," I say.

She shrugs.

Into the trash it goes.

Stupid move. Stupid fucking move. A real parenting misstep. As we make our way through the mall, she keeps trying to slip her hand out of mine and double back. On the escalator to the Tube platform, she keeps going floppy. I have to pick her up when we actually get to our station. There are looks. When Emmy calls back, we are two minutes from home. She asks if that's Coco howling in the background. I confirm it is and that the amateur dramatics have been going for over ten minutes now. Her first question is what the hell have I done to her.

"Nothing," I say.

"Is everything okay?" she asks me. "I've got a million missed calls—you scared me. I've canceled my meeting and I'm in an Uber on my way back. What happened?"

"Nothing," I say again. "There's no need to worry. Everything is fine now."

I really do not want to discuss over the phone the eight and a half minutes this afternoon when I managed to misplace our three-year-old daughter.

All the way home I have been replaying in my head my exchange with Coco, the questions I asked her, the way I framed them, the manner in which I spoke to her, wondering whether a different approach would have been more sensible. All the way home I have been trying to remember exactly what I saw from the escalator, the precise colors of the anorak, exactly what gave me the impression it was a woman. Was it the anorak that was pink, the patches on the back purple? Or was it the other way around? And if I can't even be sure about that, then what *can* I be sure about, when it comes to what I thought I saw?

Memory being what it is, it is just as likely my brain is now embroidering facts, filling in the gaps, as it is that I am actually remembering anything useful at this point.

Every time I ask Coco what happened, where she went, why she wandered off, she just says, "Bookshop."

There is a part of me that can very easily imagine myself and Emmy telling this as a story, twenty years in the future, when Coco is a writer or an academic or a literary agent; can easily imagine in a distant future the rough edges of the anecdote, any tricky questions it might raise about my parenting skills, gently rounded or glossed over. I can even imagine myself or Emmy doing Coco's inflection when we get to the word *booksop*. And there is a part of me that is secretly quite pleased it was a bookshop she was so excited about, not the Disney Store or McDonald's.

Right now, though, it is the stuffed toy on which my thoughts keep snagging.

When we get home, I take Coco through to the kitchen and make her beans on toast, which she eats sullenly in her special chair. When I ask if she wants a yogurt for dessert, she vigorously shakes her head.

"Bath time?" I ask her.

No response at all to this.

"We'll get you another . . . bear, Coco. Another teddy. A nicer one. We can go back to the bookshop another time."

She turns in her chair, pretends she's looking out at the garden. A gentle rain has begun to fall, the wet leaves glinting in the gathering gloom. Her lips are arranged in what looks very much like a pout.

"The thing is, darling, it isn't good to just wander around picking things up, is it? You don't know where they've been."

"Mine," she says yet again.

I put on a smile and assume a reasonable, soothing tone of voice.

"But the thing is, Coco, it wasn't yours, was it? I didn't buy it for you. Mummy didn't buy it for you. So the question is, where did you get it from?"

I know what she's going to say in reply to this before her lips have even finished forming the word.

I pull out a chair and sit down. Then I turn her chair so she's facing me a little more.

"Coco," I say. "I have a serious question to ask you. Will you look at me? Look at me. Thank you. Coco, that teddy. I don't suppose there is any way somebody—anybody—gave you that teddy? Like a present? Do you remember?"

She shakes her head firmly.

"No?"

She shakes her head again, more vigorously this time.

"Does that mean no, you don't remember, or no, no one gave it to you?"

"No," she says again.

I straighten up, stretch my shoulders, rub the back of my neck. It is time, I decide, to try another tack.

"Coco?" I ask her. "You know that talk we had a little while ago about telling the truth and telling stories?"

She nods her head tentatively, not meeting my gaze.

"And you know how important we agreed it was to always tell the truth?"

She hesitates, still avoiding eye contact, then nods her head again.

"Well, I'm going to ask you once again about where you got that teddy . . ."

"Found it," she says.

"You found it?"

"Found it."

Fine, I think. *Good*, I tell myself. That is a relief, a weight off my mind.

I ask her where she found it, and she tells me in a shop. "A shop?" I say. She hesitates, looks thoughtful, and then confirms this.

"What shop?"

Coco is unable to tell me.

I take a deep breath, count to twenty, announce it is time to start running a bath.

It would appear that big talk we had about always telling the truth has not perhaps sunk in as deeply as we had hoped.

*   *   *

THE NURSERY HAD SUGGESTED it might be best if both Emmy and I were present, if we all sat down with Coco to talk about things—"things" meaning, in this context, our daughter's recently developed habit of going through the bags on other kids' pegs and taking stuff and then claiming they'd given it to her as a present. Of knocking things over and letting other children take the blame. The outrageous claims she had taken to making about how rich and famous we were or where we'd been on holiday (the moon, apparently). The reason Coco's teacher had called us in, she said, was to try to find out whether Coco did the same thing at home, whether there was anything that might be upsetting her or unsettling her or why we thought she might be behaving in this way. "She's always been imaginative" was Emmy's rather defensive response. "I was exactly the same at her age."

I did not doubt that at all.

We pulled our chairs into a circle and had a very serious talk with Coco about how it's important not to make things up or exaggerate or invent stories. That there's no point trying to impress people by pretending to be something you're not. About how you shouldn't try to trick people into giving you things that don't belong to you. Coco's teacher was nodding her head very firmly through all this, very emphatically.

Don't think for a minute that either Emmy or I were unaware of the ironies of the situation. The point I kept emphasizing, every time I was given the opportunity, was that nothing Coco was accused of doing came from a place of malice. She does not have a mean bone in her body, my daughter. Nor do I believe she has any difficulty distinguishing fact from fantasy. She likes to entertain people, to make them laugh. The point I kept wanting to make is that she is a bloody clever kid. A lot cleverer than anyone else in that class. A lot cleverer than most of the people she is going to spend her childhood being taught by, if I am perfectly honest. A lot of the things they were describing were clearly jokes, obviously pranks. Like hiding her shoes and mixing up everyone else's. Like swapping plates with the person next to her and pretending she was going to eat their lunch as well.

We did laugh about some of that stuff afterward, once we'd put Coco to bed that night. We laughed, but I could tell that Emmy was secretly still pretty pissed off about the whole thing too. "That judgy cow," she suddenly huffed, apropos of nothing, about twenty minutes after I thought we'd both let the subject drop. "You realize whose benefit all that was *really* for, don't you?"

I said something bland that I hoped would be placatory.

"Do you think she'd have talked to us—to *me*—like that if I were a lawyer? If I worked in advertising? If I did literally anything else for a living? There's a kid in Coco's year with double ear piercings and a kid who craps themselves every morning and just sits there in it and a kid who only eats sausages and a kid who has had nits since last spring and *I'm* the parent who's being invited to feel shit about myself?"

"It's completely absurd," I said.

"You're absolutely right," I added.

"Kids make stuff up all the time," I observed. "All kids do that."

Another lull in the conversation followed.

There would also be more cause for concern, I pointed out, with the whole lying thing, if our daughter was actually any good at it. To be an effective liar you need to be able to remember all the things you have made up, keep track of each tiny tweak to the truth, always have your story straight. Emmy is excellent at this. Coco is not. Without blinking, she'll tell you three contradictory things in the same sentence. She'll claim she didn't do something that you've just stood there and watched her do. I wouldn't put it past her to deny she's doing something even as she's right in front of you doing it. If I say that my daughter is a terrible liar, I mean that in every sense.

To be perfectly honest, I generally find this quite funny under normal circumstances. Like when Coco tells her little friends there's a secret room at our house that is full of sweets. Or when she's telling everyone all about our holiday on the moon. Most of the time Coco's lies are so nonsensical and transparent there's nothing else you can do but laugh.

These are not normal circumstances.

As my immediate relief at finding my daughter safe and sound has ebbed, so my frustration at not knowing exactly what happened in those eight and a half minutes has grown. I still have no idea why Coco went off or where she went or how she got down to the bottom floor of the shopping center. I still have no idea where she acquired that teddy. As I give her a bath, as I'm brushing her teeth, I keep asking her questions, and I keep getting answers that are vague or can't be true or contradict the answer she gave me to some other question just two minutes ago.

I ask Coco why she wandered off in the first place, and she tells me she doesn't know. I ask her why she was going to the bookshop, and she says she can't remember that either. I ask her if anyone tried to stop her, if anyone tried to speak to her at all. She yawns. She says she doesn't remember. We're getting nowhere. It's past her bedtime. In the hall I can hear Emmy hurriedly kicking her shoes off and hanging her coat on the banister.

I shouldn't have taken my eyes off Coco. Not for a second.

The truth is, I've always been paranoid about all this stuff. About three months after we found out Emmy was pregnant with Coco, we went to the cinema. It was a film about some creep kidnapping a kid, and I actually had to get up and stumble over everyone's legs and shoes and walk out. I'm not talking about a horror movie or anything. I am talking about some stupid thriller. It was horrible. The film. The experience. I was sitting there in the cinema, and I could feel my throat closing up, my heart pounding. To be fair, I was quite hungover. But what kept going through my head was that there really are people out there in the world like that. Weirdos. Predators. Pedophiles. And this is what I was like even *before* we decided to share our family life online. Before the world was full of people who know or think they know how much money we're making from this gig, know exactly what we look like and what our son and daughter look like, what kind of life we live.

How do you impress on your child the importance of not speaking to strangers when they see Mummy greet every fan who says hi like a long-lost friend?

I suspect that in every marriage there are one or two big topics that it is impossible to discuss without things quickly getting heated. Topics that lurk beneath the surface and most of the time you both manage to navigate around or avoid entirely. Topics that you have argued about so many times or so sharply that every time they come up you find your hackles preemptively rising, your defenses going up, a series of half-repressed memories of previous fights resurfacing.

Just like the time I thought I saw someone surreptitiously taking pictures of Coco at the café in the park and freaked out, just like the time I convinced myself someone was staring at her at the pool, I already know that the discussion I am about to have with Emmy—at least the discussion we have once I explain what happened and stop apologizing—is going to go in exactly the same circles as it always does. Have we made a mistake? Are we doing something awful? Is there anything else we could do to make ourselves safer? Have we, by putting our lives and our children's lives out there on the internet for all to see, done something monumentally foolish? Are we putting Coco and Bear at risk? Is all this bad for them? Is it going to skew their sense of self, how they see the world? Is it going to fuck them up somehow, in the long term? Are we terrible people?

Round and round the conversation will go, one of us self-accusing, the other trying to reassure them, to justify what we're doing, both of us pointing out the flaws in each other's arguments, both of us wrestling with ourselves as much as each other but still quick to pick up on the other's turn of phrase or tone of voice, both of us getting tenser and tenser, the air in the room steadily thickening. And what it will come down to, after all's said and done, the horrible truth, the bottom line, the limiting factor in *all* our discussions, nutters or no nutters, qualms and quibbles or no qualms and quibbles, is this: that if we pull the plug now there's no way we can pay the bills.

Emmy

I can't say I wasn't warned.

Irene and I did sit down and have a long conversation before I signed with her about what being an influencer involves. I showed her my own personal Instagram account—emmyjackson, 232 followers, all of whom I'd met in real life, whose surnames I knew—and she used it as a show-and-tell to explain why my badly lit photos of brunch, the occasional bouquet or cupcake, unphotogenic friends and bathroom selfies with my cheeks sucked in, would not cut it. To turn this into a career, I'd need precision-planned hashtags, content streams and topical themes, fellow influencer friends I could tag and who would tag me back, photos shot weeks in advance and edited to perfection (or, as it turned out, imperfection).

She made it sound a lot like Mamabare would be similar to editing my own little magazine, each Instagram post a new page. In a way it was, back then. Followers would comment with hearts and winks. Nobody seemed to realize they could send me private messages, or if they did, they never bothered. Twitter was for sniping and snark; Instagram was a friendly space for pretty pictures and smiley faces.

The shift was imperceptible at first. Slowly, the comments stopped being total love-ins. Direct messages started to trickle in, at first mainly from happy mamas high on oxytocin during four a.m. feeds.

But they soon became a torrent, all expecting an immediate response whether they were telling me I should be ashamed of myself for selling my family online or that they liked my lipstick. Gossip sites launched. Tabloids started to report on our spats and slipups as if we were genuine celebrities.

Dan and I used to be the couple who were so in demand that we had to turn down dinner parties because our calendars were too tightly packed—the hot fashion girl and the up-and-coming author who you simply *must* meet. We would arrive looking like we might have just had sex (we usually had), with two bottles of well-chosen wine, deliver each other's punch lines all night, be first on the dance floor at the kitchen disco and then the last to leave. But we stopped going to those dinner parties long ago, knowing that I'd inevitably have my phone out by the time the second bottle of wine was opened, trying to keep on top of my messages and comments. Come to think of it, perhaps we just stopped being invited.

Eventually, Instagram felt less like editing my own personal magazine and more like hosting a daily talk radio show where a thousand listeners get to call in every episode and are allowed airtime no matter how vicious or incoherent they are. Overnight, instead of lovely little snapshots in discreet little squares, thanks to Instastories—those fifteen-second videos that gobble up our lives—now it feels like I have a GoPro strapped to my head at all times of the day and night. I can barely take a wee without feeling the need to beam the fact out for public consumption.

I sometimes look back at the private emmyjackson profile I never deleted, with those ninety-seven unplanned posts, preserved in internet aspic, and I barely recognize myself. I scroll through photos that show Emmy grinning over avocado toast, hugging Polly on a picnic blanket in the park, standing under the Eiffel Tower with Dan, or drinking shots on her wedding day, and I feel a little bit jealous of her.

Who could have predicted how big, how life-altering Instagram would become? One hundred million images uploaded a day, they say. One billion users. It boggles the mind.

Still, I'm not some ingenue who just stumbled into influencing for a living. Dan knew what we were getting into as well. We did discuss all this before Mamabare was born, but it does strike me sometimes that when he agreed I should give it a go, neither one of us really anticipated how quickly it would take off or how famous it would make us, as a family, or how exposing that would feel.

He gave himself a real scare yesterday.

I have told Dan, I have warned him, so many times, that you can't take your eyes off Coco for a second. It's one of the reasons why I'm paranoid about letting Dan's mum look after her: the thought that in the time it takes her to open her handbag and get a tissue for Coco's snotty nose, our daughter might go from riding her bike along the pavement to riding it under the wheels of a truck. And on top of the usual things that could happen to an unsupervised three-year-old— sticking a fork in an uncovered socket, say, or choking on the fifty-pence piece they inexplicably decided to suck on—there are also more than a million people out there, not all of them nice, who know Coco's face, her name, her age, her favorite food, her favorite TV program.

Of course, Dan being Dan, he was so self-flagellating about the whole Westfield thing—so dramatic about what might have happened, so emphatic about how terrible he felt—that losing my temper and shouting was not an option. And so I just had to swallow whatever irritation or anger or fear I might have been feeling about all those panicky missed calls, about having had to cancel the meeting with my agent, about not being able to leave my husband in charge of either one of our children for three fucking minutes. Instead, I found myself rubbing his shoulder, telling him it was really not such a big deal, that it could have happened whoever was watching her.

It hadn't, though, had it? It had happened on *his* watch. And just because I did not give Dan the dressing-down he deserved, that does not mean I am not furious with him about what happened—and as for what did happen, I can imagine it all too easily.

I'd be willing to bet you almost anything that he was thumbing some novel idea into his phone when she wandered off. Some plot point, some line of dialogue that had just occurred to him. I can picture the expression he would have had on his face as he did it too. The intense frown. The puckered mouth. The air of complete self-absorption.

Anyone who has two kids, and has been married for as long as Dan and I have, knows what it is like to seethe with righteous anger about something that might have happened, or to silently boil with resentment about what someone was probably doing when they should have been doing something else—especially when, as in this case, that something else was looking after *our* daughter. Which in the overall scheme of things is quite important, or so you might have thought.

Equally, I have no doubt that in his head Dan has found some way to make all this somehow my fault.

After yesterday's panicked cancellation, I hoped I could get away with just a phone chat with Irene, but she was adamant we reschedule. Because Bear the grumpy milk guzzler can't be away from my boobs for long, I bundled the tiny sling refusenik into his snowsuit and did the whole annoying journey for the second day in a row. I drew the line at lugging the Bugaboo up five flights of stairs, though, so there's currently an intern walking him around the block to keep him asleep.

To be honest, I always try to avoid Irene's office if I can. The clichéd neon art, the sketchy Tracey Emins, and the expensive mid-century modern furniture never fail to remind me how much her contracted 20 percent of my annual earnings adds up to. I would rather not know what Irene is worth, but as she is the owner of one of the most profitable influencer empires this side of the Atlantic, with a staff of forty, an office adjacent to Liberty, a mansion-block apartment in Bayswater, and a house in the South of France, it's not inconsiderable.

My mood is not improved by having spent most of yesterday evening—once I had talked Dan down off the ceiling—slogging through what felt like even more DMs than usual, replying to every single one with enthusiasm, even if an unusually high proportion were from the creepier end of my follower contingent, knowing that if I don't, they'll complain in my comments or bitch on the gossip sites that I'm getting too big for my boots. So it's a jolly response to the pensioner who has been following me ever since the Barefoot days and who asks insistently for pictures of my bare feet. *Ha ha, sorry, Jimmy, my bunions are already swaddled in their M&S slippers!* The man who sends me poems about childbirth. *Thank you so much for this, Chris, can't wait to get around to reading it properly.* The woman who wants to paint Coco's portrait in Victorian dress and keeps asking when she's free to sit for her.

I should have known better than to expect much sympathy from Irene on this front.

"Emmy, you know this stuff is just an occupational hazard." She laughs. "You'd get worse abuse, have to deal with creepier people, working at the council, or in a call center."

She can be bracingly direct, my agent.

Whatever happened yesterday, whatever impact it may have had on Dan and me, on our relationship, Irene certainly doesn't want to hear about it in any more detail—that's why she insists on paying for me to see Dr. Fairs. A trained psychotherapist that Irene also represents, Dr. Fairs has carved out a niche treating anxious influencers and angry trolls, building up an online following of a hundred thousand herself, with daily #mindfulmantras and an eponymous line of #selfcaresupplements. It's a stipulation of all Irene's contracts that her clients spend at least an hour a month on the therapist's couch.

She also makes all the talent take a personality test before she signs them.

"I like to know if my influencers are narcissists or sociopaths," Irene once joked when I asked her why. "I won't sign them otherwise." At least, I presume it was a joke.

To be honest, the therapy arrangement probably works best for all of us. I've known Irene for years, and she's always had the human warmth of a walk-in fridge—ambition is her defining characteristic. We met when I worked in magazines and she was the agent for every hot British actress you could name, feeding me a steady stream of them for shoots. That was always the best bit of my job—creating visual confections of pure fantasy with the most gorgeous women and the most beautiful clothes, every single month. Flying off to studios or locations in LA, Miami, Mustique, spending days with armfuls of couture and armies of photographers, makeup artists, and publicists, then seeing our handiwork stare back at me from the newsstands a few weeks later.

It never got old, the delight of seeing those images, of reading my name in print. Of knowing that I had created a real, permanent thing that people would see and touch and love and keep. I used to think of girls, like the teenage me, buying those magazines, taking them home to their suburban bedrooms and savoring every photograph, every word, just like I used to. Keeping them piled up by the bed and poring over the pages of beautiful people and places and things when they needed to escape their own suffocating, humdrum lives, just for a moment. But of course I know that no teenage girl does that anymore, which is why I no longer have that job.

Irene saw early on where it was all heading. She and I were tipsy together one night after a shoot when she told me about the new business she was starting. "I've seen the future, and it's social media. I've had enough of actors. Too much talent. Too many opinions. Influencers are where the money's at. And they're so malleable. They're *like* people, only in two dimensions."

She was sensible enough to know that she couldn't compete for the established fashion and beauty stars, so she built her own—what's the collective noun for influencers? An endorsement?—in niche areas. I was one of her first clients, and while she may have cheated slightly and bought my first few thousand follower bots to give me a kick-start, the rest have been real people won with pure graft. I've cultivated my prime position in the pod—my inner circle of five Instamums who play the algorithm by liking and commenting on one another's every post immediately, sending them to the top of our followers' feeds—with the same care as a CEO would chart the company's position in the FTSE 100.

Irene takes off her Chloé glasses and places them on the desk, flicks her hair from her shoulders and raises a perfectly arched brow. There's not a single strand out of place in her blunt-cut, jet-black fringe, which frames sharp features and skin so unblemished it looks like it's been run through a Clarendon filter. Not that it ever has been—like a drug dealer who won't get high on their own supply, not a single photo of Irene exists on social media. She reels off the list of Mamabare gigs in the pipeline, including a shoot with a toilet paper company, a podcast, and a day judging the You Glow Mama Awards.

"I've been chasing them, but we haven't heard back yet about the BBC Three gig. I'll keep you posted," she says, with a little shrug.

While Irene says she supports my plans to pivot into TV presenting, to use the following I've built to make a real-life name for Emmy Jackson independent of Mamabare, it's quite clear she doesn't actually think I'm cut out to be the next Stacey Dooley. Sadly, this is a view that seems to be shared by most people who work in TV. I'll admit I'm not a natural—somehow the honest mum stuff that sounds so plausible written down feels fake and forced on-screen, and it's harder to come up with it off the cuff with a camera trained on my face, so my eyes dart around wildly and I stumble over words. But I didn't get the Instagram thing right straightaway, and now look where we are. I'm playing the long game here, and every audition is a little less awful than the last, every screen test not quite as awkward.

I can't be answering 442 daily messages from strangers forever.

"There's one more thing we need to discuss. You've got a busy month coming up, and I don't think you're going to manage all your engagements, and keep on top of everything else, on your own with a newborn. So we have found you an assistant."

Irene can see I am about to object. She holds her hand up.

"Don't worry. It won't cost you a thing, I'll take care of it. She's one of my new signings, actually. I pitched it to her as an opportunity to be mentored by one of my stars. A pretty little thing. Likes hats," she says. "Her name is Winter, and she'll be at your house on Monday morning at ten a.m."

It is clear that's the end of that discussion.

Irene spends the last five minutes of our meeting rattling off my media appearances: TV and radio rent-a-mum guest slots for which I generally just have to offer a couple of uncontroversial opinions on whatever parenting topic has hit the news and then, if possible, drop in a mention of the #greydays campaign, as it's Mamabare's *thing*. For an influencer, a pet cause gives us something to bang on about when we run out of things to say about ourselves.

All the mental health stuff has been getting a bit too depressing recently, though—my downbeat posts aren't doing so well with engagement, and that's been putting some brands off. It's hard to sell shower gel the next post along from a heartfelt monologue about forgetting who you are as a human being after having a baby. We can't drop the campaign entirely in case someone else muscles in on the territory, so we've decided to introduce a #yaydays strand for some counterbalance. We need a big wow event to launch it, an authentic reason for a real party that my pod of A-list Instamums can be persuaded to come to without demanding to be paid.

There's an obvious contender: Coco's fourth birthday party.

CHAPTER FIVE

Dan

We don't often argue, Emmy and I. Very early on in our relationship, I realized there was no point. Whether or not we argue, she'll get her way eventually, and at least if we don't argue I don't find myself getting the silent treatment or having to apologize. And for the most part, I must admit that once the dust has settled, she does pretty much always turn out to have been right. About that weird thick silver wedding ring I wanted? Right all along. About the lights in the living room? So right. A great many of the things, in fact, that I have tried to dig my heels in about and made a fuss about over the years have turned out to be, in retrospect, absurd.

I guess the truth is that marriage really is about compromise. Which is not to say I always feel that we are compromising equally, or that we are meeting in the middle. Which is not to say that I always feel Emmy has necessarily fully thought through the impact that her life choices will make on the rest of us, the pressures they might place on us as a unit. Nevertheless, the fact remains that we are a unit, a team, and if you stop being a team, then a marriage stops being a marriage. If I had been allowed to write my own wedding vows—although thank God

Emmy put the kibosh on that idea—that was one of the things I would probably have said.

When it comes to my daughter's birthday party, though, I really feel like I have to put my foot down.

As usual, by the time I get around to thinking about something, it has already been on Emmy's mind for weeks. The only reason I even brought the topic up was because Mum reminded me it was Coco's birthday soon and asked what we were going to do for it. I said I wasn't sure yet but I was pretty certain Emmy had something planned, and Mum laughed, although I am unclear what part of this she thought I was joking about. The truth is, much as I might sometimes bristle at always having to ask my wife what we are doing on a given weekend, or whether I am free on a particular night, like most modern husbands I do defer to her when it comes to remembering things, organizing our social lives, making most of our plans.

It turned out what Emmy had planned for Coco's birthday was a *proper event*.

"Are you sure about this?" I asked her.

I had been envisioning something somewhat lower-key. Something personal. Something private. Something involving slightly fewer people running around with clipboards.

She and her agent had already planned it, she told me. Where it was going to be, who was going to be there, who the brand partner would be—all on account of the content, of course. They had been scouting locations and getting quotes from caterers for ages.

"So it's an Instaparty," I said to her. "An Instravaganza."

She gave me a look.

"And who's coming?"

She told me.

"What about Coco's friends from nursery? What about my friends? Am I allowed to invite any of my family along?"

She said she supposed we would have to invite my mother. Although maybe, thinking about it, under the circumstances, it would be better if we made this the official party and then had a separate thing a bit nearer to Coco's actual birthday for close friends and relatives and those sorts of people.

"Two parties?" I asked. "Like the Queen?"

Emmy shrugged.

"And I suppose all the other Instamums will be at the official party, swanning around?"

"Yes, Dan, that is kind of how it works," she told me. "We have discussed this."

I expect it was pretty obvious from the look on my face how I felt about the prospect of spending the afternoon of my daughter's birthday with that lot. Emmy's pod? Her clique, more like. What is it that swims in pods, after all, in real life? Is it not, among other things, killer whales? I swear to God you've never met a more awful bunch of people in your life. The kind of people who are always looking over your shoulder when you're talking to them and not even bothering to hide it—and half the time you find they're actually looking into a mirror. The kind of people who start talking to someone else when you're halfway through telling an anecdote. The kind of people, to cut a long story short, who I despise.

And yet somehow I seem to be stuck with them.

I probably spend more time these days with Emmy's pod than I do with any of my real friends, the people I actually like and enjoy seeing and have something in common with.

There are five of them in the inner circle, including Emmy.

I think of all of them the one I like least is Hannah Bagshott, who also happens to be Emmy's closest rival, with six hundred thousand followers. Instahandle: boob_and_the_gang. The look: blond bob, white slogan T-shirt, distressed jeans, red lipstick. Gimmick: formerly a professional doula. Posts about: leaky boobs, chafed nipples, and the endless ups and downs of her relationship with her husband, Miles (often accompanied by black-and-white wedding shots of them both). Children: four (Fenton, Jago, Bertie, and Gus). Special issue: breast-feeding in public. To promote greater acceptance of which, she organizes mass feed-ins in places where women who are breastfeeding have been asked to cover up—pubs, restaurants, once a major department store. Her husband, by the way, is an absolute bellend.

Bella Williams, aka themumpowermentcoach—the oldest of the inner circle and a part-time headhunter with a full-time, live-in nanny—is the one I least dread getting stuck in a conversation with. This isn't saying much. Single. Ismael, the father of her child, Rumi, is a Turkish painter who I think is now back in Turkey. I've never been quite sure whether he is a painter of, say, portraits and landscapes or of walls and fences. Apparently I did meet him once. Bella runs networking events for working mums and charges through the nose for them. Insta-issue: imposter syndrome—or, to be more specific, *mumposter syndrome*, a term I am pretty sure she invented, something about always feeling like you're about to be exposed as a terrible mother and a useless employee, a fraud both at home and at work. Bella is evidently not big on irony.

Next up is the_hackney_mum. Sara Clarke. Interests: interior design. Also owns a shop selling macramé hanging baskets and chunky jewelry and paintings of people in old-fashioned clothes but with animal heads. Talks a lot about the two or three months she once spent living on a canal boat. Children: Isolde, Xanthe, and Casper, who all have exactly the same haircut despite one of them being a boy. Fun fact: knows themumpowermentcoach from Cheltenham Ladies' College. Issue she thinks we should all be talking more about: maternal incontinence. I suspect that by the time she got around to trying to identify a maternal taboo to bust, all the good ones had already been taken.

Last and not quite least: whatmamawore. Suzy Wao. Distinguishing features: seems to be wearing a different pair of colorful glasses every time you see her or a picture of her. Otherwise it's exclusively vintage 1950s dresses. I'd met Suzy Wao at least ten times before she deigned to acknowledge we'd ever been introduced, and at least twenty before she remembered my name or what I do. On several occasions she has introduced me to other people as "Ian." Her husband is a very quiet man with an enormous beard, who's usually drinking a stubby beer in the corner of the room and wearing one of those collarless jackets French workmen do. It's unclear to me what he does for a living, but I think someone once told me he was a potter. Children: Betty and Etta. Starting a conversation about: body positivity.

I asked if we had to invite *all* of them.

"We have been to all their kids' birthdays," Emmy reminded me.

Exactly, I thought to myself. *Have we not suffered enough?*

At Xanthe Clarke's, we were all on a narrowboat repainted specially for the occasion in bright stripes and blobs, going up and down the canal from Islington to King's Cross and back again. This took three hours, before which it had already taken an hour for the various combinations of mums and kids to have their pictures taken in front of the boat. By the time we set off, it was raining and there was only room for half of us in the covered section. I was in my shirtsleeves. At one point the rain was refilling my wineglass faster than I was drinking. At several points I was seriously considering swimming for it.

There is a story—sadly apocryphal—that when Catherine the Great, Empress of Russia, visited Crimea in 1787, her lover, Prince Potemkin, had a series of fake villages constructed—villages one wall thick, like stage sets, to be viewed from her passing barge, complete with well-fed waving actors in peasant garb—in order to fool her into thinking that the land was flourishing and her subjects happy.

I often think of these things, these events, as Potemkin parties: pure spectacle, confected entirely for online purposes. They are not about the party games or the food or the drink or about anyone having a good time. They are entirely about the filtered photo of bunting against a brick wall—that perfect snap of someone pretending to smile as they pretend to whack a piñata; the lettering on the cupcakes, the giant foil balloons, the arty video of the entertainer blowing bubbles. Not to mention the contractually requisite number of images of the venue and mentions of its name, the carefully agreed-upon number of tags and hashtags of each sponsoring brand—the caterer, the florist, the makeup artist, the drinks company, the entertainment. It's all great exposure for them, of course.

What it isn't, for anyone, is very much *fun*.

I shall never forget the look Suzy Wao gave me when I picked up a cronut at one of her parties before she'd had a chance to have the arrangement photographed.

When I mentioned this to Emmy, she informed me—with a faint, wry smile—that fun was something people used to have in their twenties.

What I actually meant was fun for the kids. Every time you see a picture of a child having what appears to be a good time at a party on Instagram, just bear in mind how many shots it probably took to get that one perfect picture. How many times they had to pretend to be laughing at something and not get it quite right. How many times they had to pretend to be jumping with glee through a hoop, or zooming with joy down a slide. How all the time they spent pretending to do kid stuff could have been spent doing actual kid stuff.

I ask Emmy where we are having this birthday party and she tells me. I groan, and get a warning look.

"Listen, if you want to organize something yourself . . . ," she tells me.

"Maybe I will," I say. Maybe I actually will. A real party, with our real friends, and Coco's. The sort of thing a normal family might do. No specially commissioned murals, no officially sponsored goody bags, no professional photographers, none of that stuff. A birthday party like the ones I remember from my own childhood: a couple of bunches of balloons taped up around the place, a table with some snacks, a load of kids the same age hopped up on sugar screaming and shouting and having a whale of a time, a load of adults standing around drinking.

Coco is going to absolutely love it.

Emmy

I can spot an influencer at a hundred paces, and that's definitely one outside the Lord Napier right now. Yellow ditsy-print dress with buttons down the front, box-fresh white Converse, a giant wicker bag with pom-poms, and a Panama hat. So much highlighter on her cheekbones she's blinding me from across the road, eyebrows that could have been drawn on with a permanent marker, nude matte lipstick that wouldn't budge in a hurricane, and a choppy, jaw-length peroxide bob.

The dead giveaway, though, is the boyfriend dutifully snapping away with his iPhone (which means she's an amateur—serious players pay an actual photographer to use a real camera). This one is really going for it—twirling around, looking downward while she fiddles with a single strand of hair, holding his hand so it's just in shot and making out as if she's just about to open the pub door (she's not—it's nine thirty a.m.). To be fair, the Lord Napier *is* an unusually photogenic local. Outside, the walls are almost entirely covered with hanging baskets, bursting with yellow and white flowers and dripping with foliage.

If I'd remembered that my Irene-appointed assistant was starting today, I'd have been less surprised when, half an hour later, I opened the door to those eyebrows.

"Hi!" she says, holding out an arm jangling with charm bracelets. "I think you follow me, so you probably know who I am? Irene said you needed some help!"

"I'm sorry, remind me what your name is?" I say, rocking Bear back and forth in the sling to keep him asleep.

"I'm Winter! Wow, it's really nice in here. It always looks messy on your feed. And you look so, I don't know, chic? Navy is not your usual thing, is it? You're more, like, smiley rainbow mum? Oh my GOD, are all those for you? I mean, the dream!" She points at the pile of gifted glossy bags I haven't yet had a chance to go through, stuffed with clothes, beauty products, and what looks like a brand-new Nutri-Bullet.

"Just a second, I've got to WhatsApp my boyfriend and tell him this is the right house and I'll see him when I get home. Becket is just the best, so protective of me. I keep telling him he would be an amazing influencer, but he's concentrating on his music right now," she says earnestly as she types.

I welcome her in just to stop her talking, and ask her to take her shoes off, which she does. Her hat, in contrast, stays on all day.

After a brief tour of the house, I sit Winter down in the kitchen with our spare laptop and my old iPhone along with the relevant passwords she'll need. Irene calls to remind me what we agreed: Winter will manage my diary and, more important, be Mamabare when I can't—when I'm on a shoot, or at a lunch, launch, or dinner. I have to admit, I'm not hopeful that Winter's up to the task. She's already walked into the closet under the stairs thinking it's a bathroom.

Luckily, there isn't anything technical involved in the role, unless you count printing out the labels to mail the odd #greydays sweater or mug to a follower willing to part with forty-five pounds plus shipping and handling, but it is time-consuming. All my posts are photographed and written at least a fortnight in advance. But while she won't be posting, Winter will be monitoring the influencer gossip forums—it's all useful feedback, no matter how bitchy or sanctimonious—and answering my DMs, as well as liking and replying to comments. Which means I have to give her a crash course in how to speak Mamabare.

Winter takes out her notebook and puts on a serious face. I look winteriscoming up on Instagram. At a tiny eleven thousand followers, presumably at least a few thousand of which are bots Irene has bought, she's definitely at the micro end of influencer. She's already posted the shot of her outside the Lord Napier, twirling her dress while looking coquettishly at the ground. It's captioned: They Call Me Mellow Yellow, with buttercup emojis where the *o*s should be.

"Okay, the first thing to remember is that things work differently for an Instamum. *You* can get away with a coy look and a five-word caption. Look at your comments—'Your fringe is on point!' or 'Er, hallo SHOES!' Your followers just want to know where your handbag is from. *My* followers want to have a good old rummage around inside mine."

I run through the dos and don'ts. Everyone must have their comment acknowledged; every DM must have a reply. Sometimes you can't avoid getting into a longer conversation, but it's best to try and keep it light and leave it there.

You keep doing you, Mama! works well. But anything encouraging, with *mama* on the end, generally does the trick. And the trolls get as much love as the fans. "More, in fact," I explain, "because they're the ones that actually need it."

I've honed my approach over time to make sure I don't stoke the haters' rage. I am sure these are often women broken with grief for their old lives, powder kegs packed with fury at the terrible injustice of motherhood. They explode at me—not their husbands, not their health visitors, not the friends who inquire politely how they're doing with a newborn but don't really want to know the answer—because it doesn't matter if I know that they're not coping.

Another important lesson I've learned is that while I tell my followers that we're the same, I have to remember we're not, not *really*, and that I can't rub their noses in it. They're not *actually* friends, because as a rule, in the grand scheme of things, your friends are people pretty much like you: they live in the same sort of house, earn about the same, and their husbands are similar and do the same kinds of things for a living. They have more or less the same number of children, who pretty much all go to the same kind of school. There are small differences, obviously, but for the most part my friends and I and almost everyone I interact with socially in real life enjoy very much the same kind of generally comfortable, mostly contented, broadly financially stable existence. For better or worse, the same is not true of all those people who follow me online.

It's a simple case of knowing your audience—and it's astonishing how many aspiring Instamums get it wrong. Do you think an hourly employee with no benefits likes watching a well-off, middle-class white woman whine about the cost of childcare? Does a single mother like seeing you moan about your husband not taking the bins out? Does someone whose weekly grocery shop is a stretch think your complaints about the rumbling tummy that your #gifted green juice cleanse has given you are in any way charming?

Spilling stuff, exploding poos, Peppa Pig–triggered tantrums, tummy bugs. *Those* are the things I can complain about without alienating anyone. The universal *We've all been there, Mum* stuff. But even then, someone will always heckle and gripe. And when they do, I have to thank them for their valuable feedback and promise I'll learn and grow as a person.

"It's only the pervs who want to drink my breast milk and trolls who want my whole family to die in a fire that you can ignore." I laugh.

Winter looks terrified.

"Oh God, I didn't know. You never talk about them online!" she gasps.

"Irene says it's best not to make a thing of it, because they're harmless. They don't think we are real people—just avatars who only exist in a grid of tiny pictures on their phone. You couldn't do this job if you didn't believe that no matter what the trolls say, they'd never actually *do* anything—it's just sad, lonely people lurking on the internet."

It was during her pregnancy that Grace started to really spend a lot of time online. I can hardly blame her. In a lot of ways, Instagram, Facebook, Twitter—all of them—were an absolute lifesaver for her. When she first called me and told me she had an incompetent cervix, despite all the years I had spent working in a hospital I had to admit I had never heard of that before. The doctor had told her it was extremely uncommon. "And what does it mean?" I asked her, trying not to sound too obviously worried. "How are you feeling?" They had already been through so much, Jack and Grace, trying for a little one— had so many tests, such a long wait, so many disappointments and so much heartbreak. Everything this time had seemed to be going so well. Grace had not been suffering much from morning sickness so far. She was not as tired as she had been before. But until she went in for that scheduled checkup, she had no idea there was anything wrong with her cervix. It was just one of those things, the doctor had told her, a genetic quirk, that her cervix was shorter than usual, that as a result it might open too early, so she was at a heightened risk of giving birth prematurely. Did that explain . . . ? I asked her, trailing off. She said he thought it might have been a factor.

The doctor had told her there were a few things they could do. The usual procedure was a cervical cerclage, a stitch to prevent the cervix opening, to prevent her giving birth too soon. That was relatively straightforward, he told her, even if it sounded alarming. She told him she would do, would let them do, whatever it took. She had the operation at twelve weeks. It did not work—either her cervix was too short or it had already opened too far, or both—it was never entirely clear. She had already been warned that prolonged periods of time on her feet, any kind of even mildly strenuous activity, were to be avoided at all costs.

In the end, she spent almost the entire pregnancy lying down. Imagine. Just imagine. She was not allowed to walk anywhere. She was not allowed to drive. She was not even allowed to get up and make herself a cup of tea. The longest she was allowed to stand was five minutes, to have a shower in the morning.

Her work was very understanding, fortunately. Jack was brilliant. Even when she was at her lowest, her most frustrated, he could cheer her up, jolly her along. He was always thinking of nice little things to help her pass the time, picking up magazines, things for her to read and look at and do. He moved the TV upstairs so she could watch it, made sure the room looked nice, brought home flowers. He would cook the meals, do the cleaning, fetch her things. We used to joke about getting her a bell.

Of course, there were times when she got bored, fed up. There were times when she was bloody miserable. Her friends did call and email and send her little messages—but most of them were working all day or busy with their own kids and husbands and lives, and most of them were still living around here, which made it an hour's drive or even longer to Jack and Grace's, each way.

I do sometimes wonder how things might have been different if they had not moved out to the country after they got married, if they had not seen that fateful FOR SALE *sign from the motorway that day, had not gone back at the weekend to investigate, decided that out among the fields and the farms and the fresh air was where they wanted their kids to grow up. It was a gorgeous house, don't get me wrong. Beautiful views, massive great garden with a little stream at the end of it, and Grace and Jack did the whole place up something lovely. But it was not easy to get to. Not somewhere you could just pop around to the neighbors' or down to the shops; not somewhere where anybody would ever just pop in on you. Even the postman used to complain about having to drive all that way up the lane for just one house, getting his* van muddy. I used to go and see her as often as I could. We would sit and watch films, talk.

Most of the time, though, it was just her and the same four walls, the same cracks in the ceiling, the same door with the same dressing gown hanging off it, the same bit of tree and the same stretch of sky, which were all she could see out the window from her bed. Grace used to spend a lot of time on her phone. First she would check the Daily Mail, then Facebook, then Twitter, then Instagram, then her email—and then by that time there would be stuff she had not seen on the Daily Mail website and the cycle would repeat itself.

She always used to say that what appealed to her about the mums she followed on Instagram was how open they were, how honest about all the things they had been through, their struggles and disappointments and heartaches. It really made her feel less isolated, less alone, she told me. Like someone else out there understood what she was going through.

It is a gift, that way, the internet, I suppose. Sometimes it is absolutely terrible, being on your own.

Very occasionally, once or twice a month maybe, there are times when I forget for a microsecond that Grace is gone. When I am half-awake just before the alarm clock goes in the morning, for instance, when I have just had a funny dream and I find myself thinking I must tell Grace about it and then it hits me with a jolt that I can't, that I won't ever be able to tell her anything ever again. And then I think about all the other things I want to tell her and I can't. Like how much I love her. Like how proud I always was to be her mum. How much I miss her.

And that is when the anger, the real anger, comes.

CHAPTER SIX

Dan

It turns out when you are in your mid- to late thirties it is actually quite hard to get people out on a Saturday afternoon at a week's notice.

I guess in some ways what I had been hoping to recapture with Coco's party was a little of what it used to be like living on this street when I first bought the house, back when I shared it with Will and Ben and we used to drink at the Lord Napier after work every single night. When Emmy and I were first going out, we had our second date there, then our third and possibly our fourth as well. Later in our relationship, after Emmy had moved in and the guys had moved out, we would often pop across the road for a pint or a glass of wine; if there was nothing in the fridge we'd just head over to grab a burger and not even need to take our coats. We used to drift over for Sunday lunch with the papers and stay the whole afternoon.

Coco's party was not like that at all.

It was Monday before I managed to catch the right person at the pub to speak to about booking a room, and it was Tuesday before I finally got around to sending the invitations out. The first responses I got were two bounce-backs saying the email address was not recognized and an out of office. All was silent for a few hours, then steadily the apologies began trickling in. I'd invited around fifty people in total. About twenty of them already had some other London-based social commitment on Saturday—although about half offered to swing by for a quick visit if they got the chance. A dozen or so were away that weekend. One of the couples emailed back to remind me they'd moved to Dubai eighteen months ago, which triggered a vague memory of getting an email I never got around to answering about a leaving drinks thing. Three people were at the football. Two couples would either have literally just had a baby or be very overdue. One person—a writer friend of mine whose first novel came out about the same time as mine did—was reading from his latest at a literary festival in Finland. Polly had a work commitment. Several others replied enthusiastically over the next few days and said they were bang up for it but they had to check with their partner what the plans were and then never got back to me. Quite a few didn't bother replying at all.

By three o'clock in the afternoon on the day of the party, only about ten people had shown up—and two of them had already left, having some other kid's party to pop into elsewhere.

Around four o'clock, the landlord took me aside and told me he was going to have to open up our bit of the pub to other people. It was absolutely heaving downstairs, he explained apologetically.

I could hardly object, really.

At least the children seemed to be having a nice time, kicking balloons around, stamping on them—and I was glad to see that Coco was joining in and enjoying herself and screaming and shouting just as loudly as anyone else.

While the kids were playing and Emmy was handing out slices of cake, I got stuck talking to a friend from school, Andrew, who had driven down from Berkhamsted with his wife. He seemed disappointed not to see more of the old gang here, kept asking if Millsy was coming, whether I still see Simon Cooper or that bloke Phil Thornton. I do not.

I have not seen Phil Thornton since I bumped into him in a club in Clapham in 2003.

Andrew asked if I was still a writer, and with a slightly forced smile I told him I liked to think so. "Working on a novel at the moment?" he asked. I gave a nod, still smiling. I am still working on the same novel I have been working on for the past eight years, as it happens. This has at times been a source of some slight tension in my marriage. There have been occasions when Emmy has suggested I just send it out or let someone else read what I've got or asked if she can have a look and see if she can help with anything. Mostly nowadays we do not discuss the topic at all.

I am, in a sense, the victim of circumstances.

The truth is, for most of my twenties and early thirties I didn't really feel the need to earn a living. Nor did it ever feel like I was under a lot of financial pressure to finish my second book. When my father died, years ago, the summer between my first and second years at Cambridge, he left me a fairly substantial amount of money, to be administered by a trust fund until I turned twenty-five. To that money, my mother added additional funds from the proceeds of my father's life insurance. It's basically what I've been living on ever since. Quite a lot of it went into buying the house, of course. Quite a lot more went toward redoing the house. I've eked out the rest of it pretty well over the last few years. We did sell the film rights to my novel, and for a while it even looked like it was actually going to get made. I've penned a couple of screenplays on spec, had meetings with TV producers, tried my hand at short stories. I spent about six months bashing out a thriller, just to bring some cash in—my agent read it and didn't think it really played to my strengths. As for my second novel proper, the one I have spent all this time laboring over, there have been multiple occasions when I have been tempted just to scrap the whole thing and start writing something new and different and fresh instead. My laptop is full of openings of novels I was briefly very excited about and abandoned after about five paragraphs. There have been multiple occasions, usually in the middle of the night, when I have considered quitting writing entirely, retraining as a teacher or a lawyer or a plumber. Last time I checked, my life savings—all that I have left of them—consisted of about seventeen hundred pounds.

Sometimes it comes to me with a pang that I will never be one of *Granta*'s best young British novelists.

I am aware this is not exactly what Emmy would call relatable content.

By about half past four, the last of our guests were donning their coats and attempting to gather their children and wandering around making sure they had definitely got everything before they headed off, and Emmy gave me a look to indicate that it was about time we started to think about doing the same.

I guess one moral I ought to draw from all this is that there is a reason I do not usually get to do the social organizing.

All afternoon the same woman—white-haired, I would guess in her mid- to late sixties, neatly dressed—had been sitting in her coat at the same seat at the same corner table, nursing the same half-pint glass of Diet Coke and occasionally smiling indulgently as one of the kids careered into the back of her chair, watching fondly as Coco ran around the room shrieking. From time to time we would catch each other's eye and give each other a little smile of acknowledgment. I didn't have the heart to tell her the room was booked for a private function. Given the lack of other takers, I was tempted to go over and see if she wanted any cake.

Emmy's party, in contrast, Coco's "official" birthday celebration, is a complete triumph. Of course it is. Emmy has worked bloody hard to ensure that it will be.

The thing people always get wrong about influencing for a living is that they think this stuff is easy—organizing events, getting the right pictures, planning the various neat little touches and flourishes in the arrangements and the decorations and the layout of this room. That they could do it if they wanted to—which, of course, they don't. They hardly even look at Instagram, not more than five or six times a day, when they check in to see what my wife has been up to, what she has posted, what a load of other people have had to say about it.

I probably thought that myself, at the start. That influencing was easy, I mean. That all you had to do was be a bit fit and take a half-decent photo of yourself or a nice meal and say something appropriately banal once or twice a day. That as long as you were pretty enough, bland enough, I took it for granted the followers would flock in—with the only limit on your success being the value you placed on your own privacy.

This is absolute nonsense.

It's not that people should be more cynical about social media or influencers, it's that they are cynical about them in such naive ways.

One misconception it took me some time to rid myself of was that the words in an Instagram post don't matter, that anybody could write this stuff, that just because the syntax is awry and even the cliché they were aiming for has come out garbled, no thought or effort or planning was required.

This is the kind of intellectual snobbery I often find my mother falling into when we talk about what Emmy does for a living—which is something, for the record, I try to avoid. "Well, of course," she might comment, "it's not real writing like you do." Meaning, I suppose, that Emmy has never spent a whole morning hesitating over a comma, never anguished over the rhythm of a sentence, never felt her heart sink as she realizes the mot juste she's spent hours grasping for was the same mot juste she used two pages earlier. Meaning, I guess, that her readers are just normal people, looking at their phones in the car waiting to pick the kids up from school, who let her know when they like what she's saying and it resonates. My imagined readers, on the other hand, are some combination of the ghost of Flaubert, a snarky tutor I failed to impress at Cambridge, a bunch of book reviewers (most of whom I hate), my deceased father, and the agent I suspect gave up any hope some time ago that anyone connected to my literary career would be making any money. The truth is there is something genuinely amazing about Emmy's ability to find the right words (which are often, technically, the wrong words) to establish a connection with people. It is a talent. It is a skill. It is something she has put time and effort and thought into.

Because the other thing, the main thing, that people fail to understand is that this is work. *Hard* work. Planning ahead. Knowing when and where and how to mention your brand partners, finding ways of just slipping in references to Pampers, Gap, Boden, as if they're simply part of the texture of your life, the brand names that come to mind rather than ones who have paid thousands of pounds for a mention. Emmy might split the occasional infinitive, but if you think she's winging it when it comes to strategy, you are very much mistaken. There are spreadsheets of this stuff, timelines that stretch off months into the future. Possibly years. I suspect there are parts of the grand plan that even I'm not privy to.

And just like everyone else, Instagrammers put on a different persona when they are in professional mode. Just as you would if you worked in a restaurant, or a university, or a school. And when Emmy is at one of these events, she's at work. She's making sure the photographer gets the right photos, that all the people who want a moment with her get one (as long as they have something to offer in return, of course). She's thinking three steps ahead to ensure she doesn't get stuck talking to the wrong person and that whoever she's ducking doesn't even realize ("Bella, you gorgeous creature, you must talk to the fascinating Lucy! I have spent weeks telling you all about each other!") they're being ducked. She's making a mental note, when she meets someone, of that one thing they tell her she'll remember and that will make them think they really made an impression on her when they meet again—and that will remind her, when they do, of their name. She's keeping an eye on Coco—or at least keeping an eye on the person who's been charged with keeping an eye on Coco. She's keeping an eye on who is talking to who, what alliances are forming, what tensions are beginning to simmer that she might be able to exploit. She's laughing. She's joking. She's talking shop. She's listening. She is making people feel special.

Sometimes I watch my wife across the room and I am genuinely dazzled by her.

Emmy

Almost as much work has gone into making this day just right as I put into our wedding. The decorations, the guest list, the cake, my outfit—all elements have been considered and reconsidered, every angle fussed over and finessed to ensure that everything is perfectly calibrated for maximum shareability.

I can't take all the credit, of course. I may be the host, but it was Irene who managed to kick off a bidding war over the sponsorship of Coco's fourth birthday as the launch of #yaydays. So as well as covering the not-inconsiderable cost of today's event, a big fashion brand has committed to a forty-thousand-pound partnership selling T-shirts for mums, dads, and kids with #yaydays on the back and #greydays on the front, with a portion of the profits going toward helping women battle the blues.

Irene and I did agonize over whether an event this big, this obviously expensive, would be unrelatable for my followers. But a big brand was hardly going to put their name to carrot sticks and ham sandwiches and musical chairs in a drafty church hall—nor would any other influencers have turned up. We decided the charity angle, and the fact that my darling, bighearted Coco had been so happy that her birthday party could help cheer up mamas who were sad, meant it wouldn't attract too much bile.

The brand got approval on the guest list and are expecting ten influencers with followings of over a hundred thousand today. My pod is a dead cert, and the rest are hardly a stretch. There's also a handful of editors and journalists on the list—including Jess, the interviewer from the *Sunday Times*, whom I make a mental note to personally thank for the gushing profile piece—and a small swarm of micro-influencers.

They scare me a little bit as a group, these minnows, because while I'm impressed at their determination to make it and their commitment to befriending us big fish—all instantly commenting on and liking everything we post, inventing podcasts just to invite us on for an interview—some of them are borderline stalkerish. If one of us gets a new haircut, or a hot pink lipstick, or a limited-edition pair of Nikes, you can guarantee at least three will have done the same thing by the end of the week. It's one of the reasons that micro-influencers are basically indistinguishable from one another. Thank God Irene sent everyone a personalized #yaydays T-shirt with their name printed on the back or they'd be impossible to tell apart.

Polly is on the list too, as she couldn't make Dan's get-together, but was determined to come, to see Coco and meet Bear. In a way it's surprising, as Polly would usually do anything to avoid a big party. I used to have to twist her arm in our teens, coaxing her into a fancy top and chunky heels and over to whoever's house while their parents were away. It was much the same in our twenties, to be honest. Although she would usually enjoy it for a bit, she was always the one dragging me out of the door, and occasionally peeling me off the floor after that one last glass had turned into five. But she makes an effort where Coco is concerned.

Still, it was a hard-won battle persuading Irene to waste a valuable invite on a civilian, even one who can still recite my landline number from 1992 off by heart. My agent's view of female friendship is that if you've got something nice to say about someone, say it under an Instagram post, where everyone can read it.

"What's the point, Emmy? She's an English teacher who isn't even on social media—she doesn't exist, as far as the brand is concerned. And the room can only hold seventy-five." She sighed, penciling her in begrudgingly at number seventy-six. "We'd better hope someone's sick. She can't have a plus one, though," she added.

She didn't need one. Her math teacher husband, Ben, has never been my biggest fan, and I doubt very much he'd come even if he were invited. I'm sure he thinks I'm bad for Polly—the fun friend who returned his clever, sensible wife home tipsy and giggling whenever we used to go out. I did vaguely try to get him on my side when they got together, inviting them round for Sunday lunches and suggesting weekends away in seaside cottages, just the four of us. It was clear he was never that keen, and Polly's excuses got ever more vague and half-hearted.

I have also always had a strong sense that Ben disapproves of what I now do for a living, and Dan has made it quite clear he would rather spend a sunny Saturday afternoon in IKEA than stuck in yet another conversation in which Ben explains in detail one of his hobbies—which include kayaking, bouldering, and Krav Maga—in his deathly monotone. So we don't see them together often. I don't see Polly alone much either anymore, truth be told, although she knows she's still important to me, I'm sure.

Not everyone is lucky enough to have a best friend as loyal, or as low-key, as Polly.

After my mother, Polly is probably the person who knows me best in the whole world. Actually, depending on what time of day you ask my mother, Polly may know me better. She never complains no matter how many times she sees two little blue ticks on WhatsApp but gets no response for a week, or I promise to call her back then don't, or reply to one of her long emails with a couple of kisses. Somehow, she always manages to catch me just as I am heading down the steps to the Tube or about to give Coco her dinner or Bear a bath. Then I ring back later and miss her, or mean to ring back and forget.

I haven't been a great friend to her recently. I haven't been a good friend to anyone, if I'm honest. But when your entire income relies on making people you've never met feel like you know them intimately, it can be tough to find the energy to keep up with the people you do know. And when your whole *thing* is opening up, all you want to do in the bits in between is shut down.

The truth is, I have never been one of those people with a long-term gang of close friends. I don't have a WhatsApp group of girls I met twenty years ago at ballet class or Brownies, who've been together through bad boyfriends, nasty bosses, cheap holidays, and cheaper hangovers. I know this puzzles Dan, who's pretty much had the same gang of five or so close mates since university, all of whom have lived together and been one another's groomsmen and are godparents to one another's kids, even if they can't be expected to turn up to a kid's birthday party on a Saturday afternoon with less than a week's notice. The big point of difference, I suppose, is that Dan's mates are fairly straightforward and his friendships with them simple. They meet, they drink pints, they talk about books and films and podcasts. I can't imagine any of his inner circle calling him in tears because they've been belittled in a meeting, or texting to demand a heart-to-heart chat and a vat of pinot grigio when their marriage is on the rocks. Female friendships, most of them anyway, need nurturing. A lot of nurturing. And I've never much enjoyed that. Never been especially good at it, one-on-one.

Perhaps that is why my relationship with Polly has endured so long. She isn't a drama queen, nor has she ever had any desire to be the center of attention. In fact, that's probably why we worked as a teenage duo—Polly, quiet and bespectacled and eager to please, dressed by her mum in knitwear and sensible shoes, and me, all Teflon-coated self-confidence in platform trainers and frayed black satin. Very little has changed, bar the trainers.

She's the first guest through the door at the party, looking every inch the English teacher, in a navy wrap dress, cardigan, nude tights, and ballet pumps. In fact, she looks so much like she's wearing our old school uniform that I can't help but smile, especially when I see that she's clutching a badly wrapped teddy bear with one ear poking through the paper. I make a beeline for her.

"Polly Pocket!" I yell, throwing my arms around her neck. "Thank you so much for coming!"

"Don't be silly, Ems, how could I not say happy birthday to Coco? I am so sorry I couldn't make the other party; I was helping out at the school play." Polly smiles. "But I really wanted to see you, so . . ."

I lower my voice, leaning into her ear. "I just have to deal with some work people, then I promise you'll have my undivided attention." I point her in the direction of Dan, who is loitering by Bear's buggy while he naps. Sometimes I really do feel for him at these things, bored to tears trying to make small talk about engagement figures, impressions, and reach. He got in a right grump this morning, after I suggested he might want to wear an ironed shirt for the photos—I could hear him stomping around and swearing as he wrestled with the ironing board.

He'll be pleased to see someone he can talk to. Polly couldn't be more different from the stampede of Instamums in their neon Adidas trainers and denim jackets that pile in behind her a few seconds later. I take a deep breath and start to say my hellos to every single one.

"Tabitha, you legend! Do *not* tell me you only had a baby two weeks ago. You look incredible!" I say, giving her a huge hug, then realizing her T-shirt, which is emblazoned with her Instagram handle, tabbiesbabbies, is completely covered in her leaking breast milk—and now mine is too. I spot Winter, stationed by the buffet to ensure the kids keep their hands off it all until the mamas get their content, and cross the room.

"Did you bring my spare T-shirts? I'm not sure these giant milk stains scream #yaydays . . . ," I whisper.

"Oh, shit, Emmy, I'm so sorry. I totally forgot. I can go home and get them?" she says, biting one side of her bottom lip.

"Would you mind? You can jump in an Uber and do a round trip. I'll book one now," I tell her.

As she scurries off, I am pleased to see that the selfie mural by the door, with its polka dots, rainbows, and a giant speech bubble with #yaydays written in it, is being preened in front of and posed against by the guests. Nearby, there is a three-tier red velvet cake from which M&M's will spill once cut, plus COCO spelled out in the giant foil balloons and a unicorn piñata hanging from the ceiling. We also have a wall of bright pink flowers with MAMABARE picked out in yellow roses in the middle, which was my idea. Though now I see it, I have to admit Irene was right—it *does* look a little bit like a funeral wreath for poor old Gran.

Coco, in her T-shirt and tutu, her outfit accessorized with fairy wings and a fireman's helmet, is sitting on a sofa in the corner of the room playing with her dolly. I do worry that she might start thinking these sorts of parties are the norm and getting sniffy at her nursery friends' soft play and pizza efforts, but, generally, my daughter is pretty blasé about the glitzy parties and goody bags. She'd rather be on the swings or putting her teddies to bed.

Once I have done the Instamum honor guard, making sure everyone has their shot and story, I spot Polly again chatting animatedly in the corner to Jess from the *Sunday Times*. I begin to make my way over, just as my mother arrives. Even late and at the shitfaced end of tipsy, Virginia is perfectly turned out. She's spent the past week demanding the fashion brand sponsoring today's party courier a vast selection of outfits back and forth from their London HQ to her mock-Tudor pile near Winchester for approval. She's also blagged every beauty treatment she can think of ("Darling, what do you think of microblading? Instagram people all have those big, bushy eyebrows. What do you mean, it's a tattoo? Don't be silly, who on earth would *tattoo their face?*"), cold-calling PRs and introducing herself as the mother of "the world's most important Instamother" with her own following of fifty-four thousand.

The usually unembarrassable Irene actually called to ask if I could have a word, but she knows very well Virginia can't be managed.

She knows this because she's her manager.

Instagrans have turned into quite a lucrative sideline for Irene, and my mother has taken to social media like a natural. She doesn't need the money, but that doesn't stop her delightedly squirreling freebies like a survivalist stockpiles baked beans, and insisting on discounts for dinners, free nights in spa hotels, and once, memorably, a brand-new Range Rover, by waving her iPhone and demanding, "Don't you know who my daughter is?" Her dedication is impressive—it makes me sad she's never had a career to plow this much effort and energy into. With her brains and beauty, she could have done anything she put her mind to, if Dad hadn't sucked the drive out of her. I've always sworn that I wouldn't waste my life like that.

The irony, of course, is that in many ways, we're identical. Or at the very least, she's responsible for my defining characteristics. Dr. Fairs traces almost every personality trait of mine directly back to Ginny and her drinking. Trust issues? Tick. Obsessive avoidance of conflict and confrontation? Yep, that too. And a fear of abandonment and a need to control everything and everyone around me. I guess it's easy to distill an alcoholic down to their negative effects on the people who love them, but what Dr. Fairs doesn't see is what a fizzing ball of energy she is, how she can change the temperature of a room, how she draws people to her like toddlers to a tube of Smarties. She can be a complete and utter pain in the arse, but it's impossible to dislike my mother.

There's a ripple of excitement among the guests when they realize who this size-six whirlwind of Chanel No. 5 and Chablis is. She's so busy hamming it up over by the piñata that she doesn't see her granddaughter come for a cuddle and accidently bats her around the head, sending her flying. Coco picks herself up and dusts herself down, little brow furrowed and bottom lip wobbling. Finally, my mother spots me and comes over.

"Darling! I nearly chose that skirt!" she cries. "Decided it was a bit frumpy in the end. Good God, what are those hideous stains on your T-shirt? Now, where is my beautiful Coco?" She sashays across the room to the flower wall, looks it up and down disapprovingly. "Bit funereal, no?"

"Mum, this is the journalist who wrote the lovely piece about us. And you remember Polly. We were at school together. She was maid of honor at our wedding."

With some effort, Ginny's newly microbladed eyebrows knit.

"Oh gosh, yes, Polly. You've not changed a bit! Always so pretty— not that you knew it. I used to say to Emmy that *you'd* be the beautiful one if you just tried a little harder!"

Polly shoots my mother the close-lipped smile I remember well, as Virginia neatly sidesteps a floral-print toddler making a dash for the cake table.

"I am sure children used to be better behaved than this in my day," she tuts. "Where are your little ones today, then, Polly?"

"Oh, we're not . . . I don't actually . . ."

I realize, with a twinge of regret, that I don't know whether Polly and Ben are trying or not, and am about to change the subject when I spot Irene out of the corner of my eye, with her arm around the brand's PR. She's mouthing something at me and gesturing that I should join them. Thankfully, Winter finally arrives armed with my clean T-shirt a second later. I give Polly's arm a squeeze as I point at the milk stains, which have dried into chalky rings. "Sorry, Pol, excuse me, both of you. Back in a second. Just got to sort this out before we cut the cake!"

When I look for her ten minutes later, she's gone.

"Christ, what did you say to her, Mother?" I ask, as if I am joking, which I am not really.

Virginia feigns offense.

"What do you mean, what did I say? I didn't say anything at all. We were chatting away perfectly happily and then Coco came over with her doll and asked if she wanted to play babies and your friend couldn't get away quick enough. Went barreling off across the room looking like she was about to start blubbering."

Virginia indicates with a finger the direction in which Polly departed.

I eye my mother narrowly.

"Are you *sure* you didn't say something?"

She literally crosses her heart, the wine sloshing dangerously in the glass she's holding as she does so.

"You know, if you ask me, there was always something a bit odd about that girl."

Westfield was a trial run. A test for myself, to see how far I was willing to go. How far I would be capable of going.

I could have taken her. Just like that. One of the things that surprised me was how smoothly the whole thing went. I followed them from the house to the station, down the stairs to the platform, onto the Tube. We were sitting on opposite sides of the carriage. He, the dad, Dan, was reading a copy of Metro. She was watching something on his phone. At one point, she glanced up, caught me looking, and frowned slightly. I gave her a broad, friendly smile. She returned her attention to whatever she was watching.

I guess if you are Coco Jackson, you are used to people giving you funny looks, recognizing you, doing a double take. Being a woman in her sixties, of course, I get exactly the opposite treatment. For three days I ensconced myself in a corner of the Lord Napier with a cup of coffee or a pot of tea or a sandwich, watching them come and go—Emmy struggling to get the pushchair over the front doorstep, one of them taking Coco to nursery in the morning and the other bringing her back in the afternoon. Seeing the parcels come in, all the deliveries. Nobody gave me a second look. People came and sat at the table next to me and laughed and talked and drank their pints and ate their lunch and left, and I doubt half of them even noticed I was there.

Dan didn't notice either.

While he and Coco waited in the queue at Starbucks for his coffee that day, I was two people behind them. As they wandered around Foyles—he checked to see if they had his book in stock; they didn't—I was never more than one aisle over. I was pretending to check out the pirate ship in the window while he and Coco looked around in the Lego shop. When they paused for a pretzel and a sit-down in the food court, I was one booth away.

By their third shoe shop, Dan was visibly flagging. He had been checking the time on his phone about every five minutes all day. Now he was doing so even more frequently. In his defense, it did seem to take the person who went down to the stockroom an age to come back with shoes in the right size, and then there was some business with the card reader not working properly the first time they tried it . . .

Coco was standing near the door of the shop, beside a display of those trainers with the heels that light up when you walk or jump or run in them.

"Those are lovely," I commented.

She didn't look up.

"Hey," I said. "I found this lying around, just over there, and I thought to myself, Some little girl has been playing with that teddy and dropped it. Is it yours?"

She looked from me to the teddy, then back at me again. Then she thought for a bit.

"I think it might be," she said eventually.

Grace really used to love it, that teddy. You can see from the state of the thing how many times I had to wash it over the years. How many times it got dropped on the floor of the bus or dragged through a puddle or it managed to fall out of the front basket of her bike and end up covered in muddy tire prints. Even after she had grown up and left home, I always used to leave it on her bed when she was staying at mine for the night. We used to joke, she and I, about how one day she would have a son or a daughter and it would be their teddy. I can't claim that I had originally intended it that way—not consciously, anyhow—but it did strike me seeing Coco with it in her arms, holding it just the same way Grace always used to, the same way I could imagine a three-year-old Ailsa doing, that there was a certain horrible irony, a certain grim appropriateness, to that particular choice of stuffed toy, this particular use for it.

No one gave either of us a second look as Coco and I proceeded hand in hand along the gallery or when I picked her up in my arms to go down the escalator. The only person who did catch my eye was a gran wheeling a pushchair with a sleeping baby in it, and she gave me a little smile of solidarity. I smiled back, but even as I did so, it occurred to me once again—with the same abrupt, thumping sense of loss, anger, and pain as ever—that I am never going to get to do any of this. I am never going to get to spend the afternoon looking after my granddaughter, never going to get to watch her toddling about the playground, never going to get to push her shrieking happily on the swing, never going to get to see her boldly going down the slide on her own for the first time. I'm never going to get to do any of those things. And neither is my little girl.

I left Coco standing, with the teddy, outside the bookshop window. I figured if I left her there, her father was bound to find her eventually.

Originally, right at the beginning, that was the plan. Just to take her for half an hour, an hour maybe, to give them a scare. To walk off with her, go somewhere safe, and leave her for them to find, eventually. To make them experience that feeling, that sudden, sickening knowledge that someone you love is gone. The panic. The self-recrimination. The gut-twisting dread. That was all I wanted. For them to experience what I had experienced. What Grace had experienced.

Then I changed my mind.

As we were going down in the escalator, I could feel Coco relaxing in my arms. She rested her head on my lapel, playing with one of the buttons on my coat, chattering away about the different places she'd been that day, all the things she was getting for her birthday.

"You sound like you are a very lucky girl," I told her.

She has no idea. Another time, in a darker mood, I'll admit I have had thoughts about taking her and not leaving her somewhere safe to find. I know. Once upon a time I would have been as horrified by that confession as you are. Horrified that I could even consider it. Horrified that I was not a big enough person to rise above my own suffering and see that revenge solves nothing, that causing pain to someone else, someone innocent, would do nothing to put things back as they were, would probably not even stop my own hurting in the end. Maybe I have changed. I've been feeling for a long time that with what happened, something has come loose in me, that I am no longer the same person I was. I remember talking about it ages ago with one of the grief coun-selors my GP referred me to. I can remember telling them that I felt I was not a whole person or a real person or a person in the same way as everybody else was anymore. That it was like grief had blasted a hole in me and something had flowed out and I had not been able to stop it and maybe at the same time something else had flowed in.

Holding that child in my arms, feeling the gentle flutter of her pulse against me, her head close enough to my face for me to smell her shampoo—the same shampoo I can remember washing Grace's hair with—I found myself asking myself if I could really do it. If I could truly hurt an innocent human being. And the honest truth is, knowing who she is, knowing who her mother is and what she's done to me, I felt myself fully capable in that moment of chucking that child over the side of the escalator, dropping her off a balcony, hurling her headlong into traffic, without a second thought, without a moment's remorse. And the truth is the only reason I didn't do any of those things, the only reason I did leave her standing unharmed where I did, was not because I had a moment of stage fright or compassion or even doubt.

It was because I have something much worse planned for Emmy Jackson and her family.

CHAPTER SEVEN

Dan

We get back home from the party to discover our house has been broken into. As we're turning onto our road, I can hear an alarm going off and I say something like, "I hope that's not ours." Emmy looks up from her phone.

"What's that?"

I turn the radio off. In the back, both Bear and Coco are fast asleep in their seats. As we get closer to our end of the street, the alarm gets louder. I can see the bloke from across the road standing in his doorway as we approach. A couple of the other neighbors from farther down are out on the pavement.

"I've already called the police," one of them shouts as I am getting out of the car.

There are no signs of attempted entry at the front of the house. The frosted glass panes in the front door are still intact, all the windows closed. I go around to the side return and test the gate and find that's also still locked, so I hop up and look over it to see if I can see anything. I can't. "How long's it been going off?" I ask one of the people standing around.

He shrugs.

"Half an hour maybe?"

Once we've turned off the alarm and dispelled the cluster of concerned yet curious neighbors, it doesn't take us too long to put Coco and Bear down and work out what happened. The house was untouched when Winter left it, having retrieved the spare T-shirts for Emmy, so we know it happened after three p.m.—Emmy checked the time on the Uber receipt. The intruder came in through the back door, probably climbing over the gate and in via the garden. Having taped a bit of cardboard over the missing pane of glass, I secure the back doors as best I can with some twine around the inside handles and a footstool from the living room pushed up against them. Then I start wandering around the house, checking once again for anything that might have been moved or taken. Nothing seems to be missing. There are no muddy footprints, nothing disturbed in the living room or the kitchen.

There've been a lot of these sorts of opportunistic burglaries in this area recently, the police tell us, when they eventually show up. Just kids, a lot of the time. Looking for electronic goods, cash. Had we noticed anything missing, anything like that?

I tell him that as far as I can see, nothing's been taken at all. I mention I have taken photos of the back door, with its broken window, the glass on the kitchen floor, and pass him my phone. He thumbs through them without great interest.

"You were lucky," he says. "The alarm must have spooked them."

I ask him what he thinks the chances are of catching whoever did this. He tells me the police do not normally even bother investigating burglaries like this these days. Probably the best thing to do, if we're worried, is to get a camera installed; that tends to put them off. Make sure we don't leave our valuables lying around. Then he gives us a crime reference number on a slip of paper and leaves.

THE THOUGHT I KEEP trying to suppress is that this might not be just a random break-in. That whoever did this knew exactly whose house it is and what we were doing all afternoon. It wouldn't have been late when they were jumping the gate and creeping around the back garden, and putting a flowerpot through one of the panes of glass in the back door. It was still more or less light when Emmy and I were putting Coco and Bear in the car to come home.

What I keep telling myself is not to be so paranoid.

I remind myself of the rules, and how careful Emmy is to stick to them; how obsessive she is about never writing anything or posting any pictures that might give away the exact location of where we live. I tell myself to get a grip. That kind of thing might happen to a premier league footballer, their mansion cleared out on match day, but I can hardly see the average burglar having heard of Mamabare or seeing our home as an especially tempting target—unless, that is, they fancy a load of plastic toys smeared with yogurt, a bunch of beauty products, a not-very-big TV, and three laptops, none of them particularly new, mine so old and crappy I caught someone sniggering at it in a coffee shop the other day. Not a fancy hipster coffee shop, either. A Costa, I think.

Emmy scans the rooms after I'm done, trying to work out if there's anything glaring I've missed. What quickly becomes clear is that— obvious electronic goods aside—she has very little idea of what she actually owns, perhaps because she paid for so little of it. Some of the unopened bags of freebies, which may or may not have included a NutriBullet, she thinks, could have gone. A handful of the gifted jewelry she leaves tangled at the bottom of a bowl, maybe? A pair of Burberry boots that she vaguely remembers leaving by the front door to be reheeled, although she can't recollect whether she ever took them or not, and if she did, where, and a two-thousand-pound Acne sheepskin jacket that, now she thinks about it, she may have left in the back of a cab six months ago.

While she starts looking into our insurance situation online, I drift around the place, unable to settle, doing all sorts of pointless things, like checking the burglar is not still lurking on the premises in the closet under the stairs or behind the door in the downstairs bathroom. It would be horrible knowing someone has tried to get into the house at the best of times. Having a four-year-old and a newborn here makes it infinitely worse, and I feel I ought to go around washing everything, wiping it down.

There's a small part of me that would have loved to catch the bastard in the act, would have loved to get my hands on them—a part of me that, as I'm moving from room to room, is working out how I could barricade the rest of the house, planning all sorts of traps.

I decide not to mention any of this to my mother. From the very start, when I told Mum about the Instagram thing, her immediate response was to start listing all the things that could possibly go wrong. Was I sure it was safe? Was I sure it was not something we would later regret? What would happen if Coco wanted to go into politics one day? What if she resented our posting all these pictures of us when she got older? I pointed out that lots of people posted pictures of their families on Facebook. When I was a kid, I remember her always getting out books of photos of me when people came around. What if . . . ? "Enough, Mum," I had to tell her eventually.

We always used to joke about our mums, Emmy and I—that you could not get two more different people if you tried.

My mum, Sue, is thoughtful and infuriating, kind and somewhat bumbling, careful not to impose on us but always keen to offer a hand if we need one. I can see why she gets on Emmy's nerves sometimes. She gets on *my* nerves sometimes. She always seems to call at inconvenient times, and even after you've told her you're right in the middle of something, she keeps on telling you whatever she's telling you, right to the end. Sometimes I put the phone down and wander off into the next room and come back and pick it up and she hasn't even noticed. She's very bad at hiding when she disapproves of something or when the way we're doing something with Coco isn't the way she'd have necessarily done it.

Emmy's Mum is a complete fucking nightmare.

Emmy

It's always the mother's fault, isn't it?

But if you're going to point the finger at anyone, really it should be my dad. He was the one who made pretending and twisting the truth an integral part of who we were as a family. He turned lying into an art form, hiding his sexual misdemeanors with such panache that it was impossible not to be impressed. He was smart, though, funny and magnetic. I wanted to be like him, so I kept his secrets, told his lies too.

Was he crossing his fingers behind his back when he promised to be with my mother for richer and poorer, till death do us part? I doubt he'd see it like that. He was just doing what I'd watched him do time and time again: saying what he knew the person he was with wanted to hear. Better to lie and be liked than be hated for telling the truth— that's his general approach to life. He's a shape-shifter, my father. A people pleaser. Until he gets caught out. Able to be anything anyone needs him to be. Apart from a decent dad or husband.

When my mother suspected he was shagging his secretary, he managed to persuade her that she was paranoid. I knew different, as I'd been dragged on secret Saturday-morning shopping trips to buy sexy underwear and perfume, my silence bought with Barbies and Haribo. When she suspected him of having an affair with a recently bereaved family friend, he spun her a story that he was just a shoulder to cry on. I, on the other hand, overheard the breathy late-night phone calls that strongly suggested other body parts were involved too.

So the drinking isn't really Ginny's fault. Perhaps she would have been a better mum if she'd married a doctor or a teacher. Or if she'd used her law degree, and her impressive but woefully underused intellect, for anything other than checking over the divorce settlement. But when you're as beautiful as she was and marry a banker as rich and arrogant as he is, I guess you understand that contract too. Maybe you make a conscious choice to swap an actual life, one where your husband wants you to be happy, one where you have a right to complain when things aren't okay, for a lifestyle—the cars, the clothes, the holidays. Maybe she went into it knowing that it was her job to stage-manage us all into playing the perfect family—and that she could never let the act slip, even with me.

I used to study the way my friends' mothers acted with them, would consciously commit to memory all the hugs and kisses and family conversations over dinner at Polly's house about the adventures they'd had that day. I don't think I was jealous exactly, more an interested observer. I used to mentally file the best bits and construct a sort of Frankenstein's mama in my head—one who booked ballet classes and drove me to piano lessons, who didn't mind when I reached for her with grubby hands. Who was home every night to tuck me up in bed and kiss me on the forehead.

Even when Dad finally left Mum for a younger model, she couldn't bear to tell anyone—even me—that life as we knew it was over. We just moved house and started again somewhere else. I suppose the cash helped ease the pain for her. I think she was probably happier without him. Was he happier without her? Who knows? I never saw him again.

I realize I have barely paused for breath.

"And how does that make you feel?" asks Dr. Fairs.

"I'm not sure it makes me *feel* anything," I say breezily. "That was twenty-five years ago. I'm sure my dad's fine. My mother seems to be having a perfectly nice time, what she remembers of it."

"Would you say it was a happy home? Would you say yours is a happy one now?" she asks.

"Yes," I say, without hesitation. "Absolutely. Obviously it is never *nice*, being burgled, and knowing that someone has been through all your stuff and touched your things, but we're insured, and it happens to everyone, doesn't it, sooner or later? It just makes you a bit jumpier for a few days, a bit more aware of what a fragile little bubble it is you live in. I'm just thankful none of us were at home when it happened."

Dr. Fairs expresses her sympathy, although it is clear from her tone she feels I have deliberately sidestepped her question.

"We should talk more about that," she says. "And we will have time to do so later in this session. Just for the moment, though, if you don't mind, I'd like to stick with the topic we were discussing."

"Okay," I tell her.

"So let me reframe my original question. How do you think your upbringing affected your feelings about family?"

"Oh, well, that's easy. I didn't want one," I say flatly.

Never, never, never. I had a pony phase. I had a phase where I wanted to be a ballerina. I even had a short-lived goth phase. I never had a baby phase.

"What about your husband?" she asks.

"Well, Dan spent the first five years of our relationship auditioning to be a dad." I laugh at the memory.

And they do, don't they? It was endearing at first. From early on, every time we were around children Dan would make a tremendous show of how good he was with them. If we went to a wedding and there were kids there, he'd be down at their level offering piggyback rides before I'd even managed to grab a glass of prosecco. He was continually insisting on holding people's babies for them while they went to the bathroom and talking to people with pushchairs in the supermarket and asking how old the babies were. On several occasions I caught him telling someone we didn't have any children *yet*.

He'd had no idea what parenthood would entail, of course. That oppressive sense that nothing can be the same as before. That even once they start sleeping through the night, you won't be able to, kept awake by the gnawing realization that never again will you be responsible only for yourself.

I remember when Coco was tiny, Dan used to sit at the kitchen counter after she'd gone down—after he'd spent all day writing and I'd been marching the pram around the park to keep her asleep or been bored to tears at baby massage—and scroll endlessly through photos of her while I cooked us dinner. *Here's one of her burping. Here's another that might be a smile. Look at that outfit I put her in! She's a tiny penguin!* He couldn't believe we'd made a little person who was half him, half me. Then, of course, we'd go up to bed and I'd be the one doing the night feeds and the two-in-the-morning nappy changes.

Is it any wonder I put motherhood off? As a teenage girl, my mother impressed upon me how easy it was to get pregnant, that I would always need to be very careful if I didn't want to ruin my life. How *she* certainly wasn't going to be doing the childcare if I was stupid enough to accidentally make a baby with whichever hopeless heartthrob I was dating at the time. The first time I had sex was at uni. We used a condom *and* a diaphragm *and* a generous dollop of spermicidal gel. Dan was fully aware of, and highly amused by and often joked about, this procreation-related paranoia of mine (as he saw it). When we started dating, in those first few passionate months, one of his signature bedroom moves was to ask, just before the moment of penetration, whether I had remembered to take my pill. The answer was always yes.

It was only when I came off birth control—I'd decided it was responsible for the few extra pounds I couldn't shift before the wedding— that he started suggesting we "take a chance" when I reached for the condoms. Very occasionally, I was drunk enough to agree. Every time we went away for the weekend, he would spend the whole time making comments like, "Wouldn't it be fun to have a kid to take to the seaside?" and going on about the family trips he could remember from his childhood. Then when we got back to the hotel room he would have forgotten to buy any condoms.

And then one day it happened.

I knew the second I saw the blue line that there was no way I was keeping it. We'd been together long enough to have a baby, two years I think, and I probably wouldn't even have been showing at the wedding. But as much as Dan was desperate to be a dad, I was pretty sure I didn't want to be a mother. I wanted a career. I wanted to travel. I wanted to wear beautiful clothes, carry expensive handbags, eat nice meals and drink good wine in cool places and have interesting things to talk about while doing it. What exactly would Dan be giving up to have a family? Polly came with me to the clinic.

Afterward, there was an overwhelming sense of relief. Perhaps that's the only feeling I would allow in. I'm not sure.

The second time, I went alone.

I paused for slightly longer, perhaps, but I'm sure I didn't agonize. I'm still meant to be mourning, forever conflicted about my difficult decision. I know that. But I'd made a conscious choice that there would be no guilt, no grief, for those two tiny bundles of cells. Sometimes I feel an involuntary twinge when I read an Instagram post from a woman describing the pain she still bears from making the choice, but otherwise I don't let it enter my head. It is simply not something in my psyche that I choose to prod.

Perhaps Dan would feel differently, if he knew.

Dr. Fairs's expression is entirely impassive. As is the giant poster of her face on the wall behind her, advertising her self-care supplements. (Have I mentioned that my attendance at these sessions is a contractual obligation?)

She's not exactly a fraud, I don't think—even if she is always trying to sell me a bottle of her omega-three-enhanced mindfulness pills, and even if she does mention her TEDx talks and *Sunday Times* bestselling book more frequently than is seemly. She seems to have the relevant certificates framed on the wall. This isn't to say that I don't fucking resent and slightly dread having to drag myself over to Marylebone on a regular basis to spend an hour in her basement clinic, talking about the feelings she wants me to have.

"And what *did* eventually change your mind, Emmy, about having children?"

I shrug.

"Circumstances changed, I guess," I say. "It finally felt like the right time."

17,586 likes

the_mamabare: They go so quickly, don't they? The years, the tears, the am-I-doing-it-right fears. But the tiny humans don't care if you're slightly sweaty, totally knackered, and all your clothes look like someone has been sitting on you. #greydays might loom in the underbelly of your mind, but sometimes, in the most miraculous of ways, a sparkling interlude appears, unicorn-like, and the clouds lift. I call these the #yaydays— when you feel like a superhero and your circle of mama mates are your able sidekicks. The gang that reminds you that it's all about celebrating the small wins. And today, as Coco turns four, is one of those days. So with love and cake and just the best, best friends in the room, I want to know about your own #yayday. Tell me about it below and tag your mama crew to each be in with a chance of winning a £1,000 voucher. #yayday #MamaWins #CocoTurns4 #ad

They were all there, at the party. All the mamas. They seem to have posted about nothing else for the past forty-eight hours. Here are the coach one and the Hackney hipster one and the one with the boobs

and another mama I have never come across before, all holding cham-
pagne flutes and laughing with their heads thrown back. Here is an-
other one of them, posing with a child dressed as a dinosaur. Here are
some other kids with painted faces, making claws with their hands and
pretending to snarl at the camera. I click among the feeds, staring at
a single photo for a while and then checking back to see if Emmy has
posted anything new. I can spend hours doing this. Days, almost. And
what you notice if you do that is how carefully coordinated it all is.
The hashtags. The way they all like one another's posts and comment
on them. The way they are always promoting one another, mentioning
one another, tagging one another. The way they are always harping
on about the same messages, the same themes. Today the theme is ob-
viously female friendship, the importance of mums looking out for one
another. Mamabare gets the ball rolling with a picture of five or six In-
stamums from behind, arm in arm, looking over their shoulders, with
a caption about how lucky she is to have such great friends. Within
two minutes they have all responded.

Do you want to know something strange, though?

Not a single one of these people was at Emmy's wedding. That was
five years ago. She posted a picture the other month, for their anniver-
sary, and the first thing that struck me, as I was looking at it, was,
Who the hell are all these people? Her husband I recognized, of course.
But not a single one of the five or six other smiling young people gath-
ered around the happy couple on the church steps looked even vaguely
familiar. And as for the tall girl, the one holding Emmy's train, the
maid of honor, I have never seen or heard Emmy mention her any-
where, ever.

Which frankly strikes me as a little peculiar. A bit suspicious, even.

One of the things Grace found hardest, after what happened, was
the way so many of her friends dropped her, how some of the people she
thought would be in her life forever just vanished.

My daughter was always someone who would do anything for her friends, someone who had pictures of her pals on her fridge, was always the designated driver, the one who would make sure everybody got home safe. She never forgot a birthday.

Half the people we invited to the funeral didn't even bother replying.

There were some people who would make the effort to come and see her, especially at first, of course. But it was always awkward; you could see, Grace said, that they were worried about saying the wrong thing, afraid that whatever they said would upset her. There would be long silences. She would catch them looking at the clock.

The worst thing about that, I often used to think, the cruelest thing, was that after George died, when I was first on my own, Grace was the one person who always knew what to say. How to cheer me up if I was down and just couldn't see the point of it all anymore. She'd tell a story or a joke just the way he would have done to make me laugh. Or she'd say to me that her dad wouldn't have wanted me to spend the rest of my life moping and moaning and pining away. Or, if the time and the mood were right, she might remind me of all the little things he used to do around the house that would drive me up the wall. Other times, she'd just reach over and squeeze the back of my hand and let me know that she missed him too.

That I, her mum, couldn't do the same for her, could never seem to find the right words or the right gesture when she was going through her grief, that whatever I said or did always seemed to annoy her, to upset her—it devastated me. I suggested she go out—to dinner, to the cinema, even just for an errand or two to get her away from the house—but she said she didn't want to. That she didn't think it would be appropriate, that it wouldn't look right. She said she felt that whenever she went out she was being judged. She would catch someone's eye and they would look away. She would walk past people talking, and they would fall silent. Once or twice she was sure someone had actually shouted something at her from across the street. I told her not to be silly, that she was being paranoid.

It put a lot of pressure on her and Jack.

I remember one day I drove over to see them. A Sunday it was, late November, one of those days when the sun never really breaks through the clouds. I was supposed to be coming for Sunday lunch, had brought a cake with me for dessert, and when I got to the house and turned into the drive there was Jack's car halfway up it, pulled over to the side. And as I got closer I could see Jack, hunched over in the driver's seat, his head down and his arms crossed on the steering wheel, and as I got closer still I could see that his shoulders were shaking, and when he looked up his face was streaked with tears. I drove past and up to the house, and Grace heard the car on the gravel and came to the front door to let me in. We went through to the kitchen where the table was set and the food ready for dishing up and Grace did so. And about twenty minutes later, when we had both almost finished, Jack came in and said hello and sat down and joined us, and not a word was said about it.

It is strange how people come and go in life, so quickly, so easily. When you are young you think everyone is going to be around forever.

First there was me and George. Then there was me and George and Grace. Then there was me and George and Grace and Jack. Then there was me and Grace and Jack and Ailsa. Then it was just me and Grace and Jack. Then it was just me and Grace. Then it was just me.

CHAPTER EIGHT

Emmy

"Am I speaking to Holly at the You Glow Mama Awards? Hi, it's Emmy Jackson. Look, I'm running ten minutes late, we've had a bit of a situation at home. At least you don't need to worry about hair and makeup—my look is sleep-deprived and peanut butter–smeared!" I laugh, waking up a dozing Bear in the car seat next to me. I might be prepared to leave Coco with Winter, but dumping a newborn who needs to be breastfed on the hour would be pushing it.

It wasn't the best start to the day: waking up to discover someone had posted the name and address of Coco's nursery on a gossip forum. It was Irene who alerted us. Dan was in the room when I took her call and could tell from my expression it was something serious. All the time Irene was explaining what had happened, he was standing there frowning and looking concerned and repeatedly mouthing, *What?* at me.

The forum removed the post—which also featured a self-righteous rant about me having the cheek to call myself a *real* mother when I had a daughter in full-time childcare, railing against my audacity in profiting from a family I never actually spend any time with—as soon as Irene complained. The internet never forgets, though—once something's been out there, even briefly, it exists forever. Less helpfully, the forum had no information on who posted it, other than that they were a first-timer to the site. Awful as it sounds, it does immediately occur to me that it could quite easily have been one of the other nursery mums.

I know they bitch and snipe about me—I can feel the atmosphere change as I get past the gates, see the whispers behind the hands of the little gangs that congregate around the fringes of the yard. They're all perfectly pleasant to my face, but I'm convinced that at least a couple stir things up about me online. One or two may even be the trolls with no followers and no profile pictures who say mean things about my kids. Who knows? I'm sure some of them lurk on my profile without ever actually following and, after a few glasses of wine, pull out their phones to show their friends *that awful influencer mum from nursery*, while whispering, wide-eyed, that they'd found my company accounts online and *Can you believe how much she makes? They* would never sell *their* family on the internet. *I mean, that photo of Coco having a tantrum! She'll be bullied, of course, if she isn't already. Kids can be so cruel.*

Maybe, but their mums can be way worse.

Perhaps it's someone we know, perhaps not—we're hardly incognito. Anyone could have spotted us in the neighborhood. It might have been a follower whose messages Winter didn't reply to enthusiastically enough who wants their revenge and has played detective. It could have been anyone, but given the safety implications for Coco and how on edge Dan has been about things since the break-in, it's clear that we need to take immediate action.

The upshot, for today at least, is that leaving our daughter with Winter was our only option. Coco can't go to that nursery again, and Dan was absolutely adamant that he *couldn't possibly* cancel his completely vital appointment with his incredibly important editor. I would've taken her with me to the awards, but she refused to leave the house. So with a planking four-year-old teetering on the verge of a total meltdown and a howling newborn, the choices were limited.

While my assistant probably won't actually *kill* my daughter, as a childcare arrangement this solution is hardly ideal. I've been on the phone to the awards all of ninety seconds, but by the time I hang up I have five new messages from her, asking how to deal with Coco's demands for chocolate and finger paints and yet another episode of *Paw Patrol*.

It's a sunny day, just take her to the park, I quickly type as the car pulls up at the venue. I see I have a WhatsApp from Polly, flick back a wave and a kiss emoji, and make a mental note to look properly later.

My daughter is generally well behaved, although she has recently developed an obsession with my iPhone. Depending on her mood, she veers wildly between demanding I take photos while she poses—then thumbing endlessly through them until she finds one where she looks "pretty enough"—and trying to grab it out of my hand, shouting, "I want you to look at ME, Mama! Look at ME!" I'm by no means immune to that particular guilt trip, but the to-and-fro-ing is disorienting.

And while Winter may be a more competent PA than I'd initially expected, she's no Mary Poppins. She seems a bit confused by the whole concept of children and why you might want to own one, approaching Coco in the same way as one of her many hats: a useful prop to pose with. Come to think of it, I've overheard Dan's mother sniping that I do the same thing.

I apply another layer of lipstick, ruffle my hair so it looks not unlike I climbed into this cab through the sunroof, spray my face with my Evian Brumisateur, look into my phone, and press record.

"Some things I've learned about making plans when you have kids. First, *don't*. Second, get your childcare on lockdown unless you want to be a sweaty mess like me . . . I mean, look at this"—I wipe my cheek and proffer a glistening finger to the phone—"When exactly does dewy glow slip into sweaty mess? Asking for a friend . . .

"And third, if you do have an event to go to, make sure you have a spare dress on standby as someone is definitely going to give you a yogurty kiss on the way out the door. I mean, are you even a mama if you haven't had three outfit changes before leaving the house? I'm pulling off this #yaydays tee over a party dress combo, though, right? Ooh, here we are!"

We have arrived at the CubHouse, a west London members' club and boutique hotel for "media mamas and ad dads" (their words, not mine). It looks exactly as you'd imagine: a Soho House for people who've popped out a couple of kids. There are gender-neutral superheroes in tasteful shades of grey painted on the walls, neon cloud lights hang from the ceiling, and one entire room has been turned into a ball pit in millennial pink. Pale-wood toys of the sort that only child-free people give as gifts are scattered artfully on the floor. I park up the pram, and when the clipboard girls in their pastel boiler suits realize who I am, we're ushered up to the events floor and then backstage.

I spot Irene immediately. Four out of five of my pod have won awards today, and it looks like she may even have treated herself to a new outfit to celebrate—I certainly haven't seen this red velvet Gucci power suit before. I look down at my scuffed Stan Smiths and feel a pang of longing for my old life.

The rest of the gang are all here, and I give them a thumbs-up. Hannah's won Mumpaigner of the Year, and I'm happy for her (although no doubt the trolls will gripe that getting your tits out in public to feed a child old enough to pour himself a glass straight from the carton is hardly a campaign). Suzy and her frocks that time forgot have bagged Best-Dressed, and Bella's been recognized with the Mumboss award, so she can probably double the prices again for her This Mama Can career coaching days.

I feel a strange surge of pride watching them pose for photos with their statuettes (golden nappies on pink acrylic pedestals). Whatever anyone thinks of what we do, however much they judge how we make our living, it's impossible not to be impressed. We've managed to be mothers *and* businesswomen, built empires from anecdotes and selfies, fortunes from family photos and fifteen-second videos. The second- and third-tier Instamums, especially the ones who don't need the money, for whom this life is a nice little sideline, giving them a few freebies and the odd holiday, will never hit the big league like this. This is the Oscars to their amateur dramatics.

"Thank God, Emmy, I thought you weren't going to make it. Where's Coco?" Irene asks.

"I've left her with Winter," I say in a stage whisper. "We didn't really have a choice. Coco refused to leave the house."

From the look Irene shoots me, it's clear she doesn't think that was wise. "Why you won't just hire a nanny, I'll never know," she says, exasperated. "Oh, I know, I know, Dan wants her to be with *normal* children her own age, to keep her feet on the ground."

The way Irene says this last part places it in audible quotation marks—and in my own more cynical moments it has occurred to me that Coco being at nursery all day also means that Dan often has the house to himself to focus on his precious writing.

Irene frowns, her gaze resting on something on the shoulder of my T-shirt.

"You do realize that Bear has just done a milky burp on you?" She points to my son, who is happily cooing away in his custom leopard-print sling. They call my name, and I shrug and head up to the stage, smiling broadly and raising a hand to the crowd when I reach the podium.

"Firstly, let me apologize for Bear's little sicky puddle," I say, pointing at my shoulder, "but you know what? This little mishap provides me with the perfect parenting analogy. Because being a mama is all about getting on with it even when the shit hits the fan, or the vomit hits the epaulette, am I right?" I pull a muslin from the carrier with a flourish and do my best to daub off the mess. There are whoops of delight from the audience.

"What makes the perfect mama? Who knows—and really, who

cares? I'm certainly not one—and I'm not sure I've ever met one. We are all just women—women trying to do enough, be enough, have enough, without ever having it all. Women smiling through the tiny tears, trying not to add our own frustrated sobs to the screaming tantrums, hoisting these precious little humans above our own needs, every hour of every day. Doling out snuggles and antiseptic when knees get scraped, bringing home the bacon to put sausages on the table, locating the glittery angel wings from under the sofa even when your darling is being a devil. Wanting it all to stop just for a moment and crying because this"—I close my eyes and kiss the top of Bear's head—"can't last forever." I can see a woman in the front row nodding furiously as she wipes away a tear.

"I guess it's all of these things—and more. And that's what's being celebrated today. It's why I started the #yaydays campaign. It's for mums who go above and beyond, mums who inspire us all, mums who have achieved something really remarkable and whose stories deserve a wider audience. Career mums. First-time mums. Full-time mums. Diverse mums. Mums who are also dads. It means the world to me to be named Mama of the Year, but really, I am going to accept this award for everyone here. Because we're all on this crazy journey together!"

The idea that someone has given Emmy Jackson a prize for mothering makes me laugh out loud. They must be joking. She must be joking. This must be someone's sick idea of a joke. Who judges these things? Who sits in a room and decides that someone is the Best New Mama or Mama of the Year or Greatest Gran? Who nominates these people? The whole thing is being livestreamed, of course. Already the_hackney_mum and whatmamawore have chipped in with their ideas of what makes the perfect mama.

Since when did we even start calling mums mamas in this country?

Grace was a wonderful mother, just as I knew she would be. She kept saying to me, Mum, I don't know if I can do this. I don't know if

I'm going to be any good at it. I kept telling her, You are going to be wonderful. And I was not wrong. I can remember her telling me that first night after Ailsa was born, she barely slept, she was just staring at her and staring at her—she was so beautiful, so precious, such an awesome responsibility. What makes a great mum? The same thing that makes a great dad. Putting your child first—and not just when it suits or when a photo opportunity arises or when you feel like it. It means making decisions and thinking about things and being prepared to say no when you need to (and not just when it's convenient). It means worrying. It means caring. It means constantly walking a fine line between joy and terror. It means constantly asking yourself whether you are making the right decisions, and for whose benefit you are really making them. It means being a parent all day every day and all night too, no matter where you are or what else you have going on. That was what made Grace a great mum.

And then there is Emmy's approach.

The Have another glass of wine—it's probably fine approach to parenting, where the only practical advice is a cheap trick to get you five more minutes in bed in the morning or to occupy them while you get on with something else. That is continually complaining that you don't get to go to bars and drink cocktails until three a.m. or go on holiday to sophisticated places or have sex in the living room anymore. The good-enough, that'll-do, we're-all-heroes-just-for-putting-some-cornflakes-in-a-bowl-and-not-letting-them-drown-in-the-bath method of raising children. The How can I turn parenting into a profession? and let-them-eat-crisps-all-day-if-it-keeps-them-quiet-and-the-crisps-are-organic approach.

Guess which one of these people has won an award—an actual award—for their parenting. Guess who now gets paid to hold forth about parenting to other people. It is a terrible thing to say—it is a terrible thing to think—but sometimes I feel like some people don't really deserve their children.

Dan

Lunches with my publisher have been on a trajectory of steadily diminishing impressiveness over the years. They started out, after I had signed (and faxed over) the contract for my first book, at a place opposite the Garrick—all white-aproned staff and napkins you can barely fold and menus on thick card embossed with curlicued lettering, like the seating plan outside the dining area at a fancy wedding. I ordered the quail. My editor was there, my agent, several other people from the publishing company, all of them laughing at my jokes and telling me how excited they were about the book, how their boyfriend had asked them what they were laughing about when they were reading the manuscript in bed and how he had now read it and loved it too, what a buzz there was about it in the marketing department.

After lunch we all went up to the office and people kept getting called over from their desks or out from their cubicles to meet me and say hello. After the book had come out, there followed several lunches of slightly lesser grandeur, just me and my new editor, strictly lunch break only, one glass of wine each and a starter and main course before they had to get back to the office, a chance to catch up and talk about the next book and how it was going. After two or three of these lunches, I found that I was the only one ordering a glass of wine. After a while, we dropped the starter. That editor left. I got a new editor. We had a getting-to-know-you lunch—in a Pizza Express. She showed no sign of having read my first novel or of having any particular interest in my second. Almost half the lunch consisted of her telling me about a house she and her fiancée were planning to buy in Crystal Palace. That was eighteen months ago. We haven't lunched since.

Do I sound bitter? So be it.

You can imagine my surprise when that same editor suddenly got in touch out of the blue and told me they were really keen to meet up.

Was I free next Monday? "Sure thing," I said, without really checking. After all, it is not like Emmy consults with me every time she arranges a work thing. The editor suggested we meet at one o'clock at a new place serving Indian tapas near King's Cross. *Sounds intriguing*, I wrote in my email. It was only after I had replied that she asked me to send what I had of the novel so she could look at it over the weekend.

A cold fist of fear gripped my guts. I have shown snippets of the novel to people over the years. Back when I first started it, I used to read Emmy bits I'd written that day that I was especially proud of. My agent and I had talked the project over a lot, early on, and I'd sent her a couple of chapters. She had been cautiously positive, although she had added it was hard to really comment until she saw more of it. That was five years ago.

Something I should make clear is that I'm not technically *blocked* when it comes to writing. Nor am I lazy. I don't spend all day staring at a blank screen, nor do I spend my time lounging around in my underwear eating crisps. I'm actually quite diligent and industrious, as writers go. I've probably put down enough words on the page over the years to fill four or five novels. My problem is that I then go back and delete them all.

The thing no one tells you about your first novel is that it is by far the easiest one you'll ever write. You're young. You're arrogant. You have an idea one day and you sit down that evening and start writing and what you are writing turns out pretty good and so you keep going and by the end of the week you have five thousand words and by the end of the month you have twenty thousand words. You show it to some close friends, and they really like it, so you keep going. And you finish it. And you are delighted with yourself just for having finished it. And when you send it to an agent and they like it too, you are so delighted with the book and with yourself that you walk around humming for days. And then someone says they want to publish it. And then suddenly you are a writer, a real writer, a soon-to-be-published writer. And maybe that is why writing a second book is hard. Because just writing a book suddenly does not seem like such an achievement anymore. And other days you'll write something you really like but then you find yourself wondering whether it is too much like something you wrote in the first book. And some days you'll write something you like but find yourself wondering whether this new novel is going to turn out too different from the first book. And the longer you have spent on a book, the more the pressure builds up, and the higher you imagine everyone's expectations are going to be . . .

I sent off what I had at five on Friday, accompanied by an apologetic email. All weekend I've been checking to see if she's acknowledged receipt, to see if she's read any of it yet, to see if she likes it. Nothing. I'm tempted to drop her a line just to make sure she got it—and maybe, while I'm at it, to ask her casually if she has any initial thoughts—but I manage to restrain myself.

One good thing about being a parent and a writer, I suppose, is that there's always something to distract you from obsessing about things like that.

There was obviously no question of letting Coco go into nursery this morning. There is no question of letting her go back to that nursery ever again, in fact. Which is just great, given how hard it was to find a place at a nursery—to find any kind of reliable childcare—in our part of London. Nor is this the ideal day for something like this to blow up, if I'm perfectly honest. I remind Emmy that I have this lunch thing. She reminds me that she has the You Glow Mama Awards. I call my mum. She's driving her eighty-year-old neighbor Derek for a checkup on his leg at the hospital, and then waiting around to drive him home again. I suggest we call Emmy's mum. For a moment, Emmy looks as though she's actually considering this, which shows the level of desperation we have reached.

My phone pings, and it's a text from my mum saying she could make it over to the house by about four, if that would be of any help to us. The truth is no, not really.

All this time, Coco's wandering around the house kicking at things and twirling on her heel and doing big, exasperated sighs and asking why she can't go to nursery and see her friends. She's already made it very clear she doesn't want to go to an awards thing with Emmy, screwing up her face and baring her teeth and shaking her head with such vigor when Emmy suggests it that at one point she loses her balance and goes stumbling in the direction of the wall. "Be careful, Coco," I say as I step in and catch her.

"No," she tells me firmly, stomping away unsteadily. "No, no, no, no, no."

By the time Winter walks through the door, my daughter is on the verge of throwing a full-on tantrum.

"I could babysit," she suggests eventually, looking terrified.

Even as Emmy is checking that she really means it, my wife's eyes meet mine and silently ask me whether this is okay, whether this is the right thing to do, whether we are going to regret this. In reply, I offer whatever the facial equivalent of a shrug is. I mean, surely, even Winter is capable of making a sandwich and taking a four-year-old to the park up the road. We both thank her profusely and fly out the door.

I end up getting to the restaurant right on time—although this does involve my running most of the way to the Tube and then making my way from King's Cross station to the restaurant at a fairly urgent jog-trot. The greeting from my editor is encouragingly enthusiastic. I get a big wave as I am being led over to her, a wide smile. When I get to the table, I get an actual hug.

"Dan," she says, tilting her head slightly to one side, looking me up and down, still smiling.

The waiter pulls my seat back. I sit down in it.

"It has been much too long, hasn't it?" says my editor.

I answer affirmatively. Does this mean she liked what I sent? She certainly seems a lot friendlier than the last time we met, when she turned up late, informed me she needed to be back in the office in three-quarters of an hour, and spent the whole time eyeing her watch. This time around it's like she's a different person—or I am. In my chest, something a little like hope flutters. She tells me what starter she is ordering, mentions that she'll have something light for her main course because she wants to leave some room for dessert. It's really the desserts that this place is famous for, she informs me. Should we be naughty and have a glass of wine? She says she will if I will. I say I will if she will. She beckons the waiter over and orders something from quite some distance down the menu.

It is a lovely lunch. We talk about the latest changes of personnel and structure at the company, the latest trends in the book world. She mentions a couple of novels they are bringing out soon that she thinks I'll like and promises to send them to me.

It's only over the dessert menus that the editor brings up Emmy. She is, she tells me, a great admirer of Mamabare's writing. It's so funny, so fresh, so real, she says. It's so authentic. I make some joke about it being pretty different from the kind of writing I do. She smiles faintly. "How many followers does Emmy have these days?" she asks me. I tell her, rounding up to the nearest thousand, as per the last time I checked. She asks if Emmy has ever thought about writing something like a novel, or a memoir. I say I don't think so. I take a long sip of wine. Am I sure? She's convinced Emmy would be a natural at it, that it would be something people would really love to read. Maybe I should suggest it to her. Maybe I should put the two of them in touch. She'd love to hear any ideas Emmy might have.

I'm tempted to ask why, if she wants to talk to Emmy about writing, it was me she invited to lunch.

Or to ask when it was she discovered I am married to the inspirational Emmy Jackson, a slim volume of whose hastily transcribed brain farts, padded out with a load of photos and whacked out in time (I assume) for Mother's Day, would clearly be a far more commercially exciting proposition than the novel I have been pouring my heart and soul into week after week for the best part of the last decade.

I'm tempted to cry, or laugh, or scream.

Instead I simply say I'll mention it to her. My editor looks delighted. What tempts me on the dessert menu? she asks. I tell her I'll probably skip dessert, actually, that I have perhaps overestimated my appetite.

Offhand, casually, as we're waiting for the bill to arrive, I ask her what she thought of the chapters I sent through. She tells me she's not had a chance to properly look at them yet. Sorry about that.

Outside, it's raining. When I take my phone out of my pocket to summon an Uber, I see I have a WhatsApp message from Winter.

There's been an accident.

CHAPTER NINE

Emmy

The voicemail was hurried, panicked, garbled. Several seconds of muffled crying, then Winter telling me that she and Coco were in hospital, that I needed to come quickly, then Winter asking someone at the other end of the line for a reminder of the name of the hospital they're in.

An accident, Emmy. Coco. Hospital. Come now.

It's impossible to explain to anyone who does not have children quite what it feels like hearing something like that.

As I run out of the awards, as I am stepping out into the street and waving one arm over my head to hail a black cab, I keep listening to the message, over and over, for some clue as to what has happened, how Coco is. And through all of it, I'm bargaining with a God I don't believe in, promising that if Coco is okay, I don't mind dying. Anything that has happened to my baby, let it happen to me instead. Which sounds like the kind of thing people just say, but it's absolutely, viscerally true.

I lose sight of it sometimes, how lucky we are to have two happy, healthy children, when I'm treading on a tiny, spiky princess crown or she's angling for an extra story at bedtime. But the thought of my daughter—of either of my children—hurting is worse than anything that could ever possibly happen to me. She's my child, my first child, who I held in my arms before she even knew what hurt or fear was. I remember when she was a newborn and Dan and I had to clip her tiny nails and he somehow caught the end of a finger. I remember her puzzled yowl and watching that crescent of blood appearing on her fingertip and the look she gave us, as if we'd somehow betrayed her, and realizing that was the first time she'd ever experienced pain and that it was our fault.

I remember Coco twirling to impress me once on a raised platform at a play park, and stumbling and falling, and catching her chin on a bar as she fell, cutting her top lip with a tooth, and feeling just as vividly as Coco herself that abrupt transition from joy and exhilaration to sudden hurt and sadness. And nights when Coco was ill and feverish and not knowing how best to help, and whether we should take her to the hospital or just let her sleep. Knowing that something has happened to her now is like experiencing all of those moments again simultaneously, and the whole thing is worse because I don't know what has happened and I don't know how serious it is.

Every time I spot a cab approaching, I start waving more energetically before it gets closer, and I see its light is off and it's already carrying a passenger. The nearest Uber is somehow seventeen minutes away. When, finally, an available cab does stop, I then spend twenty minutes in traffic calling Winter repeatedly with no response.

Barging past the people in front of me in the queue at reception with Bear's buggy, I physically grab the first nurse I see and demand she take me to my daughter.

"Calm down, Mum. You're looking for Coco Jackson? She's fine. Come this way." She leads me down the corridor. It is only when she puts her hand on my arm that I realize I am shaking.

"Take a minute, Mum, before you see her," the nurse says, stopping by a little table with a jug on it and pouring me a plastic cup of juice. "There's no color in your face—you'll give her a fright." I take a couple of deep breaths and a few glugs of weak orange juice while the nurse explains what's happened.

When we arrive at her bedside, I find Coco happily propped up with pillows, watching *Octonauts* on Winter's phone, having apparently dispatched my PA for snacks. She has a tube bandage on her right wrist. I can't help but burst out laughing.

"Pickle, what on earth did you do?" I ask, leaning down to her and pressing my lips against her forehead. "You gave Mama a scare!"

"Mama, Winter was looking at her phone like you do, but I wanted her to look at me going high on the swings. I stood up on the seat so she could see me, but I fell off and bonked my hand," she explains. "I didn't mean to. It was a naxident."

I can tell she's secretly a bit proud of herself and is probably quite enjoying her first-ever trip to hospital.

Winter arrives back on the ward with what appears to be the entire contents of the vending machine. She stops dead in her tracks when she sees me, probably assuming that she's about to get her size-eight arse handed to her. I can see that her eyes are red and bloodshot, and mascara is streaked down her cheeks.

"I'm so, so sorry, Emmy. I don't know what happened—one second she was on the swing, and the next she was on the ground. I was only looking at my phone for a second, I promise, and then I . . . I . . . ," Winter stutters as she starts to cry.

"The nurse said she thinks nothing's broken, but they need to do an X-ray to check. She's . . ." Winter can't get any more words out before she breaks down into great big, snotty sobs.

I open my mouth to give her the epic bollocking I've been mentally rehearsing in the cab, but it won't come.

"Oh, Winter, for God's sake. You don't need to cry. Coco seems okay. You're fine, aren't you, Cocopop?" I say. With some irritation, looking at the state of Winter, I can see that I am going to have to comfort *her*.

I put my arms around the girl's heaving shoulders.

"We should never have asked you to take Coco; it's not part of your job."

"It's not that, Emmy. Well, it is that. But it's also . . . the reason I was looking at my phone, the reason I was distracted . . . Becket dumped me. He says he just wants to concentrate on his music right now. He doesn't have the headspace for anything else," she wails as she waves her phone at me. "What am I going to do? Where am I going to *live*?"

Sensitive, caring artist Becket has told Winter it's over and asked her to move out by DM. A really, really long DM. More of a poem, actually, by the looks of it. I'm going to have to dispense relationship advice while we wait for the doctor to show up, I realize. I check that Bear is asleep in his pram, let Coco pick a bag of M&M's from Winter's haul, absentmindedly stroke the nape of her neck as she shovels them into her mouth.

"Come here." I motion for Winter to sit down next to me on the end of the bed. "What happened? Did you two have a fight?"

"No, Emmy, that's just it. I thought it was all going so well. We never fight, we are—we were—totally into each other. I don't understand. I just don't know what I'm going to do." She starts hiccupping, and hands me the phone to read.

I can't bear to read the whole whiny, self-important, solipsistic thing, but quickly get the gist. Winter is trying to make a career for herself, and she isn't giving him—the artist—enough attention. She's been distracted by her new job and isn't spending enough time fawning. There is a list of gigs she missed, a DJ set she turned up late for, that time she told him that she couldn't post a picture of the cover of his EP on her Instagram feed because it interfered with sponsored content she had booked in. And he also sort of thought she'd maybe do more around his flat, like cooking or something, you know? So he could concentrate on creating?

Christ, this guy sounds like a dick.

"Winter, I know this feels like the end of the world now. But honestly, I went through the same thing as you over and over again in my twenties, and it all worked out for the best. These are just practice runs, you know, these hot idiots who break your heart? They help you work out what you want, what you actually *need*. And if you're anything like me—and I think you are, in a lot of ways—what you need is someone who has your back. Someone who is not always competing with you. Who is willing to support you fully in whatever it is you want to do— even if they don't entirely understand what that is—and who doesn't feel threatened when you do it well and people notice," I say, squeezing her knee. "And I promise, there really are men out there who don't feel that being in a relationship with a successful woman somehow diminishes or overshadows them."

She dabs away a tear. "Are you talking about you and Dan? God, I totally never thought of you guys like that. I just thought that you're, you know, a mum and dad," she says, looking at me quizzically, and I can see that in her head she is trying to imagine us as a younger couple, a young couple, trying to imagine the kind of people we used to be when we were her age.

Oh, come on, I think, *is it really that difficult?*

"You'll meet someone else," I tell her, resting a hand on her arm. "Someone who goes out of their way to make you feel special, who looks at you like you're the only woman in the world, who listens and laughs and loves you the way you deserve to be loved. You'll find your Dan."

For some reason this sets her off sobbing again. I offer her a tissue. She dabs her eyes and then blows her nose on it.

"Oh God," she moans, "that's very romantic and everything . . . it's just . . . it's just . . . Becket's parents own our flat. I haven't really earned anything from influencing since I quit my job to go full-time and I'm already in so much debt I can't look at the credit card bills. Everyone said it was easy, all this. Irene made it sound like there would be loads of money right from the start. I mean, I get sent *stuff*. But it's, like, never stuff you actually want, is it? Bags in the wrong color, dresses that don't fit. And some of the hats"—she wrinkles her nose—"they're so awful, they don't even sell on eBay.

"You can't eat free clothes, or pay your rent with them. And the holidays and the turmeric lattes and smoothie bowls for brunch with the other girls, and the giant bunches of flowers for props, the hair and beauty stuff, and you have to look different in every photo, and . . . and . . . I don't even have a proper camera . . ." She is now blowing great big snot bubbles, tears dripping from her chin. "Everyone else has an Olympus PEN!" She literally howls at the injustice of it all.

I could kiss the doctor when he arrives to give Coco a once-over, giving me the excuse I need to hug Winter one more time and send her off home. He says that he is almost certain that her wrist isn't broken but wants to check. The nurse will be back in a little while to take her down to X-ray, and until then we should just sit tight.

I take the iPad and the headphones out of my bag and hand them to Coco, who settles down again to watch *Octonauts*. Bear's still asleep, and when I pull out my phone I see I have several missed calls from Dan and one from Polly. I text Dan to let him know everything is fine, and Polly to say that I'll call her later, as Coco is in the hospital. She offers to come straight over to help, to take Bear or bring dinner or a change of clothes, but I reassure her it's just a minor sprain.

"Now, Coco," I say, "you stay there for five minutes while Mummy finds some clothes for you that aren't covered in mud!"

I push Bear in his buggy over to the gift shop, where I can only find a set of hideous and overpriced Peppa Pig pajamas in Coco's size. I buy some jumbo felt-tips too, just in case she does need a cast and we can draw pictures of princesses on it.

I arrive back at Coco's bed to find her asleep, her cheek pressed up against the iPad. A warmth fills my chest. All her big-girl attitude fades when Coco sleeps, and she's my little baby again. And along with that rush of feeling, another thought arrives. I carefully ease the iPad out from under her, pull the curtain all the way around the bed, and draw the pale blue fleece blanket up around her chin. I stop for a second, pull out my phone, and take a photo. I hold her little hand in mine and take another. Then I hop up onto the bed beside her and take another where she's lying curled up into a ball, spooning with me.

Obviously, I don't plan to ever post them, but they are a useful insurance policy. I know from a whole host of other people's Instagram scandals that distraction is always the best tactic when things go badly wrong. Say sorry for whatever the internet is accusing you of, then swiftly follow up with a personal crisis of some sort. Because who'd continue to kick a mother with a child ill in the hospital?

Dan

By the time I finally get around to checking my messages, Emmy is already at the hospital and has taken charge. "Shall I turn the Uber around and join them?" I ask. Which hospital are they at again? My driver raises his eyes to look at me in the rearview mirror. Emmy tells me not to bother, they're nearly done, Coco has sprained her wrist very mildly and they'll be back soon. "Just home," I tell the driver. "The original address, yeah?"

I'm a bit surprised, when I get home, to find the door is only single-locked. I did specifically say something to Winter about that. Ever since the break-in I've been even more fastidious than normal when it comes to making sure the front door is double-locked, setting the alarm, leaving lights on whenever we all go out. It's not just the thought that someone's been in the house, it's that someone was watching it beforehand, scoping out the neighborhood. That whoever broke in before might try the same thing again.

I go to turn the alarm off and find it's already been deactivated.

"Hello?"

As soon as I have stepped into the hall, I can tell there is someone else in the house. I don't know what it is. Some kind of animal sense. Something about the air pressure.

"Winter?"

No answer. In the kitchen, I hear something move.

"Emmy?"

The movement stops. I stop too. I hold my breath. I'm pretty sure I can hear a kitchen cupboard being closed—or a drawer opened.

Three quick steps, and I am in the doorway, ready to pounce on a burglar, ready to shout the place down, scared but also fueled by a certain sense of self-righteous excitement. My fists are clenched. My nails are digging into my palms.

My mother is making herself a sandwich.

She gives a bit of a start.

I unclench my face to assume a more normal expression.

"Hello, darling," she says. "Everything okay?"

Then it hits me that I completely forgot to call my mum and tell her not to come over.

"I hope you don't mind me making myself something to eat," she says, taking a bite.

I say, "Of course not." She eats it, apologizing—she came here directly from dropping Derek home from his appointment at the hospital and she hasn't had a chance to have a thing all day.

"Id gogo nod wid du?"

I hesitate before answering.

"No, Mum, Coco isn't with me. Don't freak out, but she's actually been at the hospital too."

She swallows and puts the rest of her sandwich on the counter, pushing the plate away from her with a flick of her fingers.

"What?"

"It's really nothing. It was silly, the person looking after her took her to the park and got distracted . . ."

Mum asks who was looking after her.

I tell her. She thoughtfully removes a bread crumb from her lower lip. "And who is Winter?"

I explain that Winter is Emmy's PA.

"And where was Emmy?"

"At an awards thing. And I had a lunch with my publisher."

My mother is looking steadily less impressed.

"Which hospital did they take her to?" she asks.

I ignore this question.

"They've just discharged her, and she's absolutely fine, Mum."

I add that Coco's on her way home now, that she'll soon be able to confirm this for herself.

My mum being my mum, the first thing she does is beat herself up about all this—if only she could've been there, if only she'd canceled Derek and told him to ask someone else to drive him in for his checkup . . . She feels awful. I keep trying to reassure her this wasn't her fault, that nothing terrible happened, that everything was fine.

"But it mightn't have been," she keeps saying. "I mean, thank God Coco is okay. But even so, just think if all those people on the internet got hold of it. The things they'd say. About Emmy, about her parenting. All the terrible, unfair things."

One of the things my mother worries a lot about is the precarity of what Emmy does for a living. How competitive it all is, the desperate struggle for paid ads and brand partners and all the things you need to turn followers into dollars (as Irene would put it). How long are we going to be able to spin this out for—until both the kids are at school? How will it work once they're both in lessons all day? What happens when they start reading and understanding what Emmy writes?

I do try—we both try, Emmy and I—to keep Coco's feet on the

ground as much as we can. We're always reminding her it's not normal to be given all this free stuff, for people to recognize you wherever you go, to have complete strangers act like they know you. I often tell her stories about what it was like when I was growing up (No iPhones! No iPads! No cartoons on demand!) and remind her what a lucky girl she is when you compare her life to the lives of lots of people around the world—and in this country too, for that matter. Once a week I try to make sure there's an evening when phones are put away and we talk over dinner and we all read a story together before bed. When she got sent a ridiculous amount of stuff last Christmas (two wooden rocking horses, several plush bears the same size as she was, a playhouse about half the size of my shed), we put some of it in the attic and redistributed or gave away most of the rest. We're careful how much we spend of it, the money Mamabare makes.

But when Mum worries about how quickly all this could come crumbling down, I have to admit she has a point.

Sure, some of the deals Irene has set Emmy up with have sounded like a lot of money for not very much actual work. If you look at the company accounts (Mamabare is, of course, a limited company), it looks like things are going pretty well for us. Then you hear the stories. Then you read about what's happened to other people. I saw a piece in the *Guardian* recently about how an influencer's entire following got stolen in the space of five minutes. Her Instagram account got hacked, her handle and password changed. That was it. Instagram wouldn't help. Nobody could ever find it again. Years spent building up a following, and bam, they simply didn't exist.

When I'm not worrying about Coco's safety, or what we might be doing to her psychologically, or that some sound I've heard downstairs is the burglars back again, what I mostly find myself worrying about in the middle of the night is this: that one false move, one fuckup, one badly judged comment, some cack-handed virtue signaling, could bring the whole thing tumbling down. The paid appearances, the shoots, the campaigns, all of it. It happens to people. It happens overnight. Remember justanothermother? I didn't think so. Eighteen months ago she was just as big as, say, Suzy Wao or Sara Clarke. Probably bigger. Eighteen months ago she was just as big as Emmy. Probably bigger. She was getting TV adverts, had a big contract lined up with Pampers, had her own (very early) morning show on talk radio. Then in a single evening she blew the whole thing up. Apart from the fact that her twins were quite cute and they all lived in the country, so there was plenty of opportunity for wholesome outdoor shots of them jumping around farmyards in muddy boots and splashing in puddles, the big thing with justanothermother was that she was really *nice*, really *wholesome*, really *sweet*. Then one night, for whatever reason—maybe it had been a long day and the kids had been playing up at bedtime or maybe she'd heard some bad news or maybe there was some particularly nasty trollish comment that had got under her skin—she sat down with a glass of wine (perhaps not the first of the evening) and started responding to her DMs and she just lost it. I mean completely lost it. Started giving the haters a piece of her mind. A dose of their own medicine. Effing and jeffing. Calling people perverts and losers and wankers. Telling people to get a fucking life. Asking them why they were such cunts. I can just imagine the satisfaction it must have given her to click send, to imagine their surprise, to really let them have it with both barrels. We've all done that, I think, during arguments, said something, thinking, *I am definitely not going to regret saying this in the morning.*

Within about fifteen minutes screenshots had started appearing— on Instagram, on Twitter, on Mumsnet. Within three hours it had been picked up as one of those little clickbait stories on BuzzFeed. By the next morning there was an account of her "four-letter fury," complete with screenshots and pictures of her from her feed, in the *Mail Online*. By that afternoon the pictures had been supplemented with grainy long-range shots of her getting into a Land Rover and the story was about her losing the Pampers partnership and being in talks with her radio bosses about whether or not they still wanted her to host one of their shows. They did not, as it transpired. Presumably she's now gone back to doing whatever it was she did with her life before she became an influencer—if that's still an option for her. The last time I looked on Instagram, she'd deleted her account. Not in the *Sorry, guys, I'm stepping away from these little squares for a few days for my mental health* way they all seem to do intermittently whenever they are getting criticized for something or want a bit of extra attention and reassurance. The way you would properly delete your account if you'd signed up to retrain as a teacher or lawyer.

And that was someone we used to see at events and say hello to and who once or twice was down to the final two or three in competition for things with Emmy, just a year and a half ago. Someone whose kids I could pick out of a lineup, whose kitchen I could describe.

I did suggest once to Emmy we drop her a line and see how she's doing, and my wife asked me why we would do that in what looked like genuine bafflement.

Twenty-three years. That is what people kept saying to me, reminding me of. Twenty-three years in the same hospital, the same department, for the last ten years the same job. It seemed to be hard for some of my younger colleagues to get their heads around. Sometimes, to tell the truth, I would find it hard to get my head around it myself.

I was not sorry to be retiring. It is tough work, being an intensive care nurse. That is the first thing most people say when I tell them what I do for a living. What I did for a living. That it must be tough. It's certainly intense, I would sometimes tell them. Knowing that when someone comes around from major surgery yours will be the first face they see. Knowing that you are going to be dealing all day with people who are scared, confused, in pain. Knowing that for every one of the people you are looking after, your diligence, your experience, your sense of when something is not quite right, could literally mean the difference between life and death.

That is something, isn't it? Not everyone can say that. That the work they do, every day, every shift, literally saves lives.

Sometimes when I think about all the people I have kept alive over the years, professionally, and of all the people who have been taken from me, personally, it almost feels like I would be within my rights to even the score a little with the universe. Just by one or two.

Sometimes I look at myself in the mirror and I wonder what I have become, what kind of person thinks like that.

Sometimes I feel like it was actually my job that was holding me together, all that time. When George died. When we lost Ailsa. When I lost Grace. Maybe that was what gave me the strength to get through the days: being able to go to work and focus on dealing with someone else's suffering, someone else's pain. There's not a lot of time for moping and introspection in an intensive care unit. There's not a lot of time to think about your own problems.

Which is not to say the sadness or the hurt or the anger go away.

I had repeatedly told everyone I did not want a retirement party. For weeks and weeks I kept dropping hints that I did not feel like a big thing, with speeches and balloons and a cake and all that. I have always hated being the center of attention at the best of times, and I had my own very good reasons for wanting to avoid the spotlight in those last few months.

They did it anyway. A surprise party, no less. Or that was the plan, anyway. I had just finished scrubbing out at the end of a shift, and someone messaged me and asked if I would pop up to the big meeting room on the seventh floor, and my heart sank and I knew before I opened the door that a load of people were going to be sitting there in the dark, all poised to turn the lights on and shout, "Surprise!" And so it was. And, as I had expected, they had all gone in together and bought me some flowers, some chocolates, a mug with a joke about retirement on it, something to do with gardening. There were speeches. And all through the speeches, as people were talking about how "kind" and "thoughtful" and "patient" and "sweet" and "lovely" I am, as they were saying things about never having seen me flustered, how they had never seen me lose my temper, never heard me snap or say a cross word about anyone, I kept looking from face to face to face, and I kept thinking, If only you knew.

If only you fucking knew.

CHAPTER TEN

Dan

There are some days when everything just seems to go wrong from the start. Take this morning. For some reason, completely out of character, Bear decides to wake up at four thirty and start screaming. I go through and check his nappy and settle him. Fifteen minutes later, he starts screaming again. Emmy goes in. For about half an hour I can hear her through the wall, jouncing him and shushing him and soothing him back to sleep. The instant she tries to put him down, he starts screaming again. From Coco's bedroom, through the door, I can hear a plaintive voice asking what's going on. It's now five fifteen, and since Emmy has a photo shoot later I get up and offer to take the baby for a few hours.

Before Bear came along I think I had forgotten what it was like, having a very young baby. The relentlessness of it. The constant stream of things to worry about. The never-ending to-do list of baby-related tasks. The amount of pressure it puts on you as a couple even at the best of times.

When I get tired, I get cranky and I get clumsy. Not a great combination. The first thing I do when I go down to the kitchen is open a cupboard door to get a bottle out to decant Bear's milk into, turn to grab something out of the fridge, then turn back to bash myself on the open cupboard door, right between the eyes.

Emmy shouts down to see what is going on. I shout back, "Nothing." She asks what all the swearing is about then.

It takes me about five minutes to find the empty plastic bottle I got out of the cupboard, which seems to have immediately vanished. Eventually I find it, right in front of me on the counter.

By this time Bear is getting hungry and whiny and irritable.

It's mornings like this when I find myself reflecting in amazement on how little childcare they did, the men of my father's generation. Did he ever change a nappy, my dad? Perhaps once, badly. I know he used to complain sometimes about the smell of the nappy bucket, the one by the back door, and there was a family story about the time he was leaving for work in his best suit (I picture it flared, acrylic, with wide lapels) and managed to kick the bucket over or step in it. But I can't remember ever hearing about him getting up in the night to do a midnight feed with a bottle or pushing a pram around the block to get me to sleep. Or even taking me to the playground or park on his own. And this is the early eighties we're talking about, not the fifties. My mum had been to college and read *The Female Eunuch* and had her own full-time job— and she still cooked all the dinners too. I just can't understand how they used to get away with it, the men in those days.

By the time Emmy and Coco get up and start going through clothes and picking an outfit for today's shoot, it's eight fifteen and I feel like I've done a full day's work already.

It is clear that Emmy and I need to get our childcare arrangements sorted, pronto.

Among the many little bits of domestic admin I've been assigned to do while Emmy's out at this shoot with Coco and Bear today is the task of finding a nanny. We have, in the end, decided to go about finding a suitable candidate in the conventional manner, after Emmy and Irene investigated without success a potential partnership with a nanny agency and I had vetoed Irene's suggestion we hold a competition to find one on Instagram. Given that Emmy's agent was probably at least half joking, I was perhaps a bit more snappish about this last proposal than the situation demanded. Emmy gave me a long, cool stare.

"Well, why don't *you* sort something out, then?" she asked.

She'd then gone to do something in the bedroom that involved quite a lot of banging around and drawer-slamming while I stomped through to the kitchen to make a cup of tea and grab my laptop. About twenty minutes later I stuck my head around the bedroom door to tell Emmy I'd signed us up with a new online matchmaking service for families in search of nannies and nannies in search of families. We sat down later that evening with a glass of wine in front of the telly and filled in an online form about who we are and the sort of person we're looking for.

While Emmy is getting Bear ready and Coco is watching cartoons at the kitchen table on her iPad I log back into the site and find we've had seven responses overnight. I cross off the one with mysteriously long gaps in her CV. Ditto the one with three typos in her personal description. I do not much like the look of the one with the nose rings and slightly divergent eyes and the purple hair. Judge me. That still leaves four promising leads. Of these, three are smiling and one looks very serious. Of the three smilers, one is twenty-two, one is forty-five, and one is in her midsixties. I can just imagine Emmy's reaction if I chose the twenty-two-year-old. The forty-five-year-old mentions in her profile that she considers herself spiritual. And so, in the space of less than ten minutes' scrolling and clicking, we have our winner. Annabel Williams, sixty-four, an Edinburgh-born, London-based childcarer with three decades' experience. Her look? No-nonsense. Nannyish, if you will. Someone reliable, trustworthy, unflappable. Just the sort of person we're looking for. She has qualifications and references. She can start immediately.

Well done, Dan, I think.

I click APPROVE and the system matches us up and invites me to submit a time for a face-to-face meeting, an interview. I do so.

I'm already imagining how casually, how smugly, I'm going to drop this into conversation with Emmy.

Two minutes later I get an automated message saying we've been rejected, with no further information.

As I am waiting for the kettle to boil and thinking about what to do next, Winter turns up. She's late, of course, as usual. Evidently not having expected any of us to be around, she clomps into the kitchen, gives a little start, says good morning, glances at the clock, pretends to be surprised by what time it is, puts her Starbucks down on the kitchen table, asks Coco how she is doing.

"Fine," Coco answers, without looking up.

It's then that the day really goes tits up.

It's then that—having shrugged her coat off and settled herself diagonally opposite me at the kitchen counter and plugged her phone in and taken a slurp of coffee—Winter asks me where her laptop is.

I ask her where she left it.

She gestures vaguely toward the corner of the countertop where all the chargers are.

At that exact moment, Emmy walks in, carrying Bear (who's wearing, I note, a bear outfit).

"What?" she asks.

I tell her.

The next half an hour is spent turning the house upside down to make sure the laptop is definitely gone. While Winter floats around looking in all sorts of implausible places (laundry basket, bread bin), I root through the boxes of toys and jigsaws and kid's books in the playroom and Emmy checks the bedrooms upstairs.

The laptop is definitely not here. The inevitable conclusion is that it was taken in the burglary—Winter, of course, what with it having been the weekend and then with all that drama yesterday, hasn't needed it since, and neither Emmy nor I ever use the thing.

While Emmy is on the phone to Irene, explaining what's happened, I keep reminding myself that things could be worse. It was not like it had been particularly expensive, that laptop. All the contents were password protected. Whoever stole it—no doubt some junkie—had probably wiped the thing and sold it by now. Irene can afford to replace it. We just need to inform the police, update our insurance claim. It wasn't Winter's fault, really. I probably should have put the thing away somewhere, in one of the drawers, before we went out.

By the time Emmy gets off the phone she's already almost an hour late for the shoot. "Right," she says to Winter and me. "Dan, you need to call the police and insurance people, okay?"

"Sure thing," I say. "That had already occurred to me, actually . . ."

"Winter?"

Winter puts her phone down.

"Irene is couriering another laptop over so you can get on with stuff here. Is that okay? Same username, same passwords as before. Once it gets here, you are good to go."

Winter looks puzzled.

"Problem?"

The problem is the passwords, says Winter.

"You don't remember them?"

She shakes her head.

"I always had them written down," she says. "I wrote them all down, all the different passwords you gave me."

"Wrote them all down where?" asks Emmy.

"On a Post-it note."

"And where did you stick that Post-it note?"

Winter tells us.

"Jesus," says Emmy.

"I'm really sorry," says Winter.

There are times, I think, when *sorry* really doesn't even begin to cover it.

Emmy

Every. Single. One.

Every single password was on that Post-it.

And so it wouldn't get lost, she stuck the Post-it to the screen of the fucking laptop.

Which means that whoever stole it has had three days' unrestricted access to everything Mamabare has ever done, all helpfully saved on my desktop or in the Cloud. Thousands and thousands of photos, emails, contracts. The task I've set Dan and Winter for this afternoon is to sit down and make a list of absolutely everything they could have got their hands on. Which is not just the stuff on the laptop itself, of course. It's every picture I have on my phone or Dan has on his phone. Every DM Mamabare has received. Text messages. WhatsApp messages. Passport scans. The guest list for Coco's party.

I literally don't have time to deal with this shit today. I don't even have time to think about it. I could have strangled Winter, I really could. If there'd been more time, I might have.

Of all the days.

In the back of the cab on the way to the shoot, I call Irene again. She promises me she'll speak to Dan and Winter, take charge, give them instructions. She thinks for a minute. "Maybe I'd better go over there myself," she says. There will be a lot of passwords to change, for one thing. There will be a lot of people to notify. She asks me how I'm feeling. She reminds me about today, how important it is. She's sure they won't mind that I am a little late, so long as I turn it on when we get there.

I tell her not to worry about that. One thing I learned very early, growing up in my family, was how to compartmentalize.

Anyway, Irene doesn't have to remind me how lucky I am to be involved in this shoot. I will be—and believe me, this is more of a coup than it sounds—one of the faces of a major toilet paper brand's #tothebottomwiperinchief Mother's Day campaign.

It's also something of a personal triumph for Irene.

She's booked all five of the pod, plus our own mothers and children, for this one. It's no accident that, as a group, we have a lot of bases covered, personality-wise, like a low-energy Spice Girls tribute act. There's Hannah with her earth mother schtick, Bella and her empowerment, Sara's small business owning, and Suzy's vintage style. Our own mothers are even more of a mixed bag—only mine has wholeheartedly embraced the influencer thing.

Virginia has been texting me for about an hour now, wanting to know where I am.

Having always been pretty sniffy about my career in magazines—not to mention my choice of a novelist over a hedge-fund husband—once she realized what was in it for her, my mother was delighted by my segue into social media. Being an Instagram grande dame suits her down to the ground and, to be fair to her, she has proven herself to be a very useful Mamabare brand extension.

It's been fascinating to see Ginny share her pearls of parenting wisdom on her own little squares (sandwiched in among an increasing number of paid-for #ads for wrinkle cream, hair dye to cover up the greys, and Windsmoor coats—although it is a personal bugbear of hers that only what she calls "old-lady labels" have been flash with the cash). Hearing her wax lyrical about all the nursery rhymes she used to sing me, all the cakes we baked together, all the fun we used to have almost makes *me* believe I had an idyllic childhood.

The photo from the family album of six-year-old me pointing at the gap where a front tooth should be with a lengthy caption about putting fifty pence and a handwritten poem under my pillow? I'm sure I'm not misremembering her, hungover, throwing a fiver in my face when I cried because the tooth fairy hadn't visited. As for the heartfelt words she shared on December twenty-fifth, about how I believed in Father Christmas until I was thirteen because she always took a bite out of the carrot and left size-ten footprints in icing-sugar "snow" on the porch? My only memories from the festive season are of her necking Santa's brandy, burning the Brussels sprouts, and accidentally showing off her red wine teeth when shushing me for the Queen's speech.

I wish I could say she's a better grandmother than she was a mother, but the photos of hugs and smiles and blowing out birthday cake candles with Coco are all for Instagram's sake. My mother has always applied what Dr. Fairs calls the if-a-tree-falls-in-the-woods approach to relationships. Even before she became an Instagran, it often felt like it was more important for her to get a photo of her and Coco to show her friends at bridge club than it was to actually spend time with Coco. She never calls to just ask how we are, never drops round unannounced to see her grandkids. If anything, she has provided me with a shining example of how not to let the optics interfere with real family life—not that I always get it right myself, by any stretch. But at least I try.

By the time we get to the studio she's been waiting around for us outside for over an hour so we can all make an entrance together. She doesn't ask me why we're late. I have to prod her to say hello to Coco, and when she does Coco's little face lights up at Granny's attention. For a split second, I see my four-year-old self in my daughter's shoes and my heart cracks a bit for both of us.

The first thing that confronts us as we walk inside is a three-foot-tall roll of toilet paper. Virginia spots it, pretends to do a double take. "Oh God, darling, did you really sign us all up for this shit?" She guffaws at her own joke. The PR looks unamused.

Today's set has been dressed to look like an enormous bathroom, with the aforementioned vastly oversized rolls, a selection of potties, and some giant toilets styled up as thrones that we'll sit on to do our interviews. We've just got to trot out the usual clichés: hardest job in the world; nothing more precious than a mama; she's always been my best friend; she told me I could do anything . . . while the assembled under-tens roll around in the four-ply like golden retriever puppies. At least that's what the director thinks will happen. I suspect he doesn't have any children himself.

With the exception of Bear, who is being fussed over by the makeup artist, all twelve kids on set are currently running around wrapped, mummy-style, in toilet paper, jacked up on *pains au chocolat* pilfered from the breakfast buffet. It is utter, earsplitting chaos. We parents are doing our best to ignore them as we mill around said breakfast buffet, recording theatrical hellos for Instastories over the avocado toast.

"Sara, you glittering marvel, I am so psyched I get to hang out with my sister from another mister all day!" Bella exclaims, filming herself going in for an enthusiastic air kiss.

I make my way over to the coffee machine to fill a #yaydays-branded mug—Irene never misses an opportunity to plug the merch. Sara heads that way too, leaving her mother stranded in conversation with Suzy Wao, whose giant earrings keep swinging perilously close to her bifocals. She gets her phone out, and I raise my mug in a cheers, throwing my head back in laughter. Sara posts it immediately with the caption: *It's a miracle: Mama drinks a cup of coffee while it's still hot!*

There *is* an art to this. I'm not saying it's one of the high arts, but it is an art.

When it's our turn to take our places on the thrones, I scoop up Bear and call Coco to come sit on Mama's lap.

She doesn't want to.

One of the assistants goes over and tries to jolly her along, points over at me and Bear, the thrones.

Coco turns her back on us, folds her arms, crouches down.

Aware I'm being watched, I keep a patient smile on my face, hand Bear to my mother, and walk across.

"Pickle," I say.

Coco doesn't respond. Understanding how many pairs of eyes are now on us, how many people are listening in, I crouch down so my face is level with my daughter's. Her bottom lip is trembling.

"What's the matter, pickle?"

She whispers something so quietly I can't hear it.

"I can't hear you, Coco. What are you saying?"

"Mummy, I don't want to. I feel shy."

"What's she saying, darling?" shouts my mother, who's managed to hand Bear off again to one of the makeup artists. "Tell her everybody is waiting."

"Just give us a minute, Mum," I shout back, as brightly as I can muster.

"Do you not remember?" I ask Coco. "We talked about how fun this was going to be. Sitting on the throne. Telling funny stories about me and Granny. You remember, we even practiced the stories."

Ages ago, when Mamabare was born, one of the first things Dan and I agreed upon was that when our daughter got old enough to say no, when she didn't want to do this anymore, that was when we'd stop. I remember we discussed it one date night, shook on it, swore. No ifs, no buts, I promised him.

The thing is, though, when you have a child, you quickly realize you're continually having to make them do things they don't want to do. Wear a nappy. Wear a coat. Get into the bath. Get out of the bath. Take their medicine. Drink their milk. Brush their teeth. Go to bed. If you never did anything your child did not want to do, you'd never leave the house. You'd just sit in front of the TV eating chocolate in a princess dress all day.

And there would not be a great deal of shareable content in that.

I can certainly remember having to do a load of things I didn't want to do when I was little: Sit through long dinners without fidgeting. An-swer promptly and clearly when anyone asked me a question. Go and say hello to all the guests at my parents' parties—a room full of men with thick voices and women with horrible laughs, a layer of cigarette smoke hanging at head height, someone with acrid breath always in-sisting on kissing me stickily on the forehead. I can remember begging not to have to go away on holiday to the same place every year, to spend two weeks in a house in Provence where I'd lie in bed listening to my parents bicker in the next room, waiting for the door to slam and the plates to smash. I can remember having to go away to boarding school at seven. I can remember coming back from my first term and finding Mum had given my guinea pig away because it was too much trouble to look after.

Did it do me any harm? Well, probably. No doubt, if you really got into it (as Dr. Fairs is always trying to), you could connect my fear of being alone in a house in the dark with that time my mum locked me in my room because I kept coming downstairs while she was entertain-ing, and you could almost definitely link my desire to make a public success of myself to both my parents' stinginess with praise and my utter, chest-swelling delight on the rare occasions I got so much as an approving nod from either. People love to find a neat psychological explanation for everything, don't they?

Nor would it take a rocket scientist to connect my choice of Dan as a husband to my confidence that he will never cheat on me or leave me. Growing up, I was fully aware that—when it came to my father—my mother and I could never be certain of either of those things. And one of the reasons I was aware of this was because she used to come into my room at night and tell me, carefully putting her wineglass down on the bedside table and raising her voice so he could hear everything she was saying, when all I really wanted was just to go to sleep. And yes, my mum was probably fucked up by her mother too, whose favorite daughter she never was, and who always found some way of telling her she wasn't the prettiest or the cleverest, and who for some reason I've never quite determined (no matter how many times I've heard the story retold) refused even to get out of the car at my parents' wedding, but just sat there in her fur coat at the end of the path up to the church while everybody waited and my grandfather tapped on the window and begged her to be reasonable.

Perhaps the truth is that I come from a very long line of very bad mothers. And that, of course, is what all this *You do you*, *Clap yourself on the back—you deserve it* crap serves to obscure. That ultimately, all mamas are not superheroes. That becoming a mum doesn't automatically confer sainthood if you were a dick before you pushed a baby out of your bits. That ultimately, all mothers are still just people. Some of us are kind and gentle and endlessly giving—others resentful and frustrated and increasingly convinced they've made a terrible mistake. Some will be getting through each day and doing their best, while others just go through the motions waiting for the seven thirty p.m. gin and tonic. There will be some mums out there who thought they were going to hate it and have surprised themselves, and others who thought they'd love it and simply don't. Some of us are wonderful. Some of us are wankers. Most of us are a mixture of all these things on any given day.

All of which, I guess, is a way of saying that while it's quite clear my daughter isn't keen on doing this commercial, I'm not about to do the heroic thing and tell everyone the deal is off, pick her up in my arms, and take her for a long walk hand in hand through a softly lit meadow. Not least because by the time we got to the car she'd have changed her mind and decided she did want to do it actually, and would then spend the whole journey home screaming and kicking my seat and demanding to go back. But also because I can only speculate how much it cost to hire this place and all the equipment, get all these people together and cater for everyone, build the set and the lighting rig and the rest. I'm not letting my family's financial future dangle and twist on the whim of a four-year-old who most of the time can't decide whether or not she wants to wear a scarf when we leave the house. And, finally, because if I know one thing for sure, it's that if we walk off this set now, we won't be walking onto one of these sets again.

Which is precisely why everyone on set is holding their breath. They know this. I know this. The only person who doesn't know this is Coco.

And so I do what any harassed working mum would do in circumstances like these.

I tell Coco if she plays ball now, we can stop at a McDonald's on the way home—somewhere we have always point-blank refused to take her—and she can have absolutely anything she wants, and then as much iPad time as she likes before bed.

She considers this for a moment.

"Happy Meal with a toy?" she says.

"It's a deal!" I tell her, wondering how she even knows what that is.

We all take our seats on the throne, my mother and me side by side, with Bear on my lap and Coco on hers. The director starts filming. My patter is polished, my gestures assured. As soon as he asks me the first question about Virginia, I reach out and grasp her upper arm. "This woman," I say, looking into the camera, welling up a little, "is my *everything*. My rock. My lighthouse." I pause. I already know this is going to be the take. "My mum," I conclude.

Somewhere out there beyond the klieg lights, there is a scattering of applause.

Then it is my mother's turn. Even though I know she had Irene write it for her and then learned it by rote, I'm mildly irritated to find that I feel a warm rush of happiness as she heaps praise onto her incredible, beautiful, smart daughter.

I see someone whisper in the director's ear, and he shouts, "Cut!"

"Can we try a take where the little girl looks a bit less miserable?" he says with an exasperated sigh.

*   *   *

There were basically three things I needed for what I was going to do. Two of them were very easy to get my hands on. The third required a little more subterfuge.

You don't spend as long as I have in an ICU without amassing a pretty thorough understanding of the practicalities of sedation. Twenty-three years I have spent monitoring pulses, checking oxygen levels, measuring levels of expired carbon dioxide, ensuring that airways are clear and drips are set up correctly and capnographs and feeds are correctly functioning, and that nothing is jammed or twisted or trapped or obstructed. Twenty-three years I have spent learning the early warning signs that something is amiss.

It is a tricky business, keeping someone alive but unconscious. No matter what you might see on your Sunday-night TV crime dramas, in your Hollywood movies, you can't just knock someone out with a massive dose of something and leave them tied up for a few days then expect them to wake up groggy but unharmed. It just doesn't work like that. First, because if you get the dose wrong and overdo things, they have a tendency to stop breathing—and if you overdo things badly, there is a good chance their heart is going to stop beating too. Second, because if you give someone a massive dose of some random sedative you have managed to get your hands on—a load of sleeping pills, say, washed down with a bottle of cough syrup, or ground up and slipped into somebody's glass of wine at dinner—then the most likely way the body is going to react is by trying to reject it, i.e., the person is going to throw up. And throwing up when you are unconscious is a great way of choking to death. It really used to exasperate Grace and her dad, when we were all watching TV together, the way I would always point out exactly where the villain was going wrong, pharmacologically, or make a point of explaining why what they were trying to do would not work.

I guess at some level I feel I owe it to all of us not to mess this up.

Even in my position, though, getting my hands on all the things I needed was far from straightforward. It was not just a matter of borrowing the keys to the relevant storeroom from the nurses' station and wandering off at leaving time with a box of benzodiazepines under your coat.

The propofol was no problem. Stockpiling that was almost worryingly easy; we use so much of it in surgery and afterward, it's just not practical to keep under lock and key. I grabbed as much of it as I could possibly need out of the drawer and wandered out of the building with it jammed into my handbag. Easy? I doubt if you had been monitoring me, I would even have displayed a quickened heartbeat. It was like walking out of the place with a bunch of pens from the stationery cupboard.

The oxygen cylinder and the mask to go with it I just took out of storage, put into a sports bag, and stowed in my locker. Then I waited until I was coming off shift late one night and carried it out to the car when there was hardly anybody around. No one raised an eyebrow. A couple of people wished me a good morning.

The infusion pump I bought online, although I probably could have sneaked one out if I had wanted to.

The midazolam was a different matter. Partly, I guess, because as a muscle relaxant and an antianxiety agent and a sedative, there are people out there who get their kicks by taking it recreationally and who are prepared to pay for the privilege. On our ward, they keep it very much under lock and key, make you sign for it. Make sure only certain people have the access code to the locked fridge.

Of course, not all of it gets used. If, say, you are an anesthetist and you need to sedate a patient and require ten milliliters of midazolam to do it, you still go (or send someone like me to go) and fetch the standard fifty-milliliter bottle.

Now, a conscientious surgeon, a diligent team, will always make sure they get rid of that other forty milliliters of midozalam before they chuck the bottle, the vial, away.

Someone who is slightly less diligent, a little less conscientious, might assume that one of the nurses will do it.

By the night they sprang that retirement party on me, I had everything I needed.

CHAPTER ELEVEN

Emmy

Hi lovely,

I've tried calling and texting a few times, but I know how busy you are. I just wanted a chat, really. I thought I might be able to steal you away at Coco's birthday, but you were so busy. I'm sorry if I seemed a bit subdued. Perhaps you guessed? You have always been so good at reading people, knowing the right thing to say—so maybe you knew, but didn't think it was the right time to ask. I don't suppose it was, really.

I have been thinking for a long time about how to tell you what I am about to—whether to share it at all. This will sound crazy, but I think I've been a bit embarrassed maybe, a bit ashamed. I have to open up now, though, as I feel like there's a huge part of my life, a huge part of me, that you just don't know about. I feel that by denying it, I am denying that those little lives we lost ever had the right to exist at all, when actually they're as important as if they were here right now.

We've had three miscarriages, Em. And that pain, and the guilt and the desperation—they just don't disappear. I can be happy one minute, or perhaps not quite happy but not achingly sad, and then it will just hit me. Three people who would have been part of our lives, just gone. The first pregnancy didn't make it past twelve weeks. A missed miscarriage, they call it. We had no bleeding, nothing. There we were at the first appointment, holding each other's hands, waiting to see the heartbeat. There was none. It's amazing how impassive the faces of the people who do the scans are, isn't it? I guess they must see it all the time. I had to have an operation for that one.

Then it happened again. We were away for the weekend in Norfolk, and I started bleeding as we were walking along the beach. The next we lost at twenty weeks. Nobody can tell us why it happened. The hope is the worst, I think. The hope that you try not to nurture from the moment that little blue line appears, but that finds its way out at night when you start to dream what it'll be like to be lying there with your baby in your arms. I haven't said anything before now because it's just so hard to find the words. Maybe there are no words. Who knows if these are even the right ones? All I know is that I have tried everything else—so maybe telling my oldest friend is the only way to heal.

The NHS doesn't fund IVF where we live, and we don't have the money to pay for it ourselves, and anyway, I don't think I can go through the heartache of losing another life. But can that really just be it? Forever?

I don't know. I don't know why I'm emailing you this. Perhaps it would feel less like mad rambling if we could talk it through face-to-face? I really miss you. Could we meet soon for a coffee or a drink?

I could really do with my best friend right now.

Polly xx

I take a deep breath, start to type a response, delete it, then read the email again as I head toward the park, a milk-drunk Bear dozing in the carrier as I walk. I had forgotten, before he was born, just how little time newborns spend awake. Feed, burp, doze, repeat. I look at his little head, topped with a cashmere beanie, beneath my chin. Feel his heartbeat against my chest. Try to imagine what it would feel like without him, without Coco. What it would be like to be in Polly's shoes. I press my lips against his head and think about all that heartache, about everything Polly must have gone through without ever breathing a word of it to me.

I also have to try to stifle a very faint sensation that feels—in a sort of queasy way—a bit like jealousy.

Sometimes I do wonder what the girls from our school think about where Polly and I are in life. When I am being kind to myself, I think they must be envious, amazed at where I've landed—a million followers, the biggest name in parenting. When I'm in a worse mood, I think that most of them probably don't have a clue who or what Mamabare is. That being Instagram famous is like being a Monopoly millionaire, and it's Polly and her husband, their pretty cottage in the suburbs and their secure jobs at a prestigious private school, that would impress them more.

The terrible irony, the thing that now stabs at me, is that I have sometimes been envious of what Polly has, or doesn't have, of how uncomplicated and comfortable her life looks. But doesn't every mother sometimes imagine what their world would be like without kids? Well, obviously I wouldn't be walking to a #greydays meetup. But what would I be doing? In a parallel universe, I'm editing *Vogue* and married to a Booker Prize winner. This—this desolate park, the low sky of unbroken cloud, the wind-scattered litter, a child strapped to my front, these fucking leggings, this slogan T-shirt—is certainly not what I thought my life would look like, but that's what happens, isn't it? You make a series of small decisions in your twenties, and they slowly bind you until they become a straitjacket. Whether or not to stay for that third drink. Whether to give that guy your number. Whether or not to answer when he rings. Whether or not you fall in love with him. Whether or not you have his babies and when.

I wouldn't say any of that to Polly, of course. But, right now, I can't think of anything to say to her. Because, really, what is there to say? I've seen it all on Instagram—all the stupid, ignorant, crass advice that people give to women who can't make babies. At least you know you can get pregnant . . . Have you thought about adoption? Tried acupuncture? Taken folic acid? Gone vegan? Done yoga? Stuck a rose quartz egg up your hoo-ha and squeezed? I can't reassure her it will all be okay, because sometimes women's bodies just don't play ball with this shit. Things do not always work out for the best.

She's not a follower expecting an emoji and a platitude—better to send something properly considered and carefully crafted than fire off a hurriedly glib or accidentally callous response. I flag the email and put my phone back in my bag.

It sometimes takes me a minute, out here in the real world, to go from being Emmy Jackson to Mamabare. To dial down the cynicism and amp up the empathy. Very slightly roughen the edges of my public-school accent. Take a deep breath and get ready for showtime. Because it's no exaggeration to say that to the kind of women I'm meeting today, I am basically a rock star.

These #greydays meetups started soon after I launched the campaign so I could meet my followers in real life, build an even deeper connection with them. I could tell by my low engagement figures that I wasn't getting it quite right on those particular posts, that they didn't ring true. Brought up as I was, taught to squash unpleasant, unwanted feelings before they made it to the surface, I found it hard to write about battling with the blues in an authentic way. But I had no choice. Women like me are expected to pick at emotional scabs for popular entertainment; we're meant to have a rich back catalogue of anxieties, insecurities, and failures that we can draw upon in podcasts and Instagram posts. It was really not until I began engaging with my followers face-to-face—hearing their stories, listening to the words they use to describe their own feelings—that I discovered how to do this in a way that connects with them, that really resonates.

The best approach, I have found, is to keep things as vague as possible, offering a suggestion of stress, a distant whiff of sadness, an oblique hint of loss. I'm careful never to go into specifics, so they can read what they need into my emotional outpourings online. Like a horoscope or a Rorschach test, they interpret the inkblots in the way that best suits them, that most helps them get through their own struggles. And I really think they do help, my posts, these monthly get-togethers, these gentle rambles around the park that have grown into a giant girl gang all sharing their battles with PND and PMT and IVF.

One harassed-looking mother with a toddler being pulled along on a scooter behind his sleeping baby sibling in a pram falls in step with me as I walk through the park gates.

"Emmy! That is you, isn't it? I'm Laura—we've met at a few of these before, when I was on maternity leave with Wolf." She points to the three-year-old angrily squishing a banana in his fists while screaming for crisps.

"This is the first time I've been out solo with him and my little Rosa," she continues breathlessly. "They say your second is easier. I mean, as you know, I had PTSD after my first birth. I thought this time round I'd be a natural, but I just can't seem to get on top of everything. I wanted to talk to you about it as I just feel you really get me." Her eyes are brimming with tears, and I know if I let her go on, they'll be spilling out in sobs, and then I'll have to spend the best part of five minutes patting her back.

I touch my shoulder to hers as we walk. "Of course I remember you, Laura. My goodness, little Wolf is so big now! He must be almost exactly the same age as Coco." I go to ruffle his hair, and he jerks his head away.

"And Rosa and Bear are nearly the same age too. It's almost like I timed it that way! Sorry to be such a fangirl, but just to know someone else is going through the exact same thing, in the exact same way, is so uplifting," she says, fiddling with a button that's about to fall off her cardigan. "It's like you see into my soul."

Pretty once, I'm sure, Laura now has huge brown patches of melasma on her face, a halo of wispy hair regrowth, and an undeflated baby bump, and is walking like someone sliced open her undercarriage and did it back up with a stapler. This baby-making business is brutal.

"That's so incredible to hear," I say, tilting my head and squeezing her hand. "It moves me so much to know my story has touched someone. You just need to remember that you are enough."

She dabs at her eyes with the sleeve of her cardigan and nods her head. The thing about these women—Laura, standing here in front of me, and the other million-odd who follow me—is that they feel like they've ceased to exist. The media, their husbands, their friends— none of them ever really acknowledge what it means to spend day in, day out mopping up puke, shit, and uneaten puree. To spend every night racking your brains trying to work out how to make tomorrow a little different to stop you going mad from boredom—not just another trip to the swings, the same baby gym that smells of feet, the café that doesn't really want you and your fussy toddler taking up space, sharing one croissant and spilling a hot chocolate on the floor.

And of course, yes, some dads do this, and go through this too. But it is not dads who follow me, and it is never men who come along to these #greydays meetups. Which used to puzzle me. Then I thought about the reaction Dan gets, walking down the street with Bear in his pram, or with Coco on her scooter. The friendly smiles, the compliments, the little nods and winks and gestures of approval and affirmation. The indisputable fact that when a man does even the very basics of childcare, however awkwardly, ineptly, or begrudgingly, he gets applauded for it. Whereas when a woman walks down the street with a baby, the only time anyone even notices is if they think she is doing something wrong.

I may be selfish. I may be cynical. But that does not mean that Mamabare does not provide a genuine public service.

I see these women, I listen to them, I understand them. I don't judge them, and I encourage them to be a bit less judgmental about themselves.

And they love me for it.

Dan

It's my mum I have to thank, really. She's the one who happened to take Coco to the park that day and strike up a conversation with the woman sitting next to her, only to find out that she was in fact a retired former nurse, now working as a nanny. She was just about to start looking for a new kid to mind, the woman (she introduced herself as Doreen Mason), because the one she was currently caring for—she gestured at a boy with longish hair on the seesaw—was about to start big school this September and wouldn't be needing her anymore. "Oh," said my mum. "That's funny."

Mum asked where Doreen lived. Doreen told her. It was about a fifteen-minute walk from our place. Mum had walked across the estate with Coco loads of times. Sometimes she pushed Coco on the swings in the little playground in the middle of it. Mum said you could tell Doreen really enjoyed spending time with children, playing with them, talking to them, from the way she spoke about the kids she had looked after over the years. She still sent them all birthday cards, she said, always got Christmas cards back. According to my mother, Doreen had a very reassuring, down-to-earth manner.

I said I hoped Mum had taken her number.

It's absurd how difficult it is to find reliable, affordable childcare. You'd think in an area full of affluent youngish working couples, an area like ours, in this day and age, it would be the sort of thing someone would do something about, wouldn't you? That if you were willing to spend a bit of money and do a bit of research then at least a couple of viable options would present themselves.

You would be wrong.

I've tried. I've spent ages online. Sent emails. Asked around. I called all the different nurseries in the vicinity. I even went to see one the other day. I turned up at the right time and no one answered the buzzer. I pushed the door and it swung right open. *Probably not the best start*, I thought to myself. There was a little row of pegs at adult waist height hung with coats in the corridor, a little row of boots lined up underneath. A child appeared at the top of the stairs, sucking on a plastic spoon. It looked down at me, then turned and wandered off. From a room to my left, I could hear a child screaming. The whole place smelled of boiled cabbage.

I didn't need to see any more.

Which left us on the waiting list for about five other places, all of which were currently operating on a one-out-one-in basis, and none of which could foresee any new spaces becoming available until the start of next year at the earliest. I did try dropping Emmy's name into at least one conversation. The woman at the other end of the line, her English thickly accented, asked me to spell it.

When Emmy last asked me how things were going I told her I was on the case. That was three days ago. Coco keeps asking when she's going back to her old nursery and when she's going to see her friends again. Did she not enjoy hanging out with me and with Gran-Gran? I asked. Coco's answer was a kind of apologetic shrug.

When I ring Doreen, she answers pretty much right away and tells me she can come over that afternoon. "And how old is little Coco?" she asks. I tell her. Doreen says she is looking forward to meeting her. The first thing, she says, will be to make sure that we all get on and understand how this is going to work. "Of course," I say, literally crossing my fingers. I tell her our address and she makes a note of it.

Thankfully, she and Coco hit it off at once. I go to make Doreen a cup of tea—two sugars—and by the time I get back, she's on her hands and knees playing with Coco and they're both having a whale of a time. Once I reappear, Doreen stands up, aided by the arm of the couch. We start chatting and, quite without prompting, Coco goes over and sits next to her and sort of curls up against her.

"Sweet little girl," says Doreen when Coco has gone off to play at the other end of the living room for a bit. "Lovely name."

"It was my wife's idea, actually," I reveal, as I always do when I get the chance.

When Doreen tells me her hourly fee, I say that sounds perfectly reasonable to me—only marginally more than we were paying the nursery. "Would you prefer cash?" I ask. She says a check is fine. "Oh," she adds, as if she has just remembered. "I'd better ask—does little Coco have any allergies?" I say not that we know of, although she does get a little sniffly on very polleny days in the summer, but she's okay with milk and nuts and penicillin. "That's good," says Doreen. "So many kids seem to have them these days, allergies." The little boy she looks after at the moment, Stephen, has to be very careful with shellfish. His mother gave her a little allergy pen to carry with her at all times. Doreen never goes anywhere without it; she wouldn't dare. "You would never forgive yourself, would you? If anything happened to one of them and it was your fault?"

I agree not.

As she's drinking her tea, her eyes are giving our bookshelves the once-over.

"I expect you'll want to know what Emmy and I do for a living," I suggest.

Doreen raises her shoulders gently.

"Is it something to do with books?" she asks.

I tell her I am a writer, and she nods, as if this explains a lot. Trying to describe what Emmy does proves trickier. I keep thinking Doreen has got it, then she asks a question like, "What is Instagram?" or expresses surprise that some people have the internet on their phones. She's pretty sure she's on the Facebook, she says. She thinks one of her great-nieces set her up an account.

We arrange for Doreen to come back and do a half day with Coco to start off with, the following morning. If you come at eight, I say, that will give you the chance to meet Emmy too.

"I'll look forward to that," she says. "And to seeing you again, Coco."

Coco looks up and smiles and waves.

"See you tomorrow!" she says.

Once I've closed the door behind her, I check the time, wondering where Emmy has got to. That thing in the park must be over by now, surely; it's nearly time for Coco's dinner. I'm looking forward to her getting home and to telling her what Coco and I have been up to and seeing her reaction.

All in all, I reckon it's been quite a successful day. My status in our relationship as a mature adult who can be entrusted with a responsible task—in this case, arranging childcare that doesn't involve Winter or my mother—has been reaffirmed. Not only that, but apparently there was another seemingly random midafternoon attempted burglary two streets over the day before last, which means that I've almost managed to put my panic about the stolen laptop out of mind entirely.

It is hardly surprising the relationship broke down, really, after what happened. I know they tried their best to get through it, to help each other through it. Neither of them ever thought they could get over it, obviously. Neither of them ever wanted to get over it. At the funeral, Grace and Jack clung to each other, keeping each other upright. All through the inquest, they sat shoulder to shoulder, holding hands tightly under the table. Afterward, she clutched the shoulder of his suit as their lawyer read their prepared statement. Death by misadventure, that was the coroner's finding.

It was only after they had got through all that, I think, that things really started to go wrong. When the funeral was over and the people had gone home and they were left to face the rest of their lives together.

The person who first noticed how oddly Grace was behaving was not me or Jack. It was my friend Angie, who hardly knew Grace at all. We were out having a cup of coffee one Saturday morning in town, and as we were sitting at our table in the window of Costa, Grace walked past. Well, that was strange, for one thing, because she hadn't said anything to me about driving over, but I guessed maybe she had arranged to meet up with some of her old friends for brunch; maybe it was a last-minute thing, something like that.

Angie spotted Grace and asked me if that was her and at first I said it couldn't be. Then I looked, and it was her and I knocked on the window. She looked up and saw me and sort of faintly smiled. I beckoned her in. She hesitated a minute. It was not until later that I found myself wondering what Grace was doing wandering around town in the middle of the morning. At the time I found myself noticing—as a mum does—that her hair looked a bit unwashed and wondering—as a mum does—whether I should say anything about it. She did seem a bit distracted, but I put that down to her having other things to think about. And while she did look a bit thin, I knew she hadn't had much appetite of late. It was hardly surprising.

Not until Angie asked me if Grace was looking after herself did I really start wondering about my daughter's state of mind. About whether she was okay. There had been a couple of times when she fazed out of the conversation completely. Admittedly, Angie is not the most scintillating conversationalist. She was telling us about a recent trip to hospital, to get some regular tests done, the trouble she had parking. But under any normal circumstances, a kind, gentle, generous girl like my daughter would at least have pretended to be listening. She got up and went to the loo. She came back again. She said she had to go. She promised she would call me. She barely even said goodbye to Angie.

That was when I started noticing things: How often, when I visited, Grace would be in her pajamas or clothes with food stains on them, or would look like she had just got out of bed. How often she was not at work. How there was never anything in their fridge when I went around but the dregs of a bottle of white wine and some milk on the turn.

It took me a long time to work up the courage to say anything about all this to Jack. He more or less told me to mind my own business. It was Grace, not him, who let slip they were not sleeping in the same bedroom anymore. It was only much later I found out she had moved into the room they had decorated for the baby, that she was sleeping on the floor in there, on a blanket.

Grace was the one who'd asked him to move out. She'd told him it hurt to look at him. That she felt guilty every time they found themselves having a conversation that was not about the baby who was gone. She felt it was all her fault, that he thought it was all her fault but would never say it and it would just fester forever. She flinched every time he touched her. Tensed every time he came into the room. Jack said she spent all her time on her phone, in a lukewarm bath, thumb scrolling, face blank.

When he did move out, he did so with the understanding that it was only a temporary thing. If she needed space, he would give it to her. When she was ready to see him again, to talk about where they went from there, he would be ready. He was only staying about half an hour down the road, with a friend, in their spare room.

One week turned into two weeks, two weeks into four. He told me she was not answering her phone, not replying to the texts he sent her.

And then one morning, very casually, very flatly, she informed me on the phone that she had decided to file a petition for divorce.

CHAPTER TWELVE

Emmy

"Oh, by the way, I meant to tell you, Irene called," says Winter, several minutes after I came back from putting Bear down for his nap. While I've been making myself something to eat, she's been sitting at the kitchen island, pouting at herself in her phone, adjusting her beret.

"Right," I say, with a glance at the clock.

"She said it was something about a TV show."

"Yeah?"

Winter nods. I smile encouragingly. The moment lengthens.

"No message?" I ask eventually.

"Oh," says Winter after a pause. "And she wants you to call her back straightaway."

Irene never calls unless she really has to. Emails, WhatsApps, DMs, yes. Picking up the phone? Almost unheard-of.

I didn't get that BBC Three job. That must be what Irene is calling to tell me. That's why she didn't want to leave a message. I can feel it in my bones.

I don't know why I even let myself get my hopes up, really. We've been here too many times before, Irene and I—been through this over and over and over. The meetings, the camera tests, the read-throughs, the waiting. The optimistic glow of that first day waiting to hear back, buoyed by memories of how friendly everybody was and how well it had seemed to go, my phone within grabbing distance at all times. The second day, anxiety starting to creep in, recurring thoughts of things I might have done better, or differently, things I wish I hadn't said. The third day. The fourth. Then the news that I was great but they've gone with someone else. I was great but someone else was even greater. They wanted someone older, someone younger; they'd decided to go with someone with more of an edge, with less of an edge. It's nothing personal, they just didn't like my hair or my clothes or my face or my voice or my personality.

Fuck it. Fuck it. Fuck it. Fuck it. Fuck them.

"Are you okay?" asks Winter. "Do you want a bit of my kombucha or something?"

"No thanks, Winter. I am afraid there are some things even a seven-quid soft drink can't fix." I smile through gritted teeth.

Something that's really begun to sink in recently, something that has really started to terrify me when I wake in the middle of the night and find myself thinking about the future, is that there may be no escape route from all this. Despite all my plotting and planning, all those years of turning up to the opening of a nappy bag, pretending to love women I'd otherwise dread getting stuck in an elevator with, of flogging bum cream and water wipes, cheese spread and chicken nuggets, of responding to every pissy DM and crazy comment—all with an eye on a bigger prize—I may have just ended up stranding myself in yet another career cul-de-sac. Canoed myself, if you will, up yet another dead-end creek. And this time, I've made reversing even harder, as I have *just enough* celebrity—like a *Love Island* contestant, say, or an *X Factor* runner-up—to make returning to normal life at best mortifying and at worst impossible. I'd be like one of those former soap stars the tabloids laugh at for working at Starbucks.

Having left behind the magazine industry as it was crumbling around my ears, it could be that I'm more aware than most about the long-term prospects of this line of work. You know those cartoons where Wile E. Coyote comes to the end of the cliff and keeps going, legs furiously wheeling away, giving it his all, and then he suddenly looks down and there's nothing underneath him? I know exactly how that coyote feels.

Anyone with any experience of the media, social or otherwise, knows this influencer stuff can't last. Just as the once-useful Twitter is now full of angry men correcting one another's grammar and swearing at feminists, like Myspace before it died along with the careers of all those Justin Bieber wannabes, Instagram is poised over a precipice. With women wising up to the fact that we are just saleswomen disguised as sisters, flogging them things they don't need, can't afford, and that won't make them feel better anyway, even if I was willing to pop out a new kid every couple of years to keep the content flowing, Instaparenting feels like a particularly precarious way to make a living. But Dan is unlikely to be finishing that second novel any time soon, so at least one of us needs to have a long-term plan. And mine has always been to make the leap from the tiny screen you hold in your hand to the slightly bigger one in the living room.

TV presenting just seems to me like the next logical step. There are times when, in my head at least, the whole thing has seemed not just natural but inevitable. Over the years, at my insistence, Irene has booked me for as many on-screen interviews as would have me, for practice in front of the camera—I've been the parental pundit on everything from *Newsnight* to *Loose Women*, with varying degrees of success. She's got me in for auditions, meetings with casting agents. The advent of Instastories helped a bit: it's been a useful training ground and a never-ending audition for the role of myself. To be honest, I was never quite as good at it as we'd both hoped, but I've improved with experience. With her contacts from the acting agent days, Irene set me up with voice coaches so I stopped swallowing my words, movement specialists so my hands don't flap awkwardly, and a media trainer who taught me how not to look wild-eyed.

I've had some paid gigs, including a kids' TV show about climate change on which I was interviewing a man dressed as a polar bear, and an influencer special of *Antiques Road Trip*. A few proper presenting projects have even looked like they were about to happen, then been canceled. The show that I'm sure Irene is calling about, a BBC Three documentary I was hoping to front, has nearly been green-lit five times before. The idea is almost as old as Coco, in fact, but while they know they want it to be about the struggles of starting a family, they keep changing their mind about the angle. There have been casual chats and hardball negotiations, only for it to all go quiet again.

The last time I was called in, they lined up an actress for a screen test, to talk me through her heartbreaking baby loss experience in all the distressing detail, the actor playing her husband holding her hand and silently weeping as she spoke. They were emoting their socks off, and all I had to do was make the right noises, come up with the right questions off the cuff. Somehow, though, I just couldn't seem to get the tone right. I could hear myself sounding fake, sounding brittle. The first few takes everyone was very supportive, the actors making encouraging comments, the director offering suggestions and trying to help me relax, loosen up a bit. By take five people were discreetly checking their watches. After take six we took a brief break. By take nine it felt pretty clear to everyone in the room that this was not a gig I was in the process of landing.

I take a deep breath and dial. "Go on, then, give me the bad news." I sigh.

"Actually, Emmy, it's the opposite. BBC Three called to say that you're down to the final two."

It takes a moment for what Irene is saying to really register. I was so braced for another knockback that by the time it does, I'm already halfway through formulating some expression of polite regret that I was not what they were looking for, again.

"The final two?" I say.

"You're up against ivfandangels—usually I'd say you're a dead cert but, well, topic-wise the show is very much on-brand for her. Obviously, though, in terms of follower count, you have a massive advantage."

She is not bloody kidding. Admittedly, ivfandangels has got two hundred thousand followers, but still, if it's sheer numbers they're going on, there's no contest.

"The thing is—and this is something they were absolutely up front about—they've changed the angle. They want whoever they choose to be able to put a personal spin on things—for the show to have an authentic human story at its heart."

Of course they fucking do. Which means, therefore, I don't stand a chance. Ivfandangels has personal tragedy coming out of her *ears*. Every time her child has a birthday she always sets out six little empty seats, lights the candles on five extra cupcakes, and posts the artfully lit pictures on Instagram.

Irene tells me they've asked us both for one more thing. They've seen all they need to, audition-wise.

"They're just asking for a brief video clip. Explaining why this is a show you *have* to make. Really opening up about your own experiences."

"Really opening up," I repeat.

"Oh, and they want you both to send your video by five o'clock today. I think they want to put you on the spot so it feels real and raw. Is that going to be a problem?" she asks.

"No problem," I reply airily. "Tell them I'll send it over by five at the latest."

The baby monitor relays a half-awake squeak from Bear's room. A series of tentative moans and mumbles follows. Jesus Christ. His nap can't be over yet, can it?

I check the time. One hour exactly until five p.m. I find myself unable to stop envisioning the minutes literally slipping away like sand through my fingers. I think about all the effort and time and energy I have put into this over the years. All the sacrifices I've made. What it would feel like to turn the TV on and accidentally stumble across ivfandangels standing by a lake and reading a poem, wandering around hospital corridors looking soulful.

The squeaks gather pace into full-on, angry screams. The baby is definitely awake.

I take a deep breath, open my email, and type the name "Polly" into the search bar.

Dan

What kind of sick fuck? That is what I keep asking myself. What kind of sick fuck?

One of the things about putting your life out there online: there is always someone who pops up and helpfully draws your attention to anything nasty, vile, or just unpleasant someone has written about you that you might otherwise somehow have missed. Some helpful fucker with nothing better to do, happy to provide a link to a terrible Goodreads review you were unaware of, to loop you into a negative discussion of your work on Twitter, or, in Emmy's case, to make sure you're kept up to speed with how a thread about you on Guru Gossip or Tattle Life titled "Has Mamabare put on more weight?" is progressing. It's not that I think Suzy Wao was delighted exactly to inform Emmy of the #rp account, but even through the three-line WhatsApp, I could feel the fizz of excitement, perhaps even a whiff of schadenfreude.

I've just read Coco her bedtime story (one from *Good Night Stories for Rebel Girls,* of which we have about twelve or so copies around the house, all presents from various people, including my mother) and wished her sweet dreams and came downstairs to grab a beer from the fridge before sitting down at the kitchen island with my laptop.

Emmy came in a few hours ago and told me her news, and I said if she was down to the last two she's bound to get it. A TV show. Not just a talking head slot, not just being part of a panel, but her own TV show. Would she have her name in the title? I asked. She said not to get ahead of ourselves; the title wasn't settled yet. We exchanged a look. Her eyes were gleaming. "I think we both know you're going to get it," I said. She smiled coyly. "All I can say," she said, "is that I have given it my best shot." While I've been sitting here, I've googled the producer's name and googled the person who commissioned it and now I am basically googling everyone involved in the whole thing. There are some serious people on board, from the looks of things. People who've worked with big names. Who have made programs even I have heard of, or at least read reviews of in the *Guardian*. It's only after Emmy has gone upstairs to check on the kids that I realize I forgot to ask what the program is actually going to be about.

Emmy is upstairs when her phone buzzes, and I glance over.

And for a moment, it feels like the bottom has dropped out of my world.

Of all the weird, disgusting, horrible stuff that happens on the internet, Instagram role-players—#babyrp is the hashtag they sometimes use, although they do it subtly, burying it toward the end of a block of hashtags so no one sees—have always seemed to me right up there. Not only in the sense that what they do strikes me as gross and insensitive and morally questionable, but in that I am wholly incapable of imagining myself into the mindset of someone who would do something like that. It's like those people who post videos of themselves doing stupid, unfunny, dangerous pranks on YouTube (drinking a bucket of puke, say, or throwing water balloons at strangers on a mall escalator and then getting beaten up). It's like deciding to troll the parents of a teen suicide or the survivors of a school shooting or spending your whole day sending hate messages to an actress of color you thought was miscast in a *Star Wars* movie. I just don't get the point. To steal pictures of other people's kids and post them on Instagram under a different name. To make up stories about them, their family situations, what they're like. Real pictures. Real children. Even if I didn't have a kid of my own, I think I'd find it unsettling in the same visceral way.

What Suzy has texted to tell Emmy is that she's stumbled across an Instagram feed that is all pictures of Coco.

Of course I unlock Emmy's phone—yes, I know her pass code; it is the date on which Coco was born—and click on the link.

In the very first picture I see, Coco is holding my hand, looking back over her shoulder at the camera. I remember that day. It was one of those late summer days, dry, bright, when there was just a hint of autumn in the air. The leaves had started falling, had started piling up along the edges of the sidewalks, because I remember Coco romping through them as we were walking down the road, laughing. We waited at the crossing next to the nursery for the cars to stop, Coco waving a chubby paw at the drivers, and I was telling Coco to be good and trying to get her excited about all the new people she was going to meet on her first day in her new room at nursery. I waited until she was playing and made a discreet exit and then sat in the Starbucks around the corner in case someone from the nursery called, in case she was upset and they needed me to come back and calm her down. She wasn't, of course. I didn't. She was not fazed by her new teacher, a whole new set of classmates, at all. I think when I came back to collect her that afternoon she was a little amazed that it was home time already.

The caption is all about little Rosie ("our DD—Darling Daughter") having trouble sleeping, and the mad thing is that all sorts of people have written comments sympathizing and offering suggestions for what got their baby to sleep.

The thought of someone making all this stuff up about *our* daughter, using her real pictures, giving her some made-up name, preying on people's gullibility, violating my daughter's privacy, makes me feel almost sick with anger.

I'm very tempted to write something under the picture myself. Something brutal, something threatening. Not physically threatening. Not really. The kind of threat I have in mind this time involves the police, and letters from lawyers.

I can hear Emmy padding around upstairs. She descends to the ground floor in her pajamas, with a face mask on, her hair piled on top of her head in a knot. She crosses to the sink, gets herself a glass of water, comes through to where I am sitting.

"How you doing?" she says.

I am not really sure how to answer. I jut my chin at the screen.

"What?" she asks.

"That," I say.

"What's that?" she asks, taking the phone from me with one hand as she rearranges her towel with the other.

"Suzy Wao found it and messaged to let you know," I tell her.

"Uh-huh," she says.

Emmy's face as she reads is expressionless. After she has clicked a few images, scrolled down a little ways, she passes me back the phone.

"I'll call Irene now," she says.

I hold her gaze, shake my head.

"No, Emmy," I say.

"You don't want me to call Irene?"

"I want her off the internet," I say. "I want Coco—I want both our children—off the fucking internet."

Emmy takes a deep breath. I know what she's about to say. That this doesn't just happen to influencers. That it could happen to anyone who has pictures of their children online. That the internet is just the internet. It's not real. It has always amazed me, Emmy's ability to shrug off online criticism, her ability to ignore all the people out there who don't like her, who rant and rave about how much they hate her, what a bad person she is; all those random strangers with their burning opinions about the way she dresses, the way she looks, the way she writes, the way she mothers.

This is different, though. This is *clearly* different. This—*this*, I think, tempted to poke the actual screen with my finger, lest the point be missed—is my child.

"Keep reading," I say. "Just look. There are loads. Fucking loads of it. Picture after picture. Post after post. Whoever this person is, they're fucking *obsessed*."

She settles down next to me with a sigh, and I can feel the heat of the shower still coming off her in waves. She starts to read. She scrolls down and stops reading. She scrolls down again. From time to time her lips contract. From time to time her nostrils flare. I watch the words reflected in her eyes, her face lit by the phone's pale glow.

All of a sudden, abruptly, she half chucks it onto the table, as if she cannot bear to have it near her, and clamps her hands to her mouth and folds her legs up under her. I reach a hand out to her and she ignores it.

"What?" I say.

She's shaking her head. Her eyes are wide.

"What is it?" I ask again.

I'm tempted to pick the laptop up and open it. I go to do so. She grabs my wrist.

"Dan," she says.

"Yes," I say. "What is it? You're scaring me a bit now."

"Those photos."

"Yes?"

"Some of those photos, the most recent ones on that account, the RP account."

"Yes," I say encouragingly.

"They're not photos that we've ever posted online."

*   *   *

I saw him the other day, Jack. Grace's Jack. I had just been over to the house, checking up on everything, mowing the front lawn and the little bit of verge in front of the hedge, trimming the foliage back around the FOR SALE *sign, checking that the place looked okay, and on the way back I popped into the supermarket, the big one on the outskirts of town, to get some milk and a newspaper. Jack looked like he was picking up supplies for the week. He was pushing a loaded shopping cart with one hand, checking his phone with his other. There is a new kid now, of course. A little boy. A new wife, or at least girlfriend. Pictures of them all pop up every so often on Facebook. A birthday party. A trip to the zoo. I'll not lie. It used to upset me to see him looking so happy, to see them all looking so happy. I thought for a while about muting him, unfriending him even. Why was he always smiling? I kept wondering. Did he never think about the baby, the daughter he had lost? The wife he had lost? And then I remembered, of course: it's just social media. Who posts a picture of themselves crying, with puffy eyes and snot on their chin? Who posts a picture of themselves feeling blue? Who posts a picture of themselves going through the slow, dull, unphotogenic business of mourning? A snapshot of one of those passing moments on the bus or waiting for one or just walking along when suddenly out of nowhere a sharp pang hits you? A reminder, the sense of something missing, the sudden realization that there are things you will never be able to tell someone, things you experienced together that you are now the only person in the whole world who remembers.*

It is a double grief in this case, of course: it wasn't just baby Ailsa who died; it was also the person she could have, would have been. The fact that she will never go to big school or university or leave home or have a boyfriend, a husband, a family of her own. That the silver christening necklace we got for her to wear when she was older will now never be worn. The baby clothes of hers that Grace kept, that I now have, that I used to look forward to showing her when she was older so she could see how little she used to be—I don't suppose I will ever show them to anyone now. They are still there, in the attic at my house, carefully wrapped up—and one day when I die and someone comes to clear out the house, it will probably puzzle them for a moment if they even bother to look inside the box.

He did not look particularly happy or sad when I saw him, Jack. Mostly he just looked tired. I watched him going up and down the baby aisle, scanning the shelves, looking for something. I did think about going over and offering to help. Perhaps that would have been the normal thing to do—but, of course, things can never really be normal between Jack and me, not now, not ever again. And so I lurked at the end of the aisle and peeked around the discounted bread and watched him pick things up and read the packet and frown and put them back again.

I'll always remember their wedding day—the dress, all the speeches. The way they looked at each other.

He must be nearly one now, the new kid, little Leon. Does Jack still think about Ailsa? He must do. It must haunt him. To know that whatever you do, however careful you are, sometimes it is just not possible to keep your baby alive. That sometimes just when it feels like you have everything, life comes and swats you and scatters you and stamps on everything you have worked for and strived toward and treasure. What can you say to someone who has lost a child? What can you possibly say? Even if the child was also your grandchild?

There is nothing to say, and you can never stop saying it.

I got my milk. I got my paper. I was heading for the checkout when Jack came around the end of the aisle right ahead of me. I practically walked straight into him.

"Oh," I said.

He looked up, raised an apologetic hand, muttered a sorry, steered the cart in a rather exaggerated way out of my path, and kept on going.

And as I turned to watch Jack making his way up the aisle, his shoulders hunched over the cart, his thoughts miles away, this person who had just looked straight through me, I found myself wondering—for a brief, silly moment—whether I had changed as much on the outside as it sometimes feels I have on the inside. Or whether the reason he had not clocked me was something to do with that sort of instinct that prompts you not to look directly at someone who is somehow out of place, damaged, broken. To avoid the eye of the beggar outside the train station. The muttering nutter on the bus. The woman who comes up and tries to talk to you on the street and needs exactly five pounds and sixteen pence to get back to Leicester. There are times when I can imagine myself ending up as one of those people all too easily.

There are times when I can imagine myself as almost anything.

CHAPTER THIRTEEN

Dan

Every day now there's another one. Another post, more made-up nonsense, another photograph not previously in the public domain. Always at the same time—seven o'clock in the evening. Just after Coco goes to bed. There have been three of them. Three new posts since we first discovered the RP account. Each of them rubbing more salt in the wound, each one slightly creepier than the last. The thing is, even now, weird as it sounds, I think that if the posts were clearly labeled #rp, if anywhere on the account the poster had acknowledged that what they were writing was fiction, I probably wouldn't be quite so freaked out by it all. Angry, sure. Disgusted, sure. A crime would still have been committed. But at least I would feel I had some clearer grasp on what they were doing, what they wanted, what their end goal might be.

The last three days have genuinely felt like being stuck in a nightmare—a nightmare that begins the moment you wake up and drags on all day and from which no escape seems imaginable.

Every time I leave the house I find myself looking over my shoulder, peering into cars, giving anyone I don't recognize a narrow stare. I spent all of yesterday evening watching a bloke in overalls put another bolt on the back door and reinforce the front doorframe only to spend half the night wide awake asking myself if I could really trust the locksmith.

This person—the one who is posting this stuff, who took Winter's laptop—*has been inside our house*. They've *touched* things in *our* kitchen. Taken things from us.

They have every photo on that laptop. Every photo on the Cloud. Private photos. Personal photos. Photos of our daughter.

And now they're posting them one by one online.

As soon as we realized what had happened, Emmy went into an immediate war council with Irene. I have to hand it to Emmy's agent: I've never known her not take a call. I'm not sure I've ever known her to keep Emmy waiting for more than three rings. Presumably she does at some point sleep, eat, use the toilet. Each of these things is more or less equally difficult to imagine.

Irene was on speakerphone. Emmy was pacing the kitchen with a glass of wine. I was sitting with my laptop on the couch.

The question Irene kept asking Emmy was what she thought the police were going to be able to do. How much help had they been, she asks, when we reported the burglary? As for Instagram, how responsive had they been to any of her previous complaints about anything?

Emmy didn't answer, so I assumed the questions were rhetorical.

Watching Emmy pace, I felt a little bit sicker and angrier than I had previously. Not just with whoever was doing this. With Emmy. With Irene. Maybe also with myself.

Yesterday's post, the second new one since Emmy and I discovered the site, was the worst of them yet. A real kick in the guts. At one point as I was reading it, I thought I was actually going to be sick, that I was actually going to hunch over on the kitchen stool I was sitting on and spatter my dinner all over the floor.

"Hello again!!" it opened. Two exclamation marks. (The whole thing, I have to admit, was a pretty convincing pastiche of the way that all the Instamums, my wife included, write. The mangled metaphors, the breathless overenthusiasm. The ingenuous clunkiness. The alliteration. It's no wonder there are people who follow this account who seem to have really fallen for it.) It was not until I got to the end of what they had written that I experienced genuine nausea.

The post ended with the news that "Rosie" had been to the hospital for some tests and that, although it had hurt at times, she had been very brave.

Oh God, so sorry to hear that was the start of the very first comment under the post, *Hope the results come back fine and she feels better very soon!* The second person to comment posted a whole anecdote about one time when their own little darling was sick. The third comment was just an emoji with a bandage around its head and a thermometer in its mouth, then a load of kisses.

The picture that accompanied the post was one I had taken of Coco in the back garden last summer, grinning on her new bike as she rides it in circles around the paddling pool.

My daughter.

My daughter.

The real girl who is asleep upstairs, in her little bed with the little ladder up to it, under her *Frozen* duvet, with her head on her pillow in its *Frozen* pillowcase. Whose floor is scattered with toys and whose walls ripple with pictures she has drawn at school every time the wind blows or the door opens and who when I last checked on her had fallen asleep still clutching her Elsa doll. Who still does not understand why she can't go back to her old nursery and see all her old friends.

By the third day I am checking the RP account once every five or ten minutes. Rereading what has been posted. Seeing what new comments have appeared. Scrolling through the latest followers. Driving myself fucking crazy.

The new post drops at seven p.m. on the dot.

Emmy and I are sitting at opposite ends of the living room couch, phones clutched tightly in our hands. The instant she sees the picture, I hear her sharp intake of breath. I stare at the screen.

"What the *fuck*?" I ask.

The photo is one of Coco curled in a ball on a hospital bed, looking sad, a drip just in shot behind her. It's not a picture I've seen before. A photo I can't really understand—where it comes from or where it was taken. It takes me a minute to work out that the drip is not actually attached to my daughter. Even then I have more questions than I know what to do with. As my brain slowly, laboriously, pieces together where the photograph was taken, and when, and by whom, and to what purpose, I feel with each realization a little sicker, a little angrier, a little more disgusted. That Emmy could do that. That Emmy could do that to our daughter. That Emmy could even think of doing that to our daughter.

I have to read the words underneath the picture several times before they start to sink in, before they start to make sense as sentences. The post begins with an announcement that it has been a difficult one to write. There follows a load of stuff about what a long day it has been but how brave and cheerful little Rosie was and how proud they are of her. There is a long section about how much it means to them both to know that they are in people's thoughts and prayers and how they are hoping to reply personally to everyone eventually.

"For the moment," it concludes, "we're just waiting for the results and taking things one day at a time."

"What does that mean?" I keep asking Emmy. "Read that. What does that mean?"

Her face, in the blue light of the screen, is drawn. Her mouth is a tight, straight line. As she reads, she's turning a bracelet on her wrist. Around and around and around.

"I don't know," she says.

She scratches at the corner of her mouth, bites a nail.

"I don't know what it means, Dan," she says again.

For the first time my wife looks like she's genuinely spooked.

*　*　*

I should have done more. I could have done more. This is what haunts me. That if I had known what to do, what to say, who to turn to for help, then Grace might still be here.

I did try to talk to her. I did encourage her to see her GP, see if he could suggest anything. I was always trying to persuade her to get out and do things, talk to her friends, see people, even just come for a walk and get some fresh air. Grace would just look at me and say nothing. Sometimes I would speak to her and it was as if she had forgotten I was there at all. Those last few weeks she looked thinner and more tired every time I saw her. Great dark bags under her eyes. Drawn cheeks. Really unwell. The shaved head did not help. Every time I saw her I asked whether she was going to grow it again, just a little, one of these days. She would get cross with me. I would let it drop.

She always used to have such long, beautiful hair, my daughter.

I just kept hoping the house would sell, that she would get a good price for it and could start over somewhere else, somewhere a bit closer to me and all her friends. Somewhere with fewer memories.

That weekend, that last weekend, Grace seemed, if anything, a bit brighter, compared to how she had been. I spoke to her on the Friday night and she even laughed once, at something I told her, something about one of my neighbors, something silly they had said to me. "I love you, Mum," she said, as she was hanging up.

It had been agreed that I would pop in on Sunday afternoon for a cup of tea.

I had my own keys to her place. I always had done, just in case she or Jack ever lost theirs, found themselves locked out, or needed me to drive over and wait in for a parcel or a repairman. I would never usually have used them, if I had known Grace was in the house.

I rang the bell for about fifteen minutes.

In the front hall, I shouted her name. I looked into the living room to see if she was in there. I checked the kitchen. Upstairs I stuck my head around the bedroom door. When I tried the bathroom door, at first I thought it was locked. Then I gave it another try and realized it wasn't locked, that it gave slightly when I put my shoulder to it, but that there was something piled up against it on the other side, stopping it from opening. I kept pushing and the door gave a little. I pushed harder and I could see something trapped under it, stuck between the bottom of the door and the floor of the bathroom. It was the sleeve of one of Grace's sweaters. I gave it a tug. It was stuck fast. I gave the door another shove. It moved another centimeter or two. I called Grace's name again. Nobody answered.

The coroner's verdict was that she had been dead since late Saturday afternoon. She had been to the shops that morning and bought some milk and bread from the co-op. As she was leaving she bumped into someone she used to work with, stopped for a chat, talked about setting a date to meet up some time, seemed in good spirits. Then at some point later in the day she put the cup of tea she was drinking down on the kitchen counter, half finished, and went to the bathroom and lined up everything she needed on the closed toilet seat lid and ran herself a bath and ended her own life. She was thirty-two years old.

Emmy

Just so you know, that little blue tick, the one that Instagram bestows upon you, the sign that you've really made it? Those discreet symbols that mark me and my pod out as the alpha mums?

Well, it turns out that little blue tick means a big fat nothing.

As soon as we found out about the RP account, Irene contacted Instagram directly, thinking the fact that I'm verified, that I earn *them* money with my paid partnerships and #ads, would lend some urgency to the request. I thought the fact that it was horrible and distressing, and made my skin crawl every time I looked at it, would prompt them to act. We hoped the account would instantly be taken down when she explained all of this, first via email and then in an increasingly irate series of voicemails to the head of influencer relations, that the photos had been stolen and that the content was, quite frankly, threatening.

They didn't do anything. They didn't even respond.

Irene didn't seem to think I should put much faith in the police being able to help either. Sure, the poster *could* be the person who stole the laptop, she said, but the police had no leads on who that was. And wasn't it just as likely that someone had hacked into the Cloud and harvested them from there? The overlapping portion on the Venn diagram between lonely, creepy stalker and very good at computer things was pretty bloody large. And anyway, I put pictures of my family online for a living; followers saved them, shared them, screenshotted them, printed them out and turned them into an elaborate shrine, for all we knew—how sympathetic would the police be to my complaints that these were just the *wrong photos*?

She was missing the point, of course. The bottom line was, whoever stole those photos is obsessed enough with us to elbow their way into our lives. Not a faceless troll or nameless hater: an actual human being who has publicly commandeered my real-life family, our private memories, as their own.

The only way I can stop feeling queasy about the whole thing is to remind myself that anyone with a public profile will find something unpleasant about themselves if they go raking through the internet for it. For all I know, the kids of every single Instamum I've ever met could have an RP account dedicated to them—I'm just unlucky enough to know about mine.

"Try not to think about it," says Irene, leaning across the back seat of the cab to pat me on the knee. "This might cheer you up: the BBC Three producers called yesterday to say they're close to a decision.

They said your story really moved them, so I have a feeling the job might be yours."

We're greeted at the recording studio by Hero Blythe, a feminist Instagram poet and the presenter of *Heavy Flow*, a period-focused podcast. She is an extremely pretty, waifish blonde, wearing a white head scarf and tasseled green kaftan over a white crop top and cutoff denim flares, wafting a bunch of smoldering sage leaves around the place.

"Well, hello, you supernova of a woman! This is just to welcome and cleanse." She gestures to her stinking fire hazard as she ushers us into a soundproof room where Hannah, Bella, Suzy, and Sara are already in their seats in front of giant microphones. "I'm just going to get us all some raspberry leaf tea, then we'll be ready to start."

I take a seat in between Suzy and Sara, and take a moment—as I do whenever I am about to record anything—to put all my distractions, all my personal problems and worries and fears to one side and focus for the next half an hour on the job in hand. One of the very few useful things my mother taught me, apart from how to mix a mean martini, is how to put on a brave face.

The way she does it, she once told me, is literally to picture a box in her head and all the things she doesn't want to think about she just puts in there, and then she forces the lid down, plasters a smile on her face, and gets on with it.

"Are you sure that's healthy?" I asked her once. "What happens when the box gets full? What happens when there are things you can't fit in it?"

Her answer was to imagine a bigger box.

Hero wafts back in with a tray of steaming #yaydays mugs. "Shall we hit record?"

I give her the thumbs-up.

"Welcome, blood sisters and regular listeners," she says, gesturing for us all to hold hands. "This week's edition of *Heavy Flow* is sponsored, as always, by Goddess Goblets, the world's most eco-friendly way of embracing your monthly blessing. These miraculous moon cups for women who truly care about the planet are available in four colorways, including a new, limited-edition rose gold, and are totally dishwasher safe.

"Today I have with me a group of game-changing mamas who are *everything*. Seriously, you are all just heroes, redefining what it means to be a modern mother. Before we start, I'd like to share with you a poem I've written called *The Blood of Creation*." She presses pause briefly. "I prerecorded that from the bathroom because of the acoustics, so I'll add that in later," she explains.

Irene looks like she wants to suffocate herself with a moon cup.

"Now, ladies, first question: Can you talk me through your first-ever period?" Hero asks earnestly.

Sara, the_hackney_mum, almost springs off her chair. "I'm so lucky that I had a wise mother who always taught me that periods were a woman's gift from the universe. That my womb is a garden where human life grows and that every month my menses were simply watering its flowers. So when it arrived, when I was eleven, she threw me a period party, celebrating with a flower-arranging class. Isolde is nearly that age now, and we are already planning hers, although we'll be making flower crowns."

Utter rubbish, of course. Like everyone else's mother in the nineties, Sara's mum had handed her a pack of those terrible sanitary pads with a single stripe of glue down the middle and all the absorbency of an umbrella, and told her she shouldn't go swimming that week. Still, Tampax has lapped it up, and as soon as poor Isolde starts bleeding, she is lined up for an #ad and a photo shoot in a white dress with a load of red roses on her head. I suppose she should just be grateful she doesn't have to roller-skate down a beach in Lycra.

"That's so moving: honoring the mother goddess in that way is just magical. Ob. Sessed. Okay, another one for you wonderful women. Do you all ever talk about your cycles together? I'm fascinated by them as, really, aren't they what defines us as women, the source of our power and strength? I like to keep a discharge diary, so I have a record throughout the whole month. I think it's so important to be honest about our hormones," says Hero.

"Oh yes." I nod, dying a tiny bit inside. Imagine thinking the most interesting part of a woman is what you mop up and flush down the toilet each month—and then building an entire bloody brand around it.

"As you know, we are all about honesty," I continue solemnly. "We want to use our platforms to lift other women up, support them to tell their own truth." I hold Sara and Suzy's hands a little tighter. "Of course, we've all managed to sync cycles too—remember when that happened in school with your BFFs?—because clearly even my womb loves these ladies to bits!" I laugh.

A thought suddenly occurs to me: It couldn't be one of them, could it, posting those pictures of Coco? Driving me off Instagram would certainly grow their share of the pie. And it *was* Suzy who'd told us. Maybe it's *all* of them? It's hard to imagine any of them actually breaking in, of course. But it's not entirely impossible to imagine them getting someone else to do it.

For goodness' sake, Emmy, just listen to yourself.

Maybe it's getting to me more than I thought, all this.

"How do you cope with the changes in your body during your time of the month? As you all know, I founded the #positiveperiod movement because I really, truly believe that celebrating the physical sensations that come along with menstruation is such a radical act of self-care. The patriarchy wants us to medicalize it, but I say we should embrace it. For example, I am wearing a moonstone, which I sell on my Etsy page—link in bio, ladies—as it has been proven to be more effective than painkillers." Hero smiles, pointing to her necklace. "Then there's lapis lazuli . . ."

As she drones on about her enchanted rocks, I can see Irene receive a text, her eyes suddenly widening. She winks and motions at me to leave the room with her, silently mouthing, *Sorry*, to Hero, who's moved onto the healing properties of sticking cabbage leaves down your pants. We quietly shut the door and, out in the corridor, Irene squeezes my arm.

"It's the BBC," says Irene. "They've asked me to call them back. Just a second."

She leaves me in the corridor while she wanders off to find better phone reception, returning moments later with a huge smile on her face. "It's a yes, Emmy. Your own show. 'Blown away by your raw honesty' were the words they used, in fact. You must have really nailed it with that video!"

"You didn't watch it before you sent it over?" I ask incredulously.

"I didn't have time! Show it to me now—I want to see what won them over."

I pull my phone out, find the clip, and press play. There I am. No makeup on, grey T-shirt that only makes me look more washed-out and tired. Eyes downcast. Clutching one of Bear's teddies, sitting in the armchair by his cot.

I'm Emmy Jackson—Mamabare to lots of you—and I have something I'd like to share. I built my platform, my following, on honesty. But I haven't been quite honest with the world, until now.

I have been thinking for a long time about how to tell you what I am about to—whether to share it at all. This will sound crazy, but I think I have been a bit embarrassed maybe, a bit ashamed. I have to open up now though as I feel like there is a huge part of my life, a huge part of me, that you just don't know about. I feel that by denying it, I'm denying the three little lives we lost ever had the right to exist at all, when actually they are as important as if they were here right now.

Three miscarriages. And that pain, the guilt, the desperation, they just don't disappear. I can be happy one minute, or perhaps not quite happy but not achingly sad, and then it will just hit me. Three people who would have been part of our lives, just gone. The first pregnancy didn't make it past twelve weeks. A missed miscarriage, they call it. We had no bleeding, nothing. There we were at the first appointment, holding each other's hands, waiting to see the heartbeat. There was none. It's amazing how impassive the faces of the people who do the scans are, isn't it? I guess they must see it all the time.

Then it happened again. We were away for the weekend in Norfolk, and I started bleeding as we were walking along the beach. The next we lost at twenty weeks. Nobody could tell us why it happened. The hope is the worst, I think. The hope that you try not to nurture from the moment that little blue line appears, that finds its way out at night when you start to imagine that you're lying there with your baby in your arms. Maybe I felt I shouldn't talk about it because I have my Bear and Coco now, and I know that should make it feel better. Maybe the reason I haven't spoken about it is that it's so hard to find the words. Maybe there are no words. Who knows if these are even the right ones? All I know is that I've tried everything else—so maybe telling my story, and helping other women to tell theirs, is the only way to heal.

Fade out to black. My voice plays over the dark screen. I allow myself a little surge of pride at my video editing skills, my eyes flitting to Irene's face and back to the phone.

"From Miscarriage to Mamabare: A Personal Look at Baby Loss. Coming soon to BBC Three."

CHAPTER FOURTEEN

Dan

Something it takes me a long time to get my head around is the idea of Emmy taking photos of our daughter in the hospital, our pale, injured, sleeping daughter. I do try to put myself in Emmy's shoes, to see things through her eyes, to piece together what the hell was going through her mind.

I can't do it.

There are moments when I am not even sure I want to.

The thought of leaving Emmy, the thought of walking out on my marriage, is genuinely not something that has ever occurred to me. Not seriously. Not even before we had children. Not for more than a furious few minutes, at any rate. What would I do with myself? Where would I end up? In some bedsit somewhere probably. Eating biscuits in bed and spending too much time on the internet. That's what I always say, jokingly, when the subject comes up, as it does occasionally. The truth is I can't really imagine it.

There have been times in the past twenty-four hours when I have seriously, and with a cold, settled fury, considered the practicalities and the logistics of such a move. There have been times when I have considered the implications of taking my daughter with me, tried to imagine the logistics of taking my son. There have been times when the only thing that has prevented me storming into the kitchen and telling Emmy I am leaving is not wanting her in sole charge of Bear and Coco. Free to use my children as props, as accessories, as sympathy grabbers whenever the fancy takes her.

Am I overreacting? I don't think so.

We are supposed to be going out for dinner tonight to celebrate Emmy's new TV show.

It is hard to think of anything I want to do less.

She does an Instastory in our hallway mirror of us ready to leave, another of the menu, takes a picture of her cocktail, takes a picture of her starter, a picture of me scowling across the table at her. Over the years I have got so used to this sort of thing that most of the time I barely even register it, but tonight, suddenly, it all seems monstrous. God knows which ones she actually posts. I've barely been able to look at her these past few days, let alone her Instagram feed.

Emmy tells me all about recording the *Heavy Flow* podcast and plays me a clip of Hero Blythe performing her period poem, and I don't even crack a smile.

I finish my first beer about the same time they are clearing our starters away and order myself another.

The line that keeps running through my head is that I used to think it was only our online life that was a lie.

"They'll be all right with Doreen babysitting, won't they?" Emmy accompanies this with a hesitant smile.

It is clear how I ought to respond to this. Everyone knows, when you are out on a date with someone and they ask you a question like that, how you are supposed to respond.

I shrug and take a swig from my bottle of beer. It was not my idea to go out, I feel like telling her.

The waitress asks if I want another and I say yes and Emmy points out I haven't even finished that one yet. I chug the last third of it and ask for the same again.

When Emmy texts Doreen to check that all is fine, she gets an answer back almost immediately. There was a bit of sleep-whimpering from Bear's room about half an hour ago, but now all's quiet on the Western Front.

We exchange platitudes about how lucky we are to have found Doreen and then fall silent again. It occurs to me that this is the first time we've been out to dinner together, have been out anywhere together, since Bear was born. I must admit, she looks beautiful. She has done her makeup carefully and has her hair up and is wearing a dress and looks like the Emmy I remember from the old days, the magazine days. They're allowed to glam up occasionally, the Instamums, if they accompany any pictures with self-flagellating captions about how rarely they get to do this, how the shoes gave them blisters and it's a special occasion because there's #bignews coming, but the baby was still up crying when they got home and they regretted it all the next morning because of the #adultheadache.

Now that we know all's well at home, Emmy is back to telling me about the TV show. I am nodding, half listening. Don't get me wrong, I'm pleased for my wife. This is big news, huge news. What I don't understand is why they've chosen her to present a program on this particular topic. I mean, it's not like this is something we have experienced ourselves. Are there going to be talking heads on it? I ask her. Is she going to be talking to doctors, or mums who have been through all that stuff, or what? She tells me they haven't really ironed out those details yet.

By the time we're looking at the dessert menu, I've remembered why it is that Emmy and I so rarely go out. We are both about ready to fall asleep in our shoes. By the time the bill arrives, I am genuinely having trouble keeping my eyes open. The lights in the room seem to get dimmer and then brighter again. The conversation trails off. Emmy starts scrolling through her messages. As I am paying, Emmy and I both yawn simultaneously and then apologize to the guy with the card machine.

I check my phone, and it is 8:47.

"That was nice," she says as we're standing outside waiting for the Uber.

I put my arm around her shoulders and give her a squeeze, but say nothing.

"Now, what route is this guy taking?" she asks, observing our driver's progress on her mobile.

I take my phone out and check the RP account.

She doesn't even need to turn her head to know what I am doing. "Anything?"

Not since seven o'clock, when there was another new picture posted (a shot of Coco asleep on the couch in front of the TV, clutching a sweater of Emmy's like a teddy or comforter), the text accompanying it something about seizing each day as it comes and treasuring each moment with your little one. Ninety-three likes and counting. Almost forty comments.

Every day they're getting worse. A little more vivid, a little more detailed, more mawkish. Almost the worst of it is, they don't just have access to hundreds of photos; there are thousands. Pictures of Coco sleeping. Pictures of Coco in the bath. Pictures of her in her swimsuit in the garden. And every day another one enters the public domain. And every day the text accompanying them gets creepier. And any day now, the person posting all this shit keeps reminding us, she and Coco will get those test results back and know the verdict. *Keep your fingers crossed*, they keep saying. *Say a prayer for us and keep us in your thoughts.*

I want to kill them.

That's the thought that comes to me as the Uber is waiting at a light and the driver asks us both again if we want him to put the window up or turn the music down, whether we've had a nice evening.

Whoever is doing this, I want to kill them.

Let me make this plain. I'm not speaking rhetorically. I want to kill them in the same way you would want to kill someone in the exact moment that they harmed or nearly harmed your child, in that immediate flash of parental rage you feel when some prick on a modified fixed-gear bike ignores a red light and swoops across the pedestrian crossing about six inches in front of the pram you are pushing. That feeling you get when some dickhead starts reversing their car at speed in your direction as you're crossing the Sainsbury's parking lot hand in hand with your toddler.

If I could get my hands on them, I'd strike them down with all the self-righteous fury of a man defending his family, of a good man pushed beyond his limit.

There are times too, when I think I would be slightly less upset, less angry, if I could work out what they were doing all this for. What kick, what satisfaction they were getting out of it. Even if it was just a financial scam, if there was a GoFundMe and they were asking for money for flights abroad and some groundbreaking operation not available on the NHS, that I think I would find less baffling—or perhaps I would be just as angry but in a slightly different way.

Emmy reaches over to pat me on the back of the hand as we're turning onto our road and she finds that my hand is balled into a fist in my lap.

"I am going to fucking kill them," I say.

She doesn't react, except to lean forward in her seat and point out to the driver where it would be best to pull over. Her hand rests on the back of mine.

"I mean it," I say. "I swear to God I mean it."

As the car pulls up, the driver puts on the overhead light to help us check we haven't left anything in the back, and we find ourselves,

Emmy and me, face-to-face, abruptly illuminated. She looks tired in the sudden harsh light. Her forehead is lined, her eyes a little puffy. Her expression is hard to read.

"Who?" she asks, quietly but with a note of exasperation and perhaps even contempt in her voice . . . "Who are you going to *kill*, Dan?"

I stare at her for a moment, then look away.

"Thanks a lot, mate," she says to the driver.

There is a brief pause at the front door as I locate my keys in the pockets of my coat, our breath hanging in the air, neither of us speaking.

I open the door as quietly as I can, gesture Emmy through ahead of me, wave silently at Doreen as her head appears from the living room, return her smile and her double thumbs-up. I slowly place my keys very quietly on the sideboard in the hall. Did we have a lovely evening? Doreen asks, and Emmy tells her it was fantastic. Wonderful food. Then Emmy sees her out and makes sure to close the door gently behind her. She tells me she's going to get a glass of water from the kitchen and go to bed.

After she's gone, I check the windows are locked and then I check the doors are locked and then I go back and check the windows again. I brush my teeth and have a pee and catch myself just before I flush the toilet and wake the baby up (old, clanking pipes). I rattle the front door one more time, just to check it is bolted as well as locked.

By the time I get upstairs, the bedroom light is off and Emmy is under the covers on the far side of the bed with her back to where I'm standing at the door. I rest my hand on the mattress to prevent myself stumbling or tripping over as I slip my socks and jeans off, then wrestle my shirt and V-neck sweater off over my head all in one go.

I fall asleep to the sound of a distantly circling police helicopter, sirens somewhere nearby.

Then the phone rings, and all hell breaks loose.

* * *

She seems like a lovely little girl, Coco. A little bit of a show-off at times, perhaps. A little bit headstrong. But basically a good kid, a thoughtful, gentle, good-natured, unselfish one. Goodness knows where she gets it from. I was expecting her to be a little monster. You know the sort of thing—always sucking on a sweetie, always screaming at someone, except when it is time to have her picture taken. A little prima donna. As far as I can see, she is nothing of the sort.

It is Grace that Coco reminds me of, more than anything. The same sweetness. The same kindness. The same generosity of spirit. On the playground, Coco is always the first one there when somebody falls over, helping them up. They even look a little alike. Sometimes as she is playing, as she is going down a slide or kicking her legs on one of the swings or just running around, I catch a glimpse of her out of the corner of my eye and it takes me straight back to Grace's childhood, all those years ago.

What strikes me most strongly, having seen what an energetic kid she is, how much she loves running around and shouting and jumping off things, is how boring she must find all this Mamabare stuff. The photo shoots. Pretending to be playing. Pretending to have fun. Being dragged around to all these events, half of them way past her bedtime. And what is it going to be like when she grows up, when she looks back at her childhood? What is she going to remember—what actually happened, or the version of what happened that Emmy posts online?

When I used to say things like that, Grace would always screw up her face and say I was being old-fashioned.

Doreen. That's the name of the nanny. She has seen me around enough—in the park, on the bus, once on the street outside the house— for us to get to the nodding stage with each other. A couple of times we have said good morning. Once we found ourselves sitting next to each other on a bench by the pond. Coco was feeding the ducks, laughing, shrieking when they started crowding up too close, waddling up over the lip of the pond and closing in on her to get the bread that she had dropped.

"How old?" I asked.

She told me.

"Granddaughter?"

She shook her head.

"Not one of mine," she said. "Just one I look after."

She does not get to see her own grandchildren as much as she would like, she told me. Two of them were up in Manchester, one over near Norwich. What about me?

I told her I did not get to see my little granddaughter as much as I would like either. Or my daughter, for that matter.

We commiserated.

"Coco," she called. "Not so close to the edge."

Coco looked back and nodded to show she had understood.

"Okay!" she shouted.

Doreen gave her a thumbs-up.

"Sweet little girl," I commented.

I am not sure whether Coco recognized me or not. If she did, she didn't say anything. But there was definitely a moment when her gaze rested on me and a little frown passed across her face as if she was trying to place me, trying to remember where we had encountered each other before. Then a duck nuzzled at the back of her coat and gave her a start, and she jumped away, shrieking.

It's all in place now. Everything I need is at the house; everything has been tested, double-tested, checked. I have taken down the FOR SALE sign, just in case, stowed it around the side of the house, by the bins. I have made sure there is enough in the fridge for me, stuff that won't go off, plenty of UHT milk and coffee in the pantry. I have made the necessary calculations. I have gone through the stages in my head. I *have asked myself if I am really capable of this, if I am really up to it, and I have thought about Grace and I have thought about Ailsa and I have found my answer.*

Now all I need is the right moment.

Emmy

It's a textbook *Mail on Sunday* sting.

A call at nine thirty on a Saturday night laying out the bare bones of a front-page story about you and asking for a response. Not that they actually want it—it's more of a courtesy call, really, letting you know that your face will be splashed all over a tabloid the next morning. There is no damage limitation to be done by that point, no time to kill the story before the sordid little thing goes to press. I know this from experience, thanks to an airbrushing scandal in my magazine days when a slapdash art director, in the process of artificially shaving a few inches off a Hollywood actress, accidentally gave her an extra elbow.

I can see that something is seriously wrong the second Dan answers the phone. A cheery "Hello?" is followed by a much more serious "Yes."

Who? I mouth with a raised eyebrow.

He ignores me.

"I see," he says into the receiver.

His expression is stern, his eyebrows almost touching. I nudge him, but he turns his back on me.

"What is it, Dan, for fuck's sake?" I hiss.

He waves my words away with the back of his hand. He was sitting down, but now he's standing, the hand that is not holding the phone covering his ear.

"Yes, I'm still here. I'm listening."

Our eyes meet in the mirror.

"No," he says, holding my gaze. "No, I have nothing to say, nothing to say to you at all. Except . . . leave my family alone."

Then he throws the phone down on the bed so hard it bounces and goes spinning off into the corner of the room.

"Dan?"

He turns, and I honestly don't think I have ever seen him look like this before.

"Let me get this right, Emmy," he says, his voice barely above a whisper. "You get an email from your best friend, a girl you've known since school, maid of honor *at our wedding*, about losing three babies. *Three*. You don't call her back. You don't even send her a text. You offer her less time, less support, than you would a total stranger online. And then, for the sake of a job presenting a documentary on a topic about which you know precisely *nothing*, you steal her story, her *actual life*, and pass it off as your own? *Our own?*"

Dan breaks off, shaking his head. "Who the fuck even are you, Emmy?"

My mouth opens. That's not what I did. At least that's not what I meant to do. It was an audition. I was acting. Nobody was meant to see it apart from them. How the hell has it made its way out into the world? How the fuck has Polly seen it? Who gave it to her? That's what I want to say. I just can't make the words come out.

"Jesus fucking Christ," Dan mutters to himself, palming his forehead, kneading his brow. "On top of everything fucking else."

Yeah, Dan, I think, *on top of everything else*. On top of a husband whose combined royalties and lending rights income in the last tax year came to £7.10 and yet who, as far as I could tell, quite enjoyed our long weekend in Lisbon and our winter week in Marrakech and our free fortnight in the Maldives. On top of being someone who pays the mortgage, pays for the childcare, pays the electricity bill, slogging away every day in an industry that constantly demands I reveal more, peel off yet another layer of skin, bare everything, share everything, just to entertain some half-interested stranger for a quarter of a minute.

My phone rings. Unknown number. I stare at it, close my eyes for a moment, hoping that when I open them again it will all have gone away. It stops for a second, then starts again. This time, it is a number I recognize. Irene.

"I've just got off the phone with the *Mail on Sunday*. We have a lot of damage control to do here, Emmy. Everything else," she says, matter-of-factly, "we can deal with later. You need to get hold of Polly now, convince her to tell them she was lying. I don't care how you do it. She's your friend—you have to make her realize what the stakes are for you. For your family. Your children."

Dan is still muttering away, so I leave him to it.

I'm shocked when Polly answers on the first ring.

"Emmy. I hear congratulations are in order." Her voice is jagged.

"Polly," I start, my voice shaking, "you know I love you. I would never want to hurt you. I am so sorry. About the email, I—"

"So nice of you to finally phone about that, Emmy. It makes me feel so valued as a friend, you know. One of your tribe. That's what you all call one another, isn't it? I learned that at Coco's party." She pauses. "Does that make you their chief?" She laughs coldly.

"You *are* phoning to check how I am doing, after my three miscarriages? The ones that I spent so long agonizing over whether I should tell you about because I didn't want to make you feel terrible about that abortion all those years ago, or burden you when you were pregnant, or overload you when you had a newborn. Or is there something else you wanted to talk about? Funny, now I think about it, this is the first time *you've* called *me* in years.

"I suppose you never felt you needed to pick up the phone," she goes on. "I could keep up with you by flicking through the little snapshots of your life you so graciously share online, like one of your followers, one of your fans, couldn't I? But did you never wonder how I was? What I was up to? Never feel the need to check in? Sorry, I don't even know why I'm asking. Clearly not.

"You know, the reason I insisted on coming to Coco's party was because it was the only way I could think of to actually see you. And those people, Emmy—those people are awful. You do know that, don't you? I only started chatting to that journalist because I couldn't bear being blanked again when whoever I was talking to realized I wasn't anybody important or useful."

"You met the person who wrote this at my party? Who?" I demand.

"Jess Watts. The freelance journalist who interviewed you for the *Sunday Times*. She saw me standing by myself and felt sorry for me, I think. She took my number because she said she's always looking for quotes from English teachers for one thing or another. Anyway, when they announced your new show, she called to say she was writing a profile piece on you for the *Mail on Sunday* and could she get some quotes. She started telling me about how your story had moved her, how important it was for other women going through the same thing that you had opened up about your own pain and grief. Had you always been such a survivor? she wanted to know. When I said I had no idea what she was talking about, she asked if I wanted to see the video the BBC had emailed her, as a bit of background, some context for the piece. I watched it cold, Emmy. Can you imagine what that felt like?"

I say nothing.

"That wasn't a rhetorical question, Emmy. I'm genuinely curious, at this point in our friendship, even after all these years. Can you actually imagine what that felt like? Or have you finally *become* 2D, like your photos?"

"I can explain, Pol, I just wasn't thinking. The director wanted to hear a personal experience, and yours was so powerful, I just knew that it needed to be shared." I can hear my tongue stumbling over the words.

"It wasn't your story, Emmy. You don't get to make that decision. They were my dead babies, not yours. Just like it would not have occurred to me for a minute to start talking to that journalist about your abortions. Not for your sake. Not for Dan's sake. Not even for Coco's or Bear's. But because I happen to believe there are still some things that are personal, that are private. Because I happen to believe there are some stories that *aren't mine to tell*.

"I always gave you the benefit of the doubt, you know. Before. I never got angry when you canceled or turned up late. Tried not to be hurt at the endless posts about your amazing crew of humans or all the banging on about the 'mamas' who changed your life, tried not to ask myself what exactly that made me. But when I saw that video . . . I mean, Jesus Christ, Emmy. And when Jess called back, I couldn't help myself. I just told her the truth. She said she knew there was something off about you that day she came to interview you and Dan. Something cold, disengaged. All your stories were too pat, too polished, she said. That's because they're just words, aren't they, to you? Just *content*—isn't that what you people call it? Nothing has any meaning anymore, unless it's public, unless it's out there for other people to read about. You're not a person anymore, Emmy. You're just a phony caption and a posed photo. A fucking invention. I hope this is a wake-up call."

"It is, Polly, it really is. But you have to know what this story will do to me—"

"I am really sorry, Emmy, but honestly, I don't give a shit."

She hung up.

My finger hovers over my phone for a moment as I wonder whether I should send a WhatsApp explaining what really happened, how I was backed into a corner, how my addled newborn-mum brain was not equipped to deal with the stress, and beg her to forgive me, convince her I'm still the same girl she's known forever. But I'm not, and she'll know that.

Then I remember justanothermother, and the damage screenshots can do.

THE INSTAMUM WHO STOLE MY DEAD BABIES: A FORMER FRIEND TELLS ALL.

That is the headline they run with.

CHAPTER FIFTEEN

"Emmy said it's fine." That was what Grace kept telling me. "She said she used to do it all the time with her little girl, Coco." I would send her links, show her the official NHS advice, make suggestions about other things they might experiment with. Grace would say she had tried everything else and none of it worked. "Tell her, Jack," she would say to him, and he would pull an apologetic face.

I used to kick myself for getting her that ticket. A birthday present, it was. Twenty-five pounds for the ticket. Plus forty-five for the Mamabare sweatshirt I bought to go with it (I have always hated giving someone just an envelope). I could not believe how much they were charging. Still, it all felt worth it when Grace's birthday came around. She put that sweatshirt on straightaway and kept it on the whole afternoon. The ticket she stuck to the fridge door, and every day for the next two weeks, she told me that whenever she went to get some milk or a bit of butter she would see it there and get another little rush of excitement. An evening with Mamabare. Doors seven thirty. A talk and a Q&A session and a chance to meet other mamas. Free glass of sparkling wine provided. She got there at quarter to seven, found them still setting up, walked around the block twice, and ended up having a glass of wine at the pub on the corner. All that week, Emmy had been posting about how excited she was to be meeting her followers face-to-face like this. It was, she said, the first time she had ever been to Guildford.

The truth was, Grace deserved a proper night out. I don't think she had really had one since Ailsa was born. I did keep offering to come around and babysit, to stay over, but her response was always the same: What was the point? Ailsa was an absolutely beautiful baby, very good-natured most of the time, and you could see they both completely doted on her, but the instant Grace tried to put her down she would start screaming. And I mean really screaming. Turning herself puce. Making the kind of noises that sounded like they were hurting her throat. Getting herself more and more and more worked up. It was okay when Jack was there. At least he could put the baby in the carrier and get her off to sleep for a bit that way, let Grace get a short nap too. Then she could catch up a little in the day on all the sleep she was missing at night. The trouble was, he couldn't always be there. He had a job to do, and quite often that job took him right to the other end of the country. I could come over sometimes for a morning or an afternoon or an evening as my shifts allowed, but I couldn't do that every weekend, let alone every night. And every night Grace was faced with the exact same problem: a baby who just would not be put down to sleep. Who would fall asleep in her mother's arms if she was sitting watching TV, but who would instantly jerk awake and start howling the moment she tried to lower her into the cot next to the sofa. She would eventually drift off if Grace sat on the bed with her and rocked her and cooed to her in the dark for hours, but would immediately stiffen and wake if you made any attempt to get her into her crib. They bought one of those things you attach to the side of the bed, like a kind of sidecar, so the baby can sleep next to you safely. Ailsa lasted about five minutes in it. They tried swaddling. They bought all sorts of ceiling lights and window blinds and white noise boxes and special cushions and God knows what else. Nothing worked.

The first thing that Grace told me when she got in the door that night, when she arrived home, was that she had asked Emmy for her advice. Had asked Emmy whether she had found it difficult when Coco used to have trouble sleeping. Whether she had ever tried cosleeping and what she thought about it.

"Oh yeah?" I said.

I don't think I really knew much about Mamabare at that stage, just the name, and that Grace thought she was funny and wise and wonderful and honest.

"And what did she tell you?" I asked her.

The whole exchange is still burned vividly into my memory. I can remember exactly where I was standing, in the hallway, and I can remember where Grace was standing, at the bottom of the stairs. She had just taken her coat off, was still standing there with it in her arms.

"She said she and Coco used to cosleep all the time in the beginning. That it was perfectly fine as long as you followed sensible precautions. That for centuries in most cultures around the world it has been the complete norm. She said that actually now that Coco sleeps in her own bedroom and they have the bed to themselves she sometimes misses her."

"Hmm," I said.

What I was thinking was: Who is this woman and what qualifies her to go around giving out advice? Was she someone with a background in this sort of thing, some kind of training? Was she a former midwife, something like that?

I was going to ask Grace, but just that moment Ailsa started crying again upstairs.

Grace let out a sigh.

"How has she been?" she asked.

"A little restless," I told her. "I've been up a couple of times to settle her and give her some milk and she went back to sleep eventually each time." Eventually being the key word. A couple of times being an understatement.

Don't get me wrong, I have every sympathy for what Grace was going through. Knowing that even after you have finally put your child down the slightest sound, or shift in temperature, or fluctuation in air pressure, will wake them up. Always on edge. Always listening out for a plaintive cry. Getting more tired and frazzled by the night, by the hour, by the minute. Feeling that this will never end and that there is nothing you can do. Resenting things. Resenting each other. Resenting the baby, sometimes.

I don't blame Grace for what happened, and I have never blamed her for a minute. She would never have done anything deliberately to hurt that baby. The truth is that she agonized about it for ages, the cosleeping, the risks, the safety issues. She researched it online and she asked her GP, and she talked to me about it and she talked about it with her friends. She ummed. She aahed. She kept reading things that put her off the idea and then reading something else that said it was absolutely fine. But it was what Emmy said that nudged her over the line. That I am sure of. That it was thanks to Emmy that Grace eventually came to the conclusion that she needed sleep and the baby needed sleep and there was only one way she could ensure that.

It was Jack who called and told me what had happened.

He had been sleeping on the couch in the living room, as I gather he had been doing quite a lot, to let Mum and baby have the whole double bed to themselves. It was six o'clock on the Saturday morning when he woke up, and he told me later the first thing that struck him as odd was that he couldn't hear Ailsa crying. He couldn't hear a thing from the bedroom. He checked the time on his phone and then he closed his eyes and when he opened them again it was seven thirty. Seven thirty! Still no sound from the girls.

This was not how he conveyed the news to me, of course. It was only afterward that I managed to piece it all together. When I answered my phone all I could hear at the other end was Jack sobbing so hard he could barely get a word out and a sort of keening noise in the back-

ground. "She's dead" was what he eventually managed to get out, and it wasn't even clear to me at first which one of them he was talking about.

He had tiptoed along the corridor, crept up to the door, turned the handle very slowly to prevent it squeaking, let the door sort of fall open in the way that it did under its own weight, that particular door. He had a bottle of lukewarm milk for Ailsa in one hand, a mug of coffee in the other, had to put one of them down to turn the handle, was still half-bent over when the door swung open enough to reveal the bed.

Later on, he told me the whole thing, talked me through it all, second by second. It seemed necessary to me to know, to understand the details, to be able to get a grip on as much of what had happened as I could. It seemed to help him to share it. Grace could not bear to hear it and left to go for a walk, closing the door with a slam behind her.

The first thing he saw was that Grace was still asleep. She looked completely peaceful, he told me. There was sunlight coming in around the curtains; she was lying on her back, out cold, as rested and relaxed as he had seen her in months. Maybe over a year, if you counted how impossible it had been trying to get a proper night's sleep late in the pregnancy. Everything was all set up just as they had left it, when he had kissed the girls good night the previous evening. The cushions arranged so that Grace could sleep with Ailsa resting against her, arranged so that there was no way she could roll over and squish the baby. The blankets were gathered and tucked so they did not ride up.

Even from the doorway, even before he took a step closer or opened the curtains, Jack said, he could tell that something was not right with Ailsa. The way she was lying. How still she was. The color of her. The sort of bruised-looking, mottled color of her little hands.

At first he thought it was just a shadow, but when he did take a step forward he could see something around her throat. Something dark wrapped around her throat.

Grace's hair.

Her long, thick hair.

Afterward, at the inquest, when they talked about how it must have happened, Jack had to walk out and stand in the corridor. Grace and I stayed. I was holding her hand tight in mine, and we were both sobbing as they described in detail how Ailsa must have snuggled in closer to her and wriggled, and snuggled in closer to her and wriggled, and snuggled in closer to her and wriggled, and each time she wriggled the bit of Grace's hair that was accidentally tucked under her chin would have wrapped itself tighter around her neck and throat. It would have started contracting her windpipe a little more and allowed a little less oxygen to her brain each time, but it was a process too gradual to wake either of them. She was too tiny to struggle. Grace was too fast asleep to know. Apparently this was a thing that happened very occasionally, the reason they sometimes advised that if you were cosleeping you tied your hair back. Grace must have known that, all the research she had done, must have forgotten that one night, or perhaps she had remembered to tie her hair back and it had somehow come undone. It was not something we ever talked about, she and I, that night, in much detail. There were some questions I could never bring myself to ask her.

Jack told me that waking Grace that morning was the hardest thing he had ever had to do in his life. It was clear Ailsa wasn't moving or breathing, and that she hadn't moved or breathed for a long time—when he felt the back of her neck it was stone-cold. Grace was still asleep and smiling, and when he first touched her arm and said her name she was still smiling. He patted her gently on the shoulder and said her name again and she mumbled something to herself—his name, Ailsa's name—and then she opened her eyes.

He must have told me the whole thing three or four times, and that was always the point at which he broke down uncontrollably.

When she came back from her walks, Grace would open the door and step inside and stay silent for a minute, listening, checking to see if he was finished talking. Then, when she was sure it was over, she would open the back door again and close it with a slam.

The funny thing is, I didn't even remember Emmy's advice to Grace, didn't even start holding her responsible, until a couple of months afterward. I was at work, actually, in the staff room, having a cup of tea and waiting for a shift to start, and I heard the name Mamabare and I looked up and there she was on Loose Women. And it just so happened that one of the topics that day was cosleeping. All the women were talking about their experiences. Emmy just shrugged and said it was never something she had tried and she didn't know a lot about it.

I thought I was going to go mad. I thought I was going mad. I could feel my brain throbbing. Even though my eyes were open I could see paisley-ish patterns swirling on the backs of my retinas.

Her laugh. That's what I remember. The little affected giggle she did, before launching into the usual spiel about doing whatever works best for you and how she wasn't setting herself up on a pedestal or claiming to get everything right. A laugh that seemed to me to be directed at anyone who had ever been fool enough to follow her, to trust her, to believe in her. A laugh that said the joke was on them, on Grace, on Ailsa, on us.

I do not regret what I am about to do to that woman at all.

Emmy

There is no such thing as bad publicity. That's what they say, isn't it? Well, "they" have a point.

Ninety thousand new followers overnight, my name trending on Twitter, the story picked up by the broadsheets, then internationally, on news websites from Manila to Milan. Offers from other tabloids and weekend supplements to give my side of things with what I presume they think is big money but wouldn't even pay for a single #ad on my grid in normal circumstances.

BBC Three, however, are not "they."

I can see that even Irene is shocked at how many BBC big boys have turned up to discuss the fate of *From Miscarriage to Mamabare*. A room full of middle-aged men all desperate to be there so they can tell the story at their next west London dinner party, smugly giving their mates the scoop on what I'm really like. I feel like a circus sideshow— *Roll up, roll up, come help knock the silly internet lady who earns far too much off her high horse.*

Josh, the director, who looks barely old enough to be in charge of an iPhone, let alone a TV series, is still gunning to get it made. It quickly becomes clear he is not going to be successful.

"What we just don't understand, Emmy, is why you would agree to present a show based on personal experience when you had none. We might as well have hired Simon bloody Cowell to tell us about his miscarriages," guffaws a man in selvedge jeans and a Supreme sweatshirt who I think may be called David, although he never introduced himself. "He'd probably have cost less too."

"That's the thing," I explain, shaking my head, allowing my eyes to fill with tears. "I would never lie about something this serious. Polly just doesn't know about what I've been through, my babies who didn't make it. I'm really a very private person. I give so much to my followers, but this is a pain I haven't chosen to share before. She just didn't know. Nobody did."

David laughs so hard that at first no sound comes out, and I am genuinely concerned that he's having a heart attack. "Listen, we aren't stupid. There isn't a single aspect of your life you haven't already sold to a million mothers; that's why we hired you."

I shoot Irene a look, silently imploring her for backup. In the process of the story breaking, not once did she ask me why I had used Polly's words when I'm usually perfectly proficient in inventing my own. I'm not even sure that I have an answer for that. I felt like an actress reading a script when I filmed it—detached from what the words actually meant, focused on doing what I'd been asked, on saying what I knew the director wanted to hear, making him like me. Not thinking for a minute what I would do if I actually got the job and had to repeat it all on national TV. But I would never have done it if I'd thought Polly would see the video. How could I have known they'd send it to a journalist?

Irene was the one who stopped me, in a split second of madness, when I saw that headline, from simply deleting my whole Instagram account permanently.

She was already at our house and had one of her PAs waiting outside a newsstand in Victoria for the first copies of the paper to be unloaded, poised to grab one, primed to send us pictures.

So at the crack of dawn, just as we were finishing our second pot of coffee, her phone rattled on the counter. She picked it up, glanced at it, and handed it to me. Her face was expressionless.

There it was. The screaming headline. A picture of Polly and her husband looking sad and angry. Me, head thrown back in laughter, standing in front of the brightly colored mural at Coco's birthday party. A picture of Polly and me together "in happier times."

I could feel Dan's eyes on me. I could feel Irene's eyes on me.

In that moment, I just wanted to kill Mamabare. Not to take Instagram off my phone for a while or go off grid for a bit, but to bury her six feet under with no chance of resurrection. Who, after all, would mourn her? Not me. Not Dan. Most of my followers would just transfer their loyalty to one of the others snapping at my heels, and the waters would close over Mamabare forever.

It took Irene to remind me, as my finger hovered over delete, quite how much money I would have to pay back, how many of the big brands I was contracted to would call in the lawyers the second I stepped away from my social media and could no longer flog their toilet paper or

T-shirts or cars. And anyway, who would it help now, to implode my entire career? Not Polly, not my family.

So while Dan continued, visibly disgusted with me, to dole out blame and recrimination, Irene spent all day Sunday helping me out of the hole, sitting in our kitchen coming up with a defense for the indefensible. I was too exhausted, too ashamed, to do anything other than limply agree to everything she said.

I could not, under any circumstances, admit that I had deliberately stolen Polly's experience as my own, or anything even approaching that. Honesty was my thing. She toyed aloud with the idea of me explaining that it was the sort of mistake you make when your heart is just *too* big. That this is the danger inherent in taking on board the trials, the struggles, the anguish of so many other mothers: their pain had become indistinguishable from my own. Then Irene had a better idea.

"She's telling the truth," says my agent icily. "Yes, the words in that clip may be Polly's, but it was an honest mistake. Emmy recorded herself on video reading Polly's email first as she needed to make sure the lighting was right, that the angle of the camera worked. She tried to rehearse with the words she had written about her own experience, but every time she tried, she broke down. She knew that it would be so emotionally draining to share her own story that she would only be able to manage one take. Sadly, her PA, Winter, emailed you the wrong video. Simple human error." She sits back in her chair, looking pleased with herself.

"We had no idea you had the wrong one, of course, let alone that you would share it with anyone, until the *Mail on Sunday* called. Of *course* Emmy has been through that heartache. There is nobody who understands the pain better—that's why she agreed to present the documentary."

"I knew there would be a simple explanation!" says Josh triumphantly, a little pathetically. "Emmy, you just need to tell everyone that, maybe on your Instagram feed?"

"You can tell everyone whatever you like, Emmy." David pulls a face as if my name has left a nasty aftertaste. "We'll be announcing that the show *will* go ahead, but with ivfandangels, and that we have no further plans to work with Mamabare because we are as appalled by your behavior as everyone else."

"And what do you think the optics of that will be, David? When you force Emmy's hand and she gives the exclusive interview that every newspaper wants? She'd have to say that she was pitted against another mother in pain, backed into a corner by a male director, male producer, and male researcher, to bare her soul to win a job she so desperately wanted," says Irene, looking genuinely interested at what his response might be. "It sounds quite manipulative when you say it like that, doesn't it? Feels like that could turn into a bit of a scandal."

Irene pauses for a moment to let this sink in.

There is a shuffling of papers, some throat-clearing, what looks like a little doodling. No one is making eye contact with anyone else. For the first time in an hour, even David seems to have nothing to say for himself.

"So how about this," Irene says as she looks about her. This tiny woman, commanding the attention of a roomful of men, some of whom are nearly twice her age. She is quite something to behold—definitely someone you want on your side in a crisis.

"If you don't want the job to go to Emmy, that is your call. But we *will* have a clean parting of the ways," she says decisively. "Which *I* will manage."

The room remains silent as everyone waits to see how everyone else will react.

It is David who eventually speaks first.

"Fine. But however you handle it, don't drop us any further in it and do it *today*," he says, getting abruptly up from his chair. "I think I've had enough of you Instapeople now."

It dawns on me as we walk back down Regent Street toward Irene's office that she never intended to save the show. It was never going to make her that much money. Her priority is protecting her bottom line.

"Right, Emmy. Here's what you're going to do," she says, sitting behind her desk and looking me up and down in the way a headmistress might after discovering cigarettes in your school bag. "And let me be honest before I even start: This is nonnegotiable. You either do what I say, or you'll have to find yourself another agent.

"You see that?" She points to her PA, who has been on the phone since we walked in. "Since Sunday morning, we have had almost every brand you work with on the line. A handful have dropped you already. Those that haven't are seriously considering it. This is not about your fans—they are so loyal they wouldn't unfollow if you committed a murder on Instagram Live—it's about the money. And unless we sort this out, you—we—will not be making any more of it. You have to serve up an explanation, make your apology, and then disappear until it blows over. No advertiser is ever going to touch you again otherwise."

Her plan is pretty simple. We use the photo, the one I have as my screen saver, of Coco holding a newborn Bear. First I share that, with a long post, written as an open letter to my oldest friend, Polly, explaining exactly what Irene told the BBC—but that I would still, for personal reasons, be backing out of the show. That I have, in fact, suffered from similar misfortunes as her but have never shared them with anyone before, apart from Dan, that the wrong video was sent, that I never meant for anybody to see it, that I deeply regret the hurt and upset I have caused, etcetera.

This will be followed up a few days later with another post, this time accompanied by one of me, walking away from the camera but looking back apprehensively. In the caption, I'll say that I've had time to reflect on these little squares and what they mean to me. That perhaps

I had come back too soon from maternity leave—that in juggling my career and looking after my darling Bear, in trying to have it all, I had simply taken on too much. Instead of pulling up the drawbridge, I had let the world across the maternal moat too soon. So I need to take stock. To have a frank and open dialogue with myself. To manage my anxiety. To work out a way forward for me and my family.

Irene has found me a digital detox retreat where, because I am still breastfeeding, they've agreed to let me take Bear. It's all taken care of, and free, of course, as long as I name-check them. Founded by a born-again tech exec, it promises five Wi-Fi-free days in a cottage so remote there's no phone signal, with a daily program of soul-searching and self-care. Apparently it's very popular with burned-out YouTubers. I didn't want to know any more details. At least the downtime might give me a moment to process it all—the humiliation, embarrassment, and pain I've caused.

I will do a series of heavily scripted stories in the car on the way there, Bear in his seat next to me, explaining tearfully how I hope time away will heal my heart and mind. How it will make me a better mother, a better wife, a better friend to Polly and to all the women— the hundreds of thousands of women—who need me.

Then I go off-grid.

Dan

What does one do in a situation like this? When you realize you can't trust your wife and you're not really sure you know her at all, but you can't be sure if everyone who has ever been married has felt this sort of feeling at one point, or whether you are in fact married to a socio-path? What can one do, as a contemporary husband, a modern father, a feminist?

I can only tell you what I do.

I identify a small, manageable task, put everything else to the back of my mind, and set myself to completing it.

Every time Emmy gets off the phone with Irene, or she returns from one of her meetings, once she has filled me in on the latest developments in the ongoing media shit storm, listed the latest brand partners who have announced they are considering breaking their ties with her, told me the latest news outlets and websites to pick up the story and run with it, I ask her the same simple, impatient, irritating question: What are they planning to do about that RP account?

There's a name for it, I've discovered. A name for what they're doing now: medical role-play, #medical #rp. Stolen pictures of sick children, reposted under different names with saccharine comments underneath, requests for prayers, accounts of how bravely they're holding up, recurring minor characters and subplots and the occasional upbeat post or two (a birthday party, a brief walk on the hospital grounds, a picture from before they got sick). In Illinois, I learn, a couple recently discovered that every picture they shared with the extended family WhatsApp group was being recaptioned by one of the cousins and then posted online. The article I read about it had screenshots, pictures to break your heart. There was a photo of their little girl, their seven-year-old, smiling bravely in a woolly hat, after the chemo. A picture of her looking terrifyingly thin, leaning on a nurse's arm. Another had her with a birthday cake, her features uplit by the candles' orange glow, her young face deeply creased and exhausted. By the time they identified the cousin (he kept requesting more photos), the RP account had something like eleven thousand followers. In the US, the UK, Europe, Japan. All over the world.

The thought that it might be someone we know who is doing this is almost too horrible to think about.

Every evening, at seven o'clock, another picture. Photos Emmy would never in a million years have shared on her actual account, now out there for all the world to see. Coco in her swimsuit at the beach. Coco playing with a hose in the garden. Coco in her pajamas being read to by my mum. Coco with a cold under a blanket in front of the telly. Coco asleep in my lap. Private pictures. Intimate pictures. All of them now telling the story of a plucky little girl suffering from an undiagnosed mystery illness, baffling the doctors, gradually growing weaker and weaker.

Every time I think about the way this story seems to be heading, I can feel my throat constrict, my stomach clenching like a fist.

Under every post now, comment after comment after comment. Public well-wishers, sending "brave little Rosie" whole bouquets of flower emojis, row after row of pink hearts and smiling faces and waving hands and poorly faces and kisses. Other mothers—real mothers? Who can even be sure?—sharing their stories. People suggesting herbal remedies. People asking what hospital she's having her tests in so they can send flowers and gifts.

Everything I write gets deleted after about five seconds. Evening after evening we go through the same loop. I post something about this not being true, this account being a fraud, "Rosie" being my daughter, threatening legal action. Almost as soon as it has popped up, it disappears again. Eventually I begin composing my messages in a Word file and copying and pasting them across, cutting and pasting and posting again and again and again. I report the account to Instagram again and again, always getting the same response: *We reviewed the account you reported for impersonation and found it does not violate our Community Guidelines.*

It's Emmy who eventually loses her patience first. She crosses the room and closes the laptop and almost catches my fingers.

I swivel on my chair, look up at her, furious.

She meets my gaze and holds it.

"What the hell do you think you're achieving, Dan?"

I suppose one of the things I am hoping for is just that I will piss them off. To feel that I have done whatever I can to spoil and frustrate whatever sick enjoyment they get out of all this. Maybe I just want to feel like I'm doing *something*.

Emmy says she's going to bed. She reminds me that she's going to be leaving at about eleven in the morning, and that Doreen is going to be picking Coco up at about nine. Have I asked my mum if she wants to come and help with teatime and bedtime a couple of the nights she'll be away? I tell her that Coco and I will be absolutely fine, that I think I can manage to chuck some pasta and tomato sauce together and tuck her in. Yes, I know where the pajamas live and which towel Coco likes, the soft one. I've got the number of the retreat if there's a real emergency.

She asks me to try not to wake her when I come up. I tell her I won't be long.

I wait until I hear Emmy's tread at the turn of the stairs, then I go through to the kitchen.

Ppampamelaf2PF4. That's the name they post under, their Insta-gram handle.

The first time I saw it, it just looked like gibberish. Then I started thinking about being at my mum's house, asking for the Wi-Fi pass-word and her producing a little scrap of paper and telling me to try this one or maybe this one. And they're all things like sjsuejackson and suejacksonSUEEJACKS. And if that doesn't work, she says, try them all again but with an exclamation mark.

I was beginning to suspect that whoever was posting these pictures of Coco was not an internet wizard either. I was also pretty sure their first name was Pam or Pamela and that their surname began with an *F*.

My first thought was to tell Emmy, see what she thought, suggest that she pass on this information, this hypothesis, to Instagram, to the police, to a lawyer.

Then a second thought occurred to me. A hunch, you might say.

Under other circumstances I might be annoyed that Winter's new laptop is just lying on the kitchen counter, pretty much in exactly the same place she left the last one. In full view of the kitchen window, as if to fucking tempt another burglar.

I suppose I should be grateful she hasn't stuck all the passwords to it this time. It doesn't take me long to work out the one I need. You don't spend as long as I have married to someone without working out the kinds of passwords they rely upon. For ages, Emmy's password to almost everything was our names and then the date we got married.

Obviously, all of the passwords have been changed since the burglary.

The password—the new password—to Emmy's mailing list is Coco's name, then her birthday. On it are all the people who have ever ordered a Mamabare sweatshirt or a #yaydays mug or attended a #greydays event. Even after I've typed in the password, the document is so massive it takes a little while to open.

Let me unpack my hunch a little.

It's long been my suspicion that you can only really understand the relationship between someone like Emmy, her fans, and her haters if you have some grasp of the Kierkegaardian concept of *ressentiment*, as popularized and expanded by Nietzsche. Meaning the projection of all one's own feelings of inferiority onto an external object, another person, someone you both hate and envy and also sometimes secretly wish to be—or at least tell yourself you could be. Could have been. Given different chances. Given their chances. Someone like Emmy, whom you either idolize because they are just like you but really successful or hate because they are someone just like you but really successful—and no doubt in a lot of ways the line between the fans and the haters is thinner than you might think.

Both kinds of people obsessively read Emmy's posts, after all. I know she and Irene have sometimes talked about how many of Emmy's followers, what proportion, are people more or less consciously hate-following her, who can't resist keeping up with each infuriating thing she posts, who loathe her yet still keep checking their phones to look at pictures of her. And one of the things that Irene has always drummed into Emmy is how quickly a fan who feels ignored or tricked or slighted can turn on the person they used to admire and identify with. And one way in which the concept of *ressentiment* is useful is that it helps us conceptualize how suppressed feelings of envy might surface in the strangest of ways.

The truth is I have pretty mixed feelings about Emmy myself at the moment.

There has been a lot of talk over the past few days about the practicalities of dealing with the fallout from this Polly business, managing the public relations angle. There have been endless meetings and phone calls and discussions between Emmy and Irene about how to play it. Emmy has talked me through her plans—their plans—and I have sat there in a corner of the kitchen nodding and nursing a beer and occasionally offering a word or proofreading something for tone as she pulls together half apologies and vaguely worded recognitions of fallibility that never quite reach the point of putting their finger on what she did wrong but instead go big on her contrition about it—even if, she implies, it's at least partly someone else's fault.

What Emmy and I have still not had is a proper conversation about what she did and why she did it. I genuinely couldn't tell you if she even acknowledges to herself that she's done anything wrong. We used to have drinks with Polly all the time. We used to hang out. I got on really well with her old boyfriend, and her husband is absolutely fine, in smallish doses, especially if you don't get stuck talking to him one-on-one. When you think about it, Polly has been part of our lives for as long as we've had a life together, and part of Emmy's life practically forever. I did suggest that Emmy reach out to her, try to apologize, try to explain what happened.

"What, so she can sell that to the papers too?"

The message I have been getting throughout this whole thing is that

I should leave Emmy and Irene to deal with it and keep my helpful suggestions to myself. This is, after all, our livelihood we are talking about here, what keeps food on the table and Bear in nappies and Coco in full-time childcare.

Which would be fine if what Emmy does for a living weren't also literally my life.

I'm sure that for all couples—modern, youngish, professional couples like us—at different times it feels like one person or the other is temporarily in the driving seat. For the last few years, with Emmy and me, it has sometimes felt like I'm in the fucking sidecar. Which isn't a problem when you're able to convince yourself you have full trust in the person driving.

Sometimes I think back to those early dates with Emmy—the dinners and long walks and kisses on park benches and the shared jokes and intimacies—and I find myself wondering how much of it was real. *Really* real, I mean. Every time I mentioned a film, she'd grip my arm and tell me how much she loved it too. Every time I referenced a book, it was one of her favorites.

Sometimes I look back on the past eight years and I get a feeling like a door has slammed and the whole set has shivered.

Sometimes I am almost grateful that the role-play account gives me something else to think about, something to focus on. Sometimes. Almost.

Pam F. Pamela F. Pammy.

I pour myself a glass of wine, pull a stool up to the kitchen island, and resettle myself in front of Winter's laptop.

There are more than three hundred *F*s in Emmy's mailing list. I try searching surnames beginning with *F* in combination with first names beginning with the initial *P*.

Eighteen names come up.

I try searching surnames beginning with *F* in combination with first names beginning with *Pam*.

Only one name comes up.

Pamela Fielding.

I click on it. Up pops her address, her email.

I was right. My hunch was right. She is not a troll or a hater, the person who's been doing all this.

She's a fucking fan.

CHAPTER SIXTEEN

Emmy

I learned early on in my Instagram career to politely decline the vast majority of the free holidays I'm offered. Would you like a night in a five-star hotel? A stay at a luxury spa? A birthday weekend in a country house with your Instamum pals? The best suite, the tasting menu, the massage, the kids' club, the babysitter? In exchange for a story, a post, a quick quote they can put on their website. Sure, sometimes they prove just too tempting, but I pick and choose, and when I do say yes, I'm sparing with the smug bikini selfies and lavish with the *Aren't we lucky, knackered mama really needed this* captions.

The rest of the pod fill their boots—and their grids—with endless #presstrips, though. Some of them even complain about packing, or moan about the jet lag, or sharing a room with their toddler twins, or that little Fenton doesn't like snow or lactose-intolerant Xanthe can't eat the ice cream. Why they don't realize that complaining about a free week away is like bemoaning having to bank your lottery win check is beyond me.

Of all the freebies I've ever been offered, I never thought one with no Wi-Fi and vegan food would be the one I'd have to jump at. I'm so irritated by the whole concept, preemptively annoyed by the sort of people I'll be forced to spend the next five days with, that I've barely asked Irene anything about it. What I do know is that they're not set up for babies, so I've spent this morning constantly adding to the enormous pile: The car seat. The travel cot, blackout blinds, white noise machine. A breast pump and bottles and sterilizer. Bags of wipes and nappies and multiple changes of sleep suits. The foldaway baby bath, the towel, the room thermometer. The baby carrier. The pram. Dan has taken himself off to work in a café so he can avoid my swearing as I stomp from room to room and dump it all by the front door over multiple trips. Doreen has taken Coco to the library.

They return within minutes of each other, to wave Bear and me off in the taxi. Dan avoids my eye even while he makes a show of kissing me goodbye in front of Coco. He takes Bear and sniffs his head, holding him tight, as I lift my daughter and balance her on my hip.

"Now, are you going to be a good girl for Doreen and Daddy? Mummy won't be gone very long. And we can do something nice when I come home—how about I take you for an ice cream at Fortnum & Mason? They're having a lovely party next week." Dan shoots me a look as I pop Coco back down on the floor.

"Fucksake, Emmy," he hisses under his breath. "You're not taking her to a press launch the day you get back. Can we just have a week off sharing our shit with the entire world?"

The taxi beeps its horn before I can answer—although I know Dan wasn't really asking. He hands Bear to Doreen and marches out to strap the baby seat into the car while the driver silently loads the bags.

All I know about the location of the retreat is that it's two hours away if the roads are clear and remote enough that my phone—and the contraband one I've brought in my suitcase in case they confiscate my first—is unlikely to work.

"You have the address, right?" I ask him.

"Yes, Madam," he says, opening the door for Dan to put Bear into the back seat. Dan takes one last sniff of Bear's little fluffy head while I climb into the car.

"Bye-bye, little man. We'll see you soon. Daddy loves you," Dan says, still avoiding my eye and instead waving at his son, who's either smiling back or about to ensure we need to immediately stop the car for a nappy change. I imagine the fact Dan will have to deal with Coco solo all weekend is the only reason he'll miss me at all right now. Dr. Fairs says five days out of contact is probably the best thing for us both.

As we drive away, I root around in my bag to double-check I have all the essentials and an emergency supply of chocolate. Within minutes, Bear's dozed off and is making the really quite extraordinary grunting sounds that got him kicked out of our bedroom and into his own at four weeks old. It's astonishing how much noise such a small person can make, even when he's fast asleep.

The driver tries to start up a conversation, but I point at the peaceful Bear and put a finger to my lips, shrugging apologetically. I settle down for a farewell scroll while we make our way through a steady stream of traffic out of town, through Chiswick, across the river, through Richmond, over the river again. Things are ticking over online as Irene had expected. The rest of the pod are pointedly ignoring the furor, hanging back to see how it plays out before speaking out in support (or otherwise). The most ardent fans have taken on the angriest trolls, and we've been watching them slug it out among themselves in the comments for days, Winter tasked with deleting the nastiest rants. Most important, the brands seem to have bought into the excuse and accepted my apology, and Irene's phone is no longer ringing off the hook with bad news.

She texts to check I'm en route and ready to start the stories. Nearly, I tell her. Once the roads start to get more rural, I pull out a mirror. Makeup-free and wearing a black polo neck, I look suitably wan and contrite. I give myself a moment, and when my eyes are visibly moist, I press record, pointing the camera first at Bear.

"If only I could sleep as soundly as him, but what's happened over the past few days has kept me awake at night," I murmur softly, panning the phone round. "I've let you all down, I know that. I've let this little man down too. I haven't been the best I could be. I should've taken time away from these little squares to really recover from bringing this new human into the world. I should have taken self-care seriously, so I could care for him—and for you all. Instead, I took on too much, and because my head was all over the place, I fucked up."

I take a deep breath, gaze sadly out of the window for a moment.

"I just really want to take a moment here to talk about kindness. There are some amazing things about this Instagram community, but perhaps we should learn to bear—forgive the pun—with each other a bit more. We need to lift each other up, not knock each other when we're down. It's so easy to fire off a comment, write a post, send a DM, without really thinking through the implications. But perhaps we should consider how what we write affects other people out there. I know that I certainly will from now on."

I take a break before pressing record again. The roads are getting more rural—I don't even think I've seen a house in the last half an hour, although I have seen quite a few distant corrugated barns, a fair number of sheep, a burned-out trailer, and a hand-painted banner about Brexit stretched across some hay bales. I record a few more emotional musings—the nature of fame, the purity of the love I have for my children, how my husband has been my rock throughout, never for a second doubting me. Then I sign off.

"As you know, I am stepping away from social media for a while to really evaluate what it means to be here. Never in my wildest dreams, when I started out with my little shoe blog, did I imagine that I would touch a million mamas. So many wonderful things have come out of my life on the grid, and I don't want to lose that, but I also know it's taking its toll on my family. We're all learning how this brave new influencer world works, kind of making it up as we go along. But I need a pause on my journey, a little metaphorical foot rub, a second to catch my breath. So Bear and I are on our way to a digital detox retreat. No social media, just me hanging out with this perfect little human and truly connecting with him, with myself. Because you can't get this magical time back, can you?"

The DMs are rolling in thick and fast by this point. *You do you, Mama! You give so much, Emmy, we're right there with you! Don't leave us, Mamabare, we need you! Such powerful words, you inspiring superhuman! Sending hugs and rainbows!*

Only the odd *Why aren't you ashamed of yourself? I hope you disappear forever* creeps in.

Bad luck, lurker. I'll be back in five days. I save the stories into my Highlights, so any followers bereft at my social media blackout can rewatch them over the next five days.

"Nearly there," says the driver, waking Bear up with a start.

As we pull up the scrubby track, it becomes clear that Irene wasn't joking when she said this would be rustic. I have no idea how many people will be at this thing—who's running it, even. Hagrid perhaps? As I am walking up to the house, the porch light comes on and a woman appears at the door. Dressed in a bobbly cardigan and cord trousers, and with her wispy white hair piled on top of her head, she doesn't look much like a former tech exec to me.

"Emmy, welcome! We are so happy to have you here. Please come in, make yourself at home. This will be your sanctuary for the next five days, the place that will disconnect you from the rest of the world, so you can truly switch off," she says, arms open expansively.

The driver helps us inside with the bags, which she instructs him to leave in the hall. He confirms the fare, and she pays it in cash. We check the boot and the back seat for any last bits and bobs that might have spilled out, and then she waves him off.

"I'm afraid we will need to search these for contraband phones and laptops before we show you to your room." She laughs. "Just take a seat here; there's a Moses basket behind the sofa for Bear. What a lovely little baby he is."

She already has a cup of tea on the table, and pours me one from a patterned china teapot while pointing to a plate of cookies. Christ, this house looks like it was decorated by a suburban housewife—there are teddies clutching hearts on the mantelpiece and one of those dreadful driftwood signs that says LOVE IS WHAT MAKES THIS HOUSE A HOME. The rug under my feet is that black-and-white faux-Moroccan La Redoute one that has its own Instagram account.

I settle into a grey velvet armchair and take a big sip from what I'm a little surprised to see is a #greydays mug.

Then, nothing.

It was so easy. That is what amazes me. How simple the whole thing was. All that creeping around, all that watching your house. All that time I spent observing your movements, as a family, as individuals, accustoming myself to the pattern of your days. The part of the plan that had always given me the most trouble was trying to work out how I was going to get you here. I had all sorts of complicated ideas, spent ages working out various elaborate machinations. I was going to snatch Coco in the park, and leave you a trail of clues. I was going to come along to one of your events, try and persuade you to let me give you and Bear a lift home. I was going to goad you online so insistently, so viciously, that you would feel compelled to unmask me, track me down—the point of the plan being that I would make this as simple as possible—and come here to confront me in person. I was going to write you a series of anonymous letters . . .

All it needed in the end was three phone calls. It came to me as soon as you announced the name of the "digital detox" retreat.

There was something typically "you" about that, wasn't there? Something typically Emmy. Announcing in advance the name of the place you are going on retreat, combining a bout of soul-searching and contrition with a free holiday.

Five days. Perfect. I could not have asked for everything to fall into place more neatly. If I am lucky, it will be several days before anyone notices anything is amiss. And even when they do, so what? There is nothing to link you to this place, you to me. Only the driver—and how will they find him?

My first phone call was last night, to the place you were meant to be staying. I told them I was your PA. Nobody questioned it. I told them I was calling to confirm the travel arrangements for today. They were sending a car, weren't they? Of course, came the reply. It was all booked. Would I like them to reconfirm that? I said if it was not too much trouble. And the car would be arriving at Emmy's at eleven a.m.? Wonderful.

My second phone call, early this morning, was to the same number, to apologize. Was this the same person I had spoken to before? Apparently it was. Was there anything I needed, they asked? "I am so sorry about this," I said. "It's the baby. The poor little thing has been up all night with a temperature and has just been sick again." We were waiting, I told them, for the doctor's to open to see if we could get an emergency appointment. Would it be possible to postpone? We were so sorry about the late notice, I told them. Emmy and Bear had been so much looking forward to it.

They were very understanding about the whole situation. I promised I would call back soon with Emmy's diary to hand to discuss alternative dates. They asked me to pass on all their best to Emmy and get-well-soon wishes to little Bear. Of course, they said, they would call and cancel the car and explain the situation.

My third call was to a local minicab company. Could they do a pickup from an address in London, at eleven a.m. today? I asked about the car, the kind of car, they would be sending. A blue Prius, they said. I told them that would be perfect. The name of the person they were collecting was Emmy Jackson. She would have a tiny baby with her. She would probably have quite a bit of luggage too. The drop-off address? I gave them the address of this place, and told them how to get here. "Once you have found the lane," I said, "you just keep going. I'll be here. I'll be keeping an eye out for you. Yes, I'll be paying cash. How much? I'll have it ready."

Isn't it strange these days, how we all just jump into people's cars, trust that they are who we assume they are, trust that they will take us where we think we are going?

And now here you are.

I could see, even as you were walking up to the front door, even before you got inside, that you were wondering if this could really be the place. I guessed you'd been expecting something a bit fancier, a bit less domestic. I could see you thinking that none of this looked much like any of the pictures on the website, could see your gaze resting on various items around the place, Grace's little decorating touches, slightly smirking.

If I had ever had a moment of hesitation about all this, that half-stifled smirk would have quashed it.

Propofol. That was what was in the cup of tea. A commonly prescribed muscle relaxant and sedative, with some retrograde amnesiac qualities. You took three sips of your tea and fell asleep midsentence. Given those amnesiac qualities, I doubt you'll even remember that.

Let me explain all this carefully. You deserve that, at least, I suppose.

The propofol was to knock you out so that I could get you upstairs (albeit with one long rest on the landing and a lot of huffing and puffing), get you into bed, get you hooked up on the drip. The drip is to deliver the midazolam. That was the stuff that was the hardest to get hold of. The stuff I had to smuggle out bit by bit, one partly used discarded vial at a time, the stuff I have been stockpiling in the fridge for some time now because I need it to make this whole thing work. It is no wonder they have to keep a close eye on it in hospitals. It is strong stuff, midazolam, a powerful muscle relaxant and antianxiety medi-

cation. That's why we give it to people before they have operations. Not just to knock them out, but to suppress their natural instinct to panic, to struggle, to flee.

In an ideal world—if this were all happening on TV, or in a movie—I would just have set you up and left you there, on the bed. Unfortunately, in the real world, for all the reasons I have already explained, that's not the way things work. I don't want to kill you, after all. And you can't just sedate someone that heavily and leave them unsupervised for that long. For this to work, for this to turn out the way I am intending, I am going to have to be here to keep an eye on you. Not all the time, naturally. I am not sure I could stand it, being in the same room the whole time, given what's going to happen over the next few days. I'll be downstairs, mostly, or outside, pottering around in the garden. It's only about once every six hours I'll need to pop back and check your blood pressure, make sure your breathing is okay, that your airways are not in danger of occlusion. At intervals I will want to measure the level of CO_2 in your blood. Every so often I'll need to dose you up again, adjust your drip. Oh, don't worry, Emmy. I am—or at least I was—a professional. You'll be very well looked after. I have some oxygen right here in case you need it. I am just about to fix you up to the finger probe, and then we're all set.

Did I mention you'll be in my daughter's room? Did I mention you are in my daughter's bed?

Were you awake, were you chemically capable of panic or even serious concern about your future, I know the question you would be asking. Don't worry, I would say. Bear will be right with you.

Now that you are all set up I am just going to go down and get him out of the Moses basket and bring him up. Don't be afraid. I am not going to do anything to hurt the baby. I am going to bring him up, and I am going to put him here right next to you. He'll be right next to you on the bed the whole time. It's a big bed. It's all set up for cosleeping. He's not going to go anywhere. I won't be doing anything to the baby at all.

I reckon a couple of days will be long enough. Three, tops. I hope you understand, Emmy, that I am going to be taking no pleasure in any of this. No doubt there are going to be some moments of doubt, some struggles with my conscience. There will be times, I am sure, when the impulse to stop all this becomes almost overwhelming, when I am seconds away from going upstairs and telling you it is all over, when I am gripping the arms of my chair to keep myself in it. I have brought earplugs, some CDs and cassettes. Things I used to listen to when Grace was a child, mostly. ABBA, the Beatles.

It will be the dehydration that does it. An adult human, a healthy adult human, can go for up to three weeks without food—but they'll only last three or four days without water. A child? They're unlikely to survive half that.

And all the time you'll be lying right there next to him.

I reckon I'll give it four days. Just to be on the safe side. Then I'll give you one last dose of the midazolam, a half dose, a twelve-hour one, and unplug everything and fold up these sheets of paper and write your name on the outside and leave them on the table downstairs and I'll go.

It should be morning when your eyes open. It's always lovely, the light in that room as the sun comes up.

Understand this, Emmy Jackson. I am not evil. I am not mad. I don't want to witness your child's suffering, or cause him unnecessary pain. I don't want to be there when he dies; I don't even know if I am going to be able to bring myself to look at him. I am not an unfeeling person. I can imagine, all too easily, all too painfully, what it will feel like to be you at that moment, to wake up groggily, staring up at an unfamiliar ceiling, and realize you are in an unfamiliar bed, and wonder with a start where the baby is, and reach for him.

I have no desire to witness what will happen next, to observe the moment your heart breaks, the moment you realize that every happy memory you have of your child will now be almost unbearably painful, forever marked by loss. The moment you begin to piece together what he went through in those last few hours, those last few days. The moment when you begin to howl and you don't know if it will ever stop.

I can remember all those feelings. I can remember seeing my daughter go through each of them in turn.

Sometimes, because I believe people should face the consequences of their actions, I have forced myself to picture what will happen next.

To imagine you groggy, distraught, stumbling downstairs, tripping over the edge of the carpet.

To imagine you clutching something to your chest. Something wrapped in a blanket but oh-so-cold; something you can't imagine ever letting go of.

I remember Jack telling me how long the ambulance crew took to persuade Grace that she would have to loosen her grip on Ailsa, just for a minute. I can remember Jack telling me how worried Grace was that she would be cold, would feel cold. Kept asking him to fetch blankets, screamed at him when he just stood there. I can remember him telling me about how Grace was babbling to Ailsa even as she finally handed her over, was telling Ailsa not to worry, that Mummy was here, that everything was okay.

And I imagine you standing in the living room at the bottom of the stairs, cautiously looking around, hesitant, unsure at this point whether I am really gone, whether you are really alone.

And when you spot the envelope I can see you crossing the room and opening it, and starting to read there at the living room table, still standing, letting each page fall as you have finished with it.

And then you'll know. What the point of all this is. Who the real villain of the piece turns out to be.

You made me, Emmy. You made me into what I am. You made me capable of doing this.

The burden I have borne, this regret and pain and sorrow and anger, I have carried long enough. I am glad to be near the end now. This is not about revenge. This has never been about revenge. It is about justice. And when it is over, all I want to do is close my eyes, and know that I have done what needed to be done, and rest.

Goodbye, Emmy.

Dan

It's a scene I have been anticipating in my head all week. As I'm seeing Bear and Emmy off. As I'm working that afternoon, typing away in the kitchen of the empty house. As I'm making Coco's dinner, giving her a bath, and reading her to sleep. As I am watching TV, watching whatever I want to watch on TV, eating whatever I want to eat and as much of it as I like. The next day, as I am sitting in a café with my laptop, occasionally checking my phone for messages from Emmy and quietly impressed by the totality of her silence (I hadn't expected her to take the whole communication-blackout thing anything like as seriously as she has) or as I'm explaining once again to Coco where Mummy is and when she's due back. As Coco and I are watching cartoons in the morning and waiting for Doreen to come and as I'm waiting in the evenings for another picture of my daughter to appear on Ppampam-elaf2PF4's feed and as I'm confirming with Doreen that it's still okay that she takes Coco on Saturday, as we've previously discussed. As I am booking my train ticket and working out how best to get from the station to Pamela Fielding's house. As I am looking at pictures of Pamela Fielding's house on Google Maps. As I am falling asleep with a whole bed to myself in the evenings and practically as soon as I am awoken each morning by Coco calling plaintively down the corridor to let me know she's ready to get up.

It's a bright day, Saturday, so I suggest that Doreen and my daughter go for a walk along the canal, then stop off at the playground next to the skate park. That should kill most of the morning. I give Doreen some extra cash for lunch, suggest they stay out to eat and check out the city farm in the afternoon. My idea is enthusiastically received.

By my calculations, what I need to do should take me six hours.

I give it five minutes after they've left, and then I depart the house as well. I didn't say anything to Emmy about any of this before she went. Far better, in my thinking, to present it to her afterward as a fait accompli. Maybe I won't tell her anything at first, just wait until she notices that the RP account has been shut down, wait until she asks how I got the stolen laptop back.

Like a lot of writers, there is some part of me that genuinely thinks I would make a pretty good detective.

All the way to the Tube I'm imagining to myself what I'm going to say to Pamela when she opens the door.

Hi there, Pam. I'm Dan. And I'm here to tell you to leave my fucking daughter alone.

Of course I've done an image search for Pamela Fielding, but the results show fifteen UK-based women (and several books about eighteenth-century literature), so I don't know which of them has been running the account and lives at the address I'm on my way to. None of them looks particularly deranged.

I arrive at Liverpool Street about fifteen minutes before my train is ready to depart. Right next to the barrier there are two policemen in helmets and luminous tabards, and I experience a brief moment of intense self-consciousness, a moment of wondering whether to make eye contact or not, whether to smile or not.

I might as well admit it. There were some mad moments when I considered taking something with me on this expedition. A hammer. A Stanley knife. A pair of scissors. Not that I would use them, of course. Just something to show I meant business. I imagined myself ramming the scissors into the doorframe. Taking the hammer to the little window in the middle of the front door. Fucking up the wheels. I spent about forty-five minutes wondering if I knew any way I could get my hands on a gun before sanity intervened. *Mental*, I told myself. *You sound absolutely mental.*

It being midmorning on a Saturday, the train is relatively uncrowded. This isn't a line I've used before, and it surprises me how quickly we're in the country, or at least what I think of as the country, how quickly we've left behind the office blocks and Victorian terraces and new high-rise developments and are passing golf courses and a field with horses in it.

I count the stops, seventeen of them, and stare out the window, my guts churning. We pass dispersed farm buildings and corrugated barns and things in fields under black plastic. All of the towns we pass through look pretty similar. An enormous IKEA. Multistory parking lots. Gardens with trampolines in them. The sky is low and grey and threatens rain.

A very tall old guy in a furry-hooded coat with a plastic bag in each hand is the only other person to get off at my station. Christ, England is depressing. The coffee shop is closed, the waiting room locked, the platform windswept and deserted. With a bit of a judder, the glass doors open to reveal an equally deserted taxi rank, the wind swirling little hurricanes of dust and burger wrappers around on the tarmac.

I have already done this walk on Street View several times, so I know what to expect. Right out of the station, past a coffee stall and an Italian restaurant straight out of the 1990s, complete with sign outside advertising paninis. Down the high street, past a pet shop and a Tesco Metro and a Costa and a bus shelter with no glass in it. A left turn at the traffic light just past the library. A long road of terraced houses.

As anticipated, the walk takes me about fifteen minutes.

It looks like a perfectly normal house, from the outside. Two bins in the front garden. The garden itself a little overgrown. Leaded windows.

When I reach the place, I don't hesitate. For weeks, I've been dreaming of the opportunity to give whoever's been posting pictures of my daughter online a piece of my mind, to shame them, to give them a scare. To stop them. All week, I've been imagining this moment. I'm startled by how hard I tap the knocker.

Then I wait.

A minute passes. Two minutes.

After a while. I begin to wonder if there's anyone home. I realize I've assumed that having come all this way, on a Saturday, Pamela Fielding is going to be here to answer the door when I knock on it.

I keep looking up and down the street to see if she's coming back from the shops or something. One or two people pass. No one gives me a second look.

Eventually, just as I am about to give up hope, I hear something in the house, and a shape appears, a white shape, in the doorway of what I take to be the living room. It moves very slowly, gradually gaining definition in the rippled glass of the little window in the front door.

They get to the door, realize it's locked, and shuffle away again. I can hear them rooting around for a key in what I assume is a bowl on the sideboard in the front hall. Eventually they locate the one they want. It's still another three or four minutes before they manage to unlock the door.

"Can I help you?"

The individual who opens the door is a man in his seventies. Seeing me, a stranger, he straightens up, brushes down his trousers, picks something (a toast crumb?) from the lapel of his cardigan. I am pretty sure this man isn't the person posting pictures of Coco. I am almost certain he's not the one who broke into my house and stole my wife's laptop. He looks like the kind of man you see collecting for the British Legion.

His expression is puzzled.

"Hi there," I say. "Is this . . . ? Is . . . ? Does Pamela Fielding live here?"

"She does," he says, literally looking me up and down. "Can I ask . . . ?"

I expect if I really was a detective I would have some kind of cover story ready to hand.

"I'm a friend," I say, eventually. "From work."

It is perhaps lucky that at exactly that minute it begins to rain. Quite heavily, in fact. It can be heard drumming on the lids of the bins. He looks at me. He looks at the rain.

"You had better come in, then," he says, after a moment.

There's a line of shoes along the hallway, several pairs of slippers next to them. The carpet itself is soft and deep, dark brown. I work my shoes off and add them to the lineup.

"Pam," he calls up the similarly carpeted stairs.

"I'm Eric," he says, offering me a soft hand to shake. I tell him my name. He gives no sign of recognizing it. "That's the living room, through there," he says.

He pauses at the bottom of the stairs, rests one hand on the banister, and calls Pam's name again. Somewhere over our heads a toilet flushes.

"Can I offer you a cup of tea?"

I say I'd love one. Milk, no sugar. I take a seat in the living room.

It has the air of a room that's not used every day, the kind that's reserved for visitors. I also sense they don't get visitors that often. The instant I sit on the couch I can feel myself sinking into it, and as this process begins, it pulls the enormous crocheted blanket that is hanging over the back of the sofa down around my shoulders. By the time I finally come to a halt, I am looking at the coffee table from between my knees, and my backside is resting at the level of my ankles.

It is hard to escape the feeling I'm not exactly going to be at my most imposing in this position. I grasp the coffee table and pull myself to standing, then rearrange the coffee table doily, scanning the room for somewhere a bit more solid and strategic to plant myself.

I end up perching on one of the soft arms of the sofa.

"Pam," Eric calls up the stairs for a third time, more emphatically now. "There's a . . . person come to see you."

As he's passing the doorway, he looks in and raises both eyebrows at me at once and says something about Pam living in her own world most of the time.

"She says she hears me calling, but I don't know she does, really," he says. "Can I take your coat?" he asks.

I tell him I'm fine.

He tells me to let him know if I want him to turn the fire on.

I give him a thumbs-up.

"One sugar, is it?"

"No sugars," I tell him, again.

Footsteps on the stairs. A moment of hesitation—Pamela checking her hair in the mirror at the bottom of the stairs? She's saying something to the man in the kitchen as she comes through, her attention in that direction. Then she sees me. Then she stops.

"Hi, Pamela," I say.

Her face stiffens. She quickly turns and closes the door behind her, and then turns back.

"I expect you know why I'm here, don't you?"

She nods, once, quickly.

"I don't imagine you thought you'd ever be meeting me in real life, like this, did you?"

She shakes her head.

"Look at me," I say.

She lifts her gaze to meet mine, very briefly, and then very quickly lowers it again.

In the other room, I can hear the man who opened the door making the tea, humming to himself. A spoon clinks against a mug. A cupboard door is opened.

"Your dad?" I ask.

She shakes her head again.

"My grandad."

Pamela Fielding is about seventeen years old.

The very first thing she tells me is that she didn't steal the photos. I ask who did, then? Someone she knows? Someone from her school? She's still at school, isn't she?

"College," she mumbles.

She looks like the kind of girl you see on the bus. She keeps tucking a strand of dark, sort-of-shiny hair behind her ear. In each earlobe is a single stud. Her cheeks, dotted here and there with acne scars, are thickly foundationed.

"Where is it?" I ask. "The laptop."

She doesn't have it, she says. She doesn't know anything about any laptop. She bought the photographs online.

"Online? What do you mean? Like, the dark web?"

She looks at me.

"I mean a website," she says. "Just a forum."

"What kind of forum?"

She fiddles with the cuff of the sweater she's wearing.

"A forum for people who do what I do, who share advice with one another, give one another tips. Sometimes we talk about all the different influencers. Sometimes we talk about how to get more followers."

"Like by pretending the person whose pictures you are using is sick?"

"I guess so."

It's at that point that Grandad comes in with the tea. If he notices any tension in the room, he doesn't mention it. He talks us both through the various treats and cookies in the tin and lets us know how many there are of each. A corner of Pamela's mouth twitches impatiently. When he leaves, Pamela's grandfather sets the living room door slightly ajar. Both of us glance at it. Neither of us gets up to close it.

I'm aware of being in a very strange position at this point. I'm trying very hard to avoid raising my voice, losing my temper. This is not easy.

"So, this forum," I say, "What's it called?"

She tells me. I ask her to spell it.

"And is it open or closed?"

"Some of it's open and some of it's closed."

"And it is someone on this forum you have been buying photographs from?"

She nods.

"Who are they?" I ask. "What do they call themselves?"

"The Mad Hatter," she says.

"The Mad Hatter? As in Alice?"

She looks blank.

"Their avatar is a picture of a hat," she tells me.

"And what else do you know about them? Anything? How did you get them the money?"

"PayPal," she mutters.

"Show me."

Reluctantly she brings her phone out from her pocket, unlocks it, and holds it up.

"Which one is it? Which transaction?"

She shows me.

"You're sure?"

She nods.

"That was the account you paid the money into? The account this Mad Hatter wanted credited?"

She nods again.

The PayPal account into which she paid the money is in the name Winter Edwards.

Winter?

It takes a minute or two for me to get my head around this, for it even to start to sink in.

I ask Pamela whether this person, the one on the forum, said anything about how they got the photographs and why they were selling them. Was it just about the money? Was it from jealousy, from spite? Do they think we have wronged them in some way?

Pamela shrugs.

"I didn't really ask."

"And what about you? Why do *you* do it?" I ask her. "That's what I can't understand. What's the kick?"

"I don't know."

"I want you to take the account down, and I want you to delete those pictures. All those pictures. And I want to watch you doing it. And maybe then I won't call the police and I won't tell your grandfather. But only if you promise me never to do this again. To speak to someone about why you feel the need to do this, what compels you. I mean, I don't know what your family situation is, or whatever. If you want me to find you someone to speak to, a number to call, I can do that."

She says something that sounds like *okay*, very softly.

"I mean, you do get that it's weird, don't you, what you've been doing?"

"I guess so."

"You guess so. Taking someone's pictures and making up stories about them and posting them for all the world to see? Someone who has not given you their consent? Who doesn't even know you're doing it? It's fucking disgusting. It's sick."

There follows a long pause.

She's staring hard at the carpet, her hair hanging down in front of her face, and when she speaks it is so quiet I can't even hear her.

"Sorry?" I say.

"I said, 'How is it any different?'" she says.

"Different from what?" I ask.

As I'm waiting for an answer, my phone starts ringing and at first I ignore it but it just keeps buzzing and buzzing in my pocket and eventually I take it out to see who's calling. It's Irene, and I answer it and say something fairly brusque like, "What?" and she says, "Emmy," and from the way she says it I can tell she's trying to keep her voice calm and steady.

"Dan," she says. "I think something has happened to Emmy."

Emmy

I think it is possible that I am dying.

Have I said that already?

For quite some time now, I've been trying to work out if I'm awake or asleep, watching patterns swirl and dissolve on the insides of my eyelids, trying to keep up with the twists and turns of the conversation I am conducting in my head with somebody who is sometimes Dan, sometimes my mum, sometimes Irene, sometimes a complete stranger. I keep trying to make my thoughts go in a straight line, but it's like attempting to walk on a dead leg. As soon as I feel I've got something straight in my head, I immediately forget it. How I got here, for instance. Where I am.

Have I been in an accident? Has something happened to me? In my more lucid intervals I get the distinct impression I am lying in a hospital bed somewhere. Every so often I seem to sense that I am not alone, that there is someone leaning over me, checking something, making little adjustments to whatever equipment they have got me hooked up to here, inspecting whatever monitors I can hear occasionally beeping. Sometimes I hear them clucking to themselves, muttering, moving things around. Sometimes I can feel them arranging my head, my shoulders, the pillow.

I could be dreaming or imagining all of that, of course. I remember Dan once telling me about the tricks the mind plays when you've been alone in the dark too long, when it has been starved of sensory input. The sorts of things long-distance truck drivers start seeing swirling out of the darkness after being behind the wheel for days. For ages, for instance, I was convinced I could hear ABBA's greatest hits playing somewhere nearby, just loud enough to hear, over and over on repeat until I could have told you without hesitation as soon as one song ended what the next one was going to be.

For ages too I have been sure that I can hear a baby crying, really close and really loud. For a while I was convinced it was Bear, then I remembered where I am and realized it must be someone else's baby, someone else on the ward, someone in another nearby bed, but by God it sounds unhappy and by God it sounds like mine—so much like mine it is making my own milk-swollen breasts throb and ache. On and on and on it goes. Inconsolable, unbroken howling for what feels like hours with just the occasional intermission while they gulp in more air.

Why is no one comforting it? That is what I don't understand. Why does no one seem to be to trying to calm it down, giving it a cuddle, taking the poor thing for a quick walk up and down the corridor or into another room for a bit? *Here*, I feel like saying, *let me show you. Have you tried burping them, maybe? That's the way my little one always cries when he is feeling gassy.*

And in my head, I am composing a very long post about all of this, adding in what a fantastic job they are doing, all those nurses and doctors, how wonderful our NHS is, but also mentioning how incredibly thirsty I am and is there not anything anybody can do about this baby . . . and then I realize I am not actually composing a post, I am just mentally dictating it to nobody, and all this time the baby keeps screaming.

And then it stops, in the abrupt way that babies do stop crying, eventually, after they have howled themselves into exhaustion, and in that sudden silence I find myself wondering if I really heard anything, whether there was a baby, whether there is even a ward.

Time passes. The silence continues.

Thank God for that, I think.

Then the screaming starts again.

Dan

I can remember every detail of that phone call as if it happened yesterday. Wandering down the street, not really able to take anything in, asking Irene questions over and over again that she'd already told me she didn't know the answer to. I just couldn't get my head around it. Emmy and Bear had never arrived at the retreat. The retreat had never sent a car. No one had seen or heard from my wife or my son for over seventy-two hours.

After that, things get kind of fuzzy, fragmented.

I can remember calling Doreen from the train and telling her not to panic, and she offered to give Coco her dinner and a bath and put her to bed, to wait there until I got home, and then the train went into a tunnel and we lost our connection for about five minutes.

I can remember trying Emmy's phone, frantically, pointlessly, again and again and again. Then trying the other one, the one she said she was going to try to hide from the hippies and hang on to. Both of them went straight to voicemail.

I can't remember telling Irene where I was or how long it would take me to get to London, but I must have done, because when I got to the ticket barrier at Liverpool Street, there she was.

She'd just spoken to the hospital, she said. Emmy's mother was going to be fine. No signs of concussion.

That's why she'd been trying to contact Emmy, the reason she'd called the retreat. To tell her that Virginia was in the hospital. That she'd tripped coming down the stairs of a Mayfair members' club after the launch of a limited-edition gin and landed backward on the marble floor of the lobby, knocking herself out cold. Irene told me this in the back of a taxi on the way to the nearest police station, but to be honest, not much of it registered. Every time we hit traffic, Irene would lean forward and enter into a brief exchange with the driver, then we'd pull a sudden U-turn or take a sharp detour. "They let me speak to Ginny half an hour ago," Irene informed me. "She insists her shoes were the problem." The whole time Irene was talking, she had one eye on her phone, her thumb constantly moving.

"Right," she said, glancing up as the taxi pulled to a halt outside the police station. "Here we are." Irene and I made our way into the building and identified ourselves at the front desk. As we were waiting for someone to come down and collect us and take a statement, she talked me through all the steps she was going to take, and explained those she had already taken. I was barely listening, or, if I was listening, I was not capable of taking any of it in.

All I can remember thinking about was Emmy and Bear, Bear and Emmy, out there somewhere, missing.

The very first thing I told the police was that I had seen the car. The one Emmy left in. I had seen the car pull up, seen her get into it, seen the thing drive away. They asked me to describe it. I told them it was blue, the kind of car Uber drivers always have. A Prius, maybe? I don't drive, don't know or care much about cars. The driver? I said I hadn't really got a good look at him. No, I couldn't remember the license plate number. And my wife, they said. Did my wife seem in any way upset as she was getting into the car? Concerned? "No," I said. "But she thought she was getting into the car the retreat had sent," I reminded them. She had no way of knowing someone had canceled that car. She didn't have any idea what car she was getting into. They asked if I was able to remember the last thing we talked about.

I could.

The last thing Emmy had said to me was whether I'd put Bear's change kit in the duffel bag and whether the duffel bag was in the trunk and I said yes and she asked if I was sure and I said I had literally just double-checked. Fine, she said. Then she'd tried to slam the car door but caught the corner of her coat and had to open the door and slam it again as they were driving away, but she didn't look back.

It suddenly struck me that I might never see my wife again, that my last ever memory of her might be that moment, her silhouette as she fiddled around, half turned in her seat trying to get her seat belt plugged in.

The police asked about the retreat. I told them everything I knew. They asked why I hadn't raised the alarm sooner. I repeated quite a lot of what I had already told them.

"So you weren't surprised that she didn't get in touch with you?"

"Like I said," I reminded them, "I wasn't expecting to hear from her for another two days."

The thing that kept going through my head was that statistic about most people who go missing turning up within forty-eight hours. It was a statement that kept coming up in the stuff I had looked at on the train when I was trying to work out how to file a missing person report, trying to work out what it was the police actually did in a situation like this—and I suppose for most people it was a statistic that would have been reassuring.

But Emmy and Bear had been missing now for three whole days.

The most likely explanation, one of the officers suggested, was that Emmy had just needed to get away and clear her head for a bit. That happened. People did that. Had I checked our joint bank account for transactions? She was probably having a lovely time at some spa in the West Country or something, with no idea about all this hullaballoo going on at home.

Irene looked unconvinced.

I suspect what she was thinking was that if Emmy was going to pull a disappearing act like that, the old Agatha Christie routine, she'd have discussed it and cleared it and planned it out with her first.

I found it hard to dispute this logic.

What the police seemed most worried about was whether Emmy was depressed, whether she had expressed to me any self-harming impulses or feelings of low self-worth, whether she has been showing any signs of postnatal depression.

I shook my head firmly.

They asked me a lot of questions about my whereabouts over the past few days, questions I didn't fully grasp the significance of until I went over it all in my head again later.

Were we experiencing any financial worries currently? Did I think there was any possibility she had met someone else?

"Listen," I said. "I am really sorry, I know you are just trying to eliminate the most obvious explanations first, but please listen to me. My wife didn't leave or run off or decide to disappear. She's been taken by someone. That man, the driver. You need to find that man. Just look at her feed. There are pictures, videos. She thinks she's going to a retreat for five days. That's what she told everyone. She was behaving completely normally."

Half the computers in the building turned out to have social media automatically disabled. At least two of the others didn't switch on at all. Finally Irene pulled out her phone and we talked them through Emmy's feed, standing in the one corner of the room where she got decent reception.

I think it was only when Irene logged into Emmy's account and started showing them the kinds of direct messages that people would send her that they really started to take what we were saying seriously.

"Just look," she told them, her thumb bending and straightening, message after message after message scrolling by. Of course, there were the usual fawning ones, but interspersed with real, spine-chilling nastiness. These were anonymous, for the most part, although not all of them. The same words cropped up again and again. Threats. Abuse. Irene clicked on one of the messages to show who had sent it. Their profile picture showed a woman, a perfectly pleasant-looking middle-aged woman in a polo shirt holding a glass of white wine on a balcony, somewhere sunny. The message she had sent was about what a shit parent Emmy was and how Coco deserved to choke on an uncut grape. There was someone with no followers and no posts and no profile picture telling Emmy that she hoped her whole family—my whole family—would perish in a car accident. A little farther down, a picture of some guy's balls, taken from behind. It took me a moment to work out how he'd even managed to take a photo at that angle. Then a load more gratuitous personal bile and spite, on every possible topic from the color of her hair to the names of our children.

It genuinely felt like a glimpse of some version of hell. All that fury. All that malice. All that jealousy. All that hate.

"She never . . . ," I said. "I didn't . . ."

I kept saying I had to take a minute, try to process all this, and then I realized there was just too much to process, that it wouldn't matter how many minutes I had.

On Irene's screen was a message from a woman who literally kept sending my wife pictures of dog shit. A silhouette in a grey circle who kept demanding to debate her in person about mental health issues. A man who wanted her to mail him a bottle of her breast milk.

Emmy could be in the hands of any of these people. Emmy and Bear. Two of the people I loved most in the world. My little boy, an eight-week-old baby who couldn't quite lift his head or even turn it, who'd barely even learned to smile. The most helpless, beautiful, placid, innocent creature in the world. My wife. The woman with whom I'd chosen to spend the rest of my life, the person I'd known I was going to marry the moment I met her. Who was still, in spite of everything, my best friend.

And then it hit me that the last thing I had said to Emmy as she was leaving was not *I love you* or *I'll miss you* or *Let's talk about things properly when you get back*—it was some snippy little comment about her luggage.

And for the first time in several days, the only thing I thought about when I thought about Emmy was nothing to do with how complicated our lives had become or the problems in our marriage or whether there was anything we could do to save it.

Instead I thought about the night I first met Emmy. Her smile. Her laugh.

I thought about our first date, about the color of the sky that late summer evening as we walked back from the zoo along the canal, hand in hand.

I thought about all our private in-jokes, all the secret references no one else in the world would ever get, all the catchphrases and funny names for things that Bear and Coco would grow up thinking were normal and would one day realize were peculiar to our particular family unit.

I thought about our honeymoon, the first night, when we got so drunk at that place on the beach we had to carry each other back to the hotel, and the next morning we woke up fully dressed and facedown in a tangle of unraveled towel animals on a bed covered in rose petals. I thought of the morning we discovered that Emmy was pregnant with Coco, the tears of joy, the fierceness with which I could feel her hugging me, the test stick still in her hand. I thought of all those nights in front of the TV, a whole winter of Netflix and hospital visits and scans and alcohol-free beers. I remembered the day Coco was born, that first moment they handed her to us to hold, the look on Emmy's face, the glow. I remembered that afternoon, after we got home, alone in the house with the baby for the first time, that terrifying feeling of not having a clue what to do.

At least then I'd had somebody else to share that feeling with.

The police said they'd host a press conference the following morning. Did I have a picture of Emmy and Bear and me together, a picture of all of us smiling? they asked.

I told them I thought I could probably find one. I don't think they even realized the irony of their question.

Irene and I left. I assumed we were heading home, and we'd been in the cab for about ten minutes before I realized we were going in the wrong direction.

I said something like, "Hey," and swiveled in my seat.

"Settle down, Dan," said Irene. "We haven't got time to fuck about."

She'd put up a post on Emmy's feed before we had even left the police station. It was a simple, straightforward message saying when Emmy had vanished, describing the car and the driver, describing what she was wearing and asking if anyone had seen her and Bear.

It took us about fifteen minutes to get to Irene's place. All the way there we were both glued to our phones. I was aware of the driver asking us a friendly question at one point and getting no answer and muttering to himself. We both ignored him. Under Irene's post on the Mamabare account, comments were flooding in more quickly than I could even scroll through them. A lot of them were lengthy rambles about how much they hoped Emmy was safe and sending her love and letting her know they were thinking of her. Within about five minutes there were loads of people announcing the whole thing was a *Hoax!!!!* Within ten minutes all sorts of people were speculating wildly about what was going on, on the basis of absolutely nothing.

It can really rob you of your faith in the human spirit, sometimes, the internet.

On the other hand, by the time we got to Irene's flat, someone had already spotted a road sign in one of Emmy's Instastories, expanded it, and identified the bottom half of the letters *enham*. There was a lot of buzz about Cheltenham for a bit. Then someone mentioned Twickenham. That seemed more likely, given how long Emmy would have been traveling by the time she'd posted it.

Irene's car was parked around the side of her building. I had never seen where she lived before. It was an art deco block, somewhere in Bayswater, with brass handles on the front door and a marble desk in the lobby with a bloke behind it. The car was a classic two-seater MG, pale blue. Inside, it smelled strongly of old cigarettes.

It was getting dark by the time we hit the A316. I'd spoken to Doreen. Coco was in bed, and Doreen had agreed to stay the night. We passed Chiswick. We crossed the river. By the time we hit Richmond, someone had identified a service station in the background of one of Emmy's Instastories as the one off the A309, just before you pass through Thames Ditton.

If that was the case, it made sense in terms of the direction we were already heading.

What makes you so sure it was that service station? someone asked.

They pointed out the waving artificial man on the forecourt, the mannequin in overalls with the painted smile and the bobbing arm. They noted his distinctively chipped head, his weather-beaten features. They listed all the things you'd see if you reversed the shot 180 degrees—the chip shop across the road, the paper place, the closed-down Chinese restaurant with newspaper over all the windows.

It was good enough for us.

We didn't speak much, Irene and I. She was driving, I was trying to keep up with what was going on online.

What was going on online was that the whole community was assembling. Already—I wasn't sure whether at Irene's bidding or of their own volition—the rest of the pod had amplified our call for help.

Not just the pod, either. All the small fry, all the followers. People in Scotland, people in Wales, people in the US. As it turned out, it was lucky they did. It was a woman in Arizona, an expat, who first suggested that a stretch of trees and open green in the back of Emmy's next Instastory was Claremont Park at the point where it runs along the A307, who noted that if we looked carefully we could see a glint of lake in the distance.

At that very moment I spotted a National Trust sign with the name of the park on it, approaching on our left. A few minutes later, we passed another sign indicating where to turn into the park.

As we drove, the landscape was darkening around us. We'd been on the road now for at least an hour and a half. The last of Emmy's Instastories had been posted at about twenty to one on the day she and Bear vanished. It had shown the car turning off the main road onto a narrower, hedge-lined road with a ditch running alongside it. The caption to the Instastory had been *Where the f*ck . . . ?* It was deeply unsettling watching the videos as we drove through the same landscape, knowing what we knew now. What kept bringing a lump to my throat was the thought that if something awful had happened to Emmy, this would be the footage that would be on the news, poignant and fascinating, like someone's last grainy CCTV appearance before some awful tragedy or horrible crime.

I swear there were times that afternoon when a ransom note would have been a relief.

"There," I said suddenly, almost as we were passing the turnoff.

Irene hit the brakes hard, looked behind us, put the car into reverse. "You're sure?" she asked me.

I nodded.

We both peered down the long, narrow, hedge-lined road. I checked once again the paused image on my phone.

"This is it," I said.

It was one of those country lanes I hate driving down at the best of times, the kind you find yourself on when you're on holiday, where you dread anything coming the opposite way because there's nowhere to pass or pull over and one of you is just going to have to back up and back up and eventually try to nudge into a tiny space next to a gate or where the road slightly widens and hope you don't end up scratching the rental car or reversing it into the ditch.

Irene was taking it at about fifty miles an hour. You could hear thorns scraping along the paintwork, branches slapping against the side mirrors.

We passed several gaps in the hedge, several gates opening onto what looked like empty fields. It was nearly ten minutes before we reached the house. Irene slowed the car almost to a halt as we both peered up the drive. No lights on. No sign of a car.

"What do you reckon?" she said.

"I don't know."

We kept going. Up ahead, the road began to curve. Two minutes later it came to a halt at a gate. I got out of the car first. The gate was closed. On the far side of it was a field, which sloped away downhill. Standing on the lowest rung of the gate, I could look down across it as far as the little stream that marked its far boundary. Somewhere in a clump of nearby trees, a wood pigeon was burbling. I could hear the faint hum of the electricity lines strung from pylon to pylon across the middle of the field.

I looked back at Irene and shook my head.

There was only one place a car—as opposed to a tractor—coming up this road could have gone.

Irene turned the car around.

It was a strange feeling, knowing that Emmy and Bear had been here, knowing they had driven up this very road, looked out at these very bushes. I wondered at what point Emmy would have realized something was wrong, that this was not where they were supposed to be going. That was almost the hardest thing to picture, to think about.

I had no doubt her first thought would have been for Bear, to protect Bear. Would she have tried to get away? Would she have tried to reason with them? To bargain?

Halfway up the drive, Irene pointed out that the garage door was ajar.

She pulled up in front of the house, left her headlights on. I had my door open and was stepping out of the car before it had even come fully to a halt. It was one of those garages that had been built into the house, with a bedroom over it, some time after the rest of the house. The double doors of the garage were wooden, old, losing their paint in places. I pulled one open and then the other.

Apart from a refrigerator and a square of carpet with some oil on it in the middle of the cement floor, the garage was empty. Two tiled steps led up to the rest of the house. I tried the door. It opened.

Behind me I could hear Irene talking to someone on the phone. The police, I presumed.

The room on the far side of the door was in darkness. Some kind of storage room, it felt like. The window onto the back garden was frosted, letting in little light. I got an impression of piled chairs and tables under sheets, stacks of plastic boxes. I felt for a light switch but couldn't find one. There was a sort of path through the middle of the room that I groped my way down, and at the far end of it I fumbled around in the dark until I found a door handle and then opened it.

"Emmy?" I whispered.

The house was silent. Remembering the flashlight function on my phone, I took it out of my pocket. I was in a living room. In front of me was a couch and a pair of armchairs, and beyond that a door presumably leading to a kitchen. To my right was a dining table, bare apart from what looked like some old, unopened mail. To my left was a staircase.

"Emmy?"

I flashed the light from my phone around the kitchen once, detected nothing out of the ordinary. A glass-windowed door to the back garden. A single plate on the worktop. The kitchen curtains, like those in the living room, were closed. Outside on the gravel I could hear Irene pacing, calling my name, calling Emmy's. That was when I saw them, next to the door.

Emmy's shoes.

I was halfway up the stairs, shouting my wife's name at the top of my voice, before I even really knew what I was doing. Three steps at a time, crashing into the wall where the stairs turned halfway, I charged up in the dark. I was fucking lucky not to break my neck, especially at the top where the last step caught the end of my trainer and almost sent me flying. The first door I opened was a bathroom. I checked the bath. I pulled the curtain back on the shower.

Nothing there.

The second room I tried was painted pink, with a light shade done up to look like a little hot-air balloon, a little teddy bear in the basket underneath. There was a crib in the corner. The crib was empty.

The third door I opened revealed a bedroom with closed curtains and a bed in the middle of it. I took a step back. The smell was appalling. From downstairs, I could hear Irene stumbling around in the living room in the dark, swearing.

"Up here," I tried to shout, then realized that my throat was so dry I could barely croak.

In the corner of the room, blinking, was some kind of medical drip with a monitor attached. From it ran a tube. I could see its silhouette running down to whatever was under the pile of blankets on the bed.

Shit. That was one of the things I could smell. Old shit. Also vomit.

I listened. I could not hear breathing. I ran the light over the blankets—brown, woolen, thick. I could see nothing moving.

"Emmy?" I said.

No response.

I found the light switch and flicked it on. I took two steps forward and threw the blanket back.

Emmy was lying on her back with her mouth open, something attached to her arm, very pale, the bedsheets sodden, the clothes she was wearing soaked through.

"Irene!" I shouted. "Up here!"

I think I probably shouted something about calling an ambulance too. Something about checking the other rooms.

I tried to remember how they had taught us to check for a pulse in the Boy Scouts. I could feel nothing. Emmy's skin was cold, clammy.

Then I felt it. Faint, very faint. It was so faint that at first I wasn't sure if I was just imagining it, just feeling the pulsing of my own heart throbbing in my own fingertips.

She was out cold.

I touched her cheek gently.

No response.

I leaned over her, said her name, shook her by the shoulder. Nothing happened. I shook her harder, tried lifting her up a little. Her head slumped forward. I tried lifting one of her eyelids with my thumb. She offered no resistance. I shone the light from my phone directly into the open eye.

She gave a very faint groan.

I became aware that Irene was standing in the doorway. She seemed uncertain whether to cross the threshold, what to do next. She asked me if Emmy was okay.

"She's alive," I said. "She is definitely alive."

"Bear?" she asked.

I shook my head.

"Not here," I told her.

There was a little pile of whitish vomit on the pillow. There was more of it in Emmy's hair. I turned her arm to look at where the tube had been taped to her, to see where she was hooked up to it. Whatever had been in the bag was finished now.

"Bear? Bear?"

I could hear Irene opening the remaining doors on the corridor, swinging open cupboard doors and peering under beds and trying wardrobes, crashing around.

Emmy will know, I thought. *Emmy will be able to tell us what had happened, who did this, what happened to Bear.* Digging my fingers into her shoulders, I gave her a shake, harder and more urgent than I'd shaken her before.

Emmy let out another little groan. Her lips were chapped and cracking. Her face looked drawn. She was barely breathing. But she was alive.

"Emmy? Emmy, can you hear me?"

A sound that might have been almost anything passed her lips.

Her tongue looked swollen, sore.

"Emmy, where is Bear? What happened to Bear, Emmy?"

It was only as I was trying to lift her out of the bed, trying to swing her legs over the side and get her upright, that I realized I didn't need Emmy to tell me where my son was.

My baby son, grey and unmoving, lay curled up on the mattress next to her. He was so small, so still, that I hadn't even noticed him, had been practically kneeling on him.

I'd never seen him looking so tiny.

When I picked him up, he was so light it was like picking up something hollow, a husk.

His eyes were closed tight, his swollen lips parted, almost purple. I lifted him to my ear, and I couldn't hear him breathing. I kept checking his wrists, his neck, for a pulse, for the faintest flickering of a pulse. Nothing.

It was easily the worst moment of my life.

Irene was talking to me from the doorway, but it was like someone trying to make themselves heard over a howling wind across a wide river.

When I opened my son's eyes and shone a light into them, they were as dull and lifeless as the eyes of a fish on a slab.

Emmy

He always pauses at that point, Dan. Shuts the book. Takes a deep breath. Closes his eyes. As if reliving that moment. As if overcome by emotion.

There must be three hundred people in this tent. It feels as if every single one of them is holding their breath.

Dan looks around, locates his glass of water, takes a swig from it. His thumb is still inserted at the spot he left off reading in the book he is holding to his chest. I can see the photo of us holding hands, looking meaningfully into each other's eyes, on the back of the dust jacket. *These Little Squares: The Bare Truth*, by Mamabare and Papabare. Half a million copies sold in the first six months.

"I'm sorry," he says, his voice cracking a little, addressing his words somewhere over the top of the audience, up toward the roof of the tent. He puts his glass down as he clears his throat.

Christ, what a ham.

On every face I can see is the same look of sympathetic concern. The same look I used to get when I shared my maternal struggles with a room of paying mums. Shit, he might actually be *better* at this than me. I'd say 80 percent of the eyes focused on my husband are at the very least a little misty. In the third or fourth row a woman is blowing her nose loudly. One girl in the front row has an arm around her friend's shaking shoulders.

Am I imagining it, or does Dan make a quick little gesture as if he is wiping a tear away from his eye? If so, that's a new flourish. I wonder how long he's been planning that. He certainly didn't do it the last time we did one of these festival readings in Edinburgh two weeks ago.

Don't get me wrong. I think both Dan and I found that part of the book hardest to write. To force ourselves to go through it all again. Actually, if I'm honest, I barely remember being in the hospital, let alone that horrible house. While it is permanently etched into Dan's memory, I have only the vaguest sense of those terrible hours.

They tell me the very first thing I did, when I woke up in that stinking bed, and then again on the hospital ward, was ask where Bear was. I can remember the brightness of the room, the unfamiliar ceiling, the expression on Dan's face. They were doing all they could, he said. Bear was *very* malnourished, *very* weak, *very* dehydrated. Thankfully the ambulance had got there quickly. Thankfully Dan and Irene had not arrived even an hour or two later.

The police found the woman's car, abandoned, in a parking lot somewhere on the south coast, about a ninety-minute drive away. Her wedding ring was in the glove compartment. Her shoes were on the floor in the front. Jill, her name was. They found it on a hospital parking pass on the dashboard.

"In my darker days, the harder nights, I have cursed these little squares, questioned whether I should really be sharing my life with what is now nearly two million of you, as Papabare. Of course, I understand my wife's urge to switch off from social media entirely, and I totally respect it.

"But as a writer, I felt compelled to do the only thing I know how to, to process those dark moments—which is write my story, *our* story, alongside my incredible partner, my wise and luminous wife. In part, we have our talented editor to thank for that too." Dan smiles at her as he says this. She is standing just stage left, clutching what I notice is a *very* expensive Prada handbag.

"I know that it would be easy to blame social media for what happened to us—for the suffering that terrible woman inflicted on our family," Dan says, shaking his head, biting his lip. "Perhaps—and I know this is an awful thing to say—the fact I know *that woman* is dead and can't hurt us any more than she already has makes it easier.

"But what I also realized in the process of writing this book—now, extraordinarily, a *Sunday Times* and *New York Times* bestseller—is that when we really needed them, this amazing community came together. That for every evil soul like Jill, with an axe to grind for no reason at all, there are a thousand hearts brimming with kindness."

I survey the tent—clocking my mother at the back grabbing another glass of prosecco from the penned-off VIP area, tottering slightly on her heels—and wonder what they would think if they knew the truth. The reason that lunatic woman blamed me for her daughter and granddaughter's death.

I didn't know it for a long time. Dan didn't tell me about the letter until I'd regained some of my strength. With the eagle eye she usually reserves for contracts, Irene noticed my name on a brown envelope sitting on the living room table, and before the police arrived at that house—while Dan was screaming, cradling our son's limp body in his arms—she pocketed it.

She really is unflappable, my agent.

She didn't even tell Dan about the letter for a fortnight, presumably while she watched how the media storm panned out, how the situation would work out for us. Whether we were worth sticking with at all. She watched as the story turned me into a genuine, bona fide celebrity— not just Instafamous, but *famous* famous. There were Indonesian radio stations, Australian talk shows, American cable news, *Newsnight* and *Panorama* and even *Ellen* all clamoring for interviews.

More important, she monitored Dan's reaction to the global acclaim—how he handled the endless news stories about the novelist-turned-detective who, when the situation demanded it, turned into a cross between Sebastian Faulks and Sherlock Holmes to save his wife and child from certain death. The fact Irene gave them his author's photo from a decade ago wouldn't have hurt. Anyway, all the international interest, the world's attention? It turned out Dan fucking loved it.

By the time they showed me Jill's typed pages, her confession, her whole life story practically, my husband had already pitched a book, a memoir, based on the events surrounding my abduction, using it as a springboard to explore the darker side of internet fame. Jill's personal motives were not to feature.

Winter's, on the other hand, are fully picked over. Dan kept what she did a secret for a while—to be honest, I think he forgot about the stolen pictures until I asked why she hadn't visited us in hospital. I have to admit that staging the break-in showed a level of competence that I'd never have given her credit for, not to mention keeping up the act when Dan was exploding over that RP account—even if the moron did use her own PayPal account to pocket the cash for the photos.

It started off, Winter said, with taking little things, mostly gifts, that she knew I didn't care about and wouldn't miss, but that she could easily sell on eBay. When it snowballed and she thought I'd start to notice—the two-thousand-pound Acne jacket and the Burberry boots were the tipping point—she decided to cover her tracks with the smashed window and the stolen laptop. Only when Becket kicked her out of their love nest, when she was completely and utterly broke and up to her fedora in credit card bills, did she hit upon the idea of selling my photos as special fans-only content, through one of the forums I had asked her to monitor. She didn't think a few pictures were a big deal, she said; they were just the spare ones we hadn't used.

There is a long interview in the book with Pamela Fielding too, practically a chapter by itself, all about her problems at home, her troubles at school, the validation she found she could get online, the elaborate fantasies of family life she constructed. I found myself feeling quite sorry for her in the end, really. I think we both did.

It was decided—probably rightly—that my glorious reentry into the world of social media would look too cynical after all that had happened. Much better to let Dan take over my account, renaming it the_papabare, have custody of my followers, promote the book online, and chronicle our family's slow and ongoing recovery from almost unimaginable horror. Irene knew, by that point, with offer after offer

rolling in from ITV, Sky, NBC, that my career was about to go strato-
spheric. She'd already tentatively accepted my family talk show, *Mama
Bare*, by the time I was out of hospital.

Luckily, Dan is better at all of this than I could ever have imagined.
He likes to joke that for social media, he just writes as if someone has
shaved twenty points off his IQ, or dropped a brick on his head. It's
also astonishing how much easier everyone goes on him—his comments are all hearts and winks and racy DMs about how he can save
them from a murderous stalker any time he likes.

Would Dan have two million followers today if those people knew
what really drove that woman to do what she did? Probably not. On
the other hand, who knows if it was even my advice that her daughter
took? She could just as easily have read it on Mumsnet or heard it from
some other influencer. I'm sorry for what happened to her, to her baby,
of course I am, but why should I feel guilty? I've never claimed to be
an expert on anything—least of all parenting. The truth is, all I have
ever done is tell people what they want to hear.

Irene certainly did not think the whole messy story worked for Dan
and me, brand-wise. Better to keep Jill vague, she reckoned, a motive-
less online bogeywoman made flesh. Slightly to my surprise, Dan very
quickly came around to the same point of view. It was certainly, he
reckoned after some reflection, in some ways a more resonant story
that way, a whydunnit for the social media age, a timely invitation to
reflect on all our online behavior, a reminder of the dangers that lurk
in the shadows of the everyday. It was also, of course, a good way to
ensure that we emerged as the untarnished heroes of our story.

On similar grounds, it was maybe a good thing that Polly didn't
want to be interviewed for the book. I was asleep when she came to
visit me in the hospital, still hooked up to drips and beeping monitors.
She brought flowers and left a card to say she was glad I was safe, that
Bear was okay. I haven't heard from her since, despite emailing and
calling many, many times.

Dan reckoned that was probably all for the best too. Better, he suggested, to keep all that Polly stuff as elusive and indirect as possible, for her sake as much as ours.

He was the storyteller, he said. Let him take the lead.

Five hundred thousand books sold so far suggests he wasn't wrong.

I watch him up onstage, looking more like that author's photo than he has in years, and I feel a little flutter in my stomach.

"Even after everything that has happened, my wife and I," he says, gesturing toward the back of the tent, where I'm standing between the stall with the signed copies of our book and a whining Coco, "are eternally grateful." I see three hundred necks crane to see me, and hear an audible gasp—one or two people even clap here and there—as they notice my six-months-pregnant belly.

Doreen, who's been standing by the front of the stage the whole time, allows Bear to toddle over to climb onto his father's lap. Our boy, our darling boy, just a few months shy now of his second birthday and as healthy and rambunctious as anyone could wish for.

When the heads turn back around, I don't imagine there is a dry eye in the house.

It is a lot harder than you would think, being dead.

Legally dead, I mean. Missing, presumed.

For one thing, you can't just ring up and book a ticket for a talk at a literary festival and pay for it with a credit card.

Mine is very much a cash-only existence, these days. Cash-only, cash-strapped, and strictly hand-to-mouth.

Sometimes it does tempt me, the thought of all my life savings just lying there in my bank account. Sometimes I wonder what would happen if I tried to withdraw them. You'd have been tempted too, with some of the places I have found myself staying these last eighteen months, some of the jobs I have found myself doing to keep body and soul together.

I meant to do it. That was always the plan. As soon as I was sure, as soon as I had achieved what I had set out to.

All I needed was a little more time. A few hours probably would have done it. Half a day, at most. When I looked in on Emmy and Bear one last time, there were no signs of movement, no stirrings among the bedclothes.

I had been keeping a close eye on her Instagram account, of course. I saw the announcement that she was missing. Then I saw all the people chipping in, helping identify the landmarks in her video. I could see them piecing together the route, getting closer.

It was all so fast. The whole thing fell apart so quickly.

Even when I got to the beach, I thought I was still going to do it. I parked and took my rings off and put my phone and purse in the glove compartment, as if I were going for a swim. It was a place I always used to notice when I drove past, years ago, because of all the signs about the currents, all the warnings about the undertow. An eerie place, desolate, with a greyish beach that appears to stretch almost to the horizon at low tide, then seems to disappear within minutes as soon as the tide starts coming in.

It would have been so easy. I got there just as the tide was turning, just as night was beginning to settle. All I would have had to do was walk out onto the sand and keep walking.

It was not a love of life that stopped me. It was not fear.

It was the thought that I had let Grace and Ailsa down again. That justice had not been served.

It was the knowledge, from watching it all unfold on social media, that this whole thing was going to make you bigger than ever.

I tried to destroy you. Instead I turned you and your family into front-page news. Emmy the victim. Dan the hero. I could picture it all. There you would be discussing your ordeal on breakfast television. Holding hands on the sofa. Talking about how much stronger it had made you as a family.

I can remember staring out across the beach and screaming with all the power in my lungs, and the wind was buffeting me and deadening the sound and I could feel sand or maybe rain battering my coat. My face was wet and cold with tears, and I kept screaming until I was just coughing and crying and coughing, my throat raw and aching.

I have never in my life felt rage like that, such all-consuming anger—with myself as well as everyone and everything else now. Such utter despair. And that was before I knew how you would portray me in the book.

As a stalker, a loner, someone "whose true motivations may never be known." I am quoting your actual words. There is no mention of the envelope I left for you, no attempt made to connect what I did to the suicide of my daughter or the death of my granddaughter. Nothing like that. Instead there is just a load of pious guff about how jealous people are of those in the public eye, how naive you and Dan were, and how the whole experience had taught you some tough lessons, followed by an absolutely stomach-churning passage about how even if it is impossible for anyone to know what was going through my head, you both one day hope to be able to find it in your hearts to somehow forgive me.

I was tempted to buy a copy of the book when I arrived this afternoon, join the queue afterward, ask you both to sign it. It's not exactly likely you would recognize me—not after all that propofol, Emmy; even if my picture was splashed all over the news for a couple of days, Dan. Not with my new hair, my new clothes, these glasses. The picture they kept using was one from my hospital ID card—an old image, pixelated and washed out, several years old now. "Face of Evil," was the headline in one of the tabloids. Another one managed to find—somewhere on the internet—an old holiday photograph of me and George and Grace on holiday in Majorca in about 1995, all smiling, all in our beachwear. I am currently carry-

ing a canvas bag with the name of a bookshop on it, wearing a long skirt, a turquoise linen shirt, sandals. I do not look like the woman in either of those photographs. Nor do I exactly stand out in this crowd.

Even so, there is no sense taking pointless risks.

I have already achieved what I set out to achieve today. All through the reading, all through the Q&A, here I was, not more than twenty feet from you. There in the fourth row, in the sunglasses, with the program. Watching you. Listening. Reminding myself of all the pain and damage and hurt you have caused in the world. Reminding myself this is not over.

One of these days we'll see each other again, Emmy. Our eyes will meet and you will look away and you will not give me a second glance.

I could be the woman sitting next to you on the bus, the woman squeezed up against you on the Tube. I could be the woman who stops to let your shopping cart past at the supermarket. I could be the person who brushes past you on the escalator, who pulls faces at your children across a table on the train, asks if they are allowed sweets. I could be the person pressed apologetically up behind all of you on a crowded Underground platform. I could be the person who offers to help carry your pushchair up a very steep flight of stairs. The person your husband and your children are standing next to at a busy pedestrian crossing. The person who with an accidental nudge of their elbow could send your child's bike swerving off the pavement into the incoming traffic. The person you don't even notice in the park. The one waiting for that single moment your attention is diverted from the new baby as you turn your back on the pram, just for a moment, to see to one of the other children.

One of these days.

ACKNOWLEDGMENTS

A holiday spent with our baby daughter and close friends by an exceptionally cold swimming pool, with donkeys braying by the bedroom windows, was the birthplace of *People Like Her*. Thank you, Susan Henderson and Alicia Clarke, for putting up with the plotting and Matt Klose for keeping us all excellently fed.

Thank you to Holly Watt for nagging us to actually write it—and providing a shining example of how to get it right, sharp pointy awards and all, with *To the Lions* and *The Dead Line*. Catherine Jarvie, you also did not let up telling us we had to finish it and for that we are so grateful—as we are for your plot pearls of wisdom, your excitement about the book in general, and your close reading with an eagle eye. Kaz Fairs, you proved yet again you are much more than a Beaty face; thank you for your brilliant suggestions and feedback. To Lesley McGuire and Zu Rafalat too, some of our first readers. Zu, we miss you endlessly.

The hard work, kindness, and generosity of many people has been indispensable in bringing this project to fruition.

For their help, advice, friendship, encouragement, and support over the years, Paul would like to thank: Cara Harvey, Dorothea Gibbs, Florence Gibbs, Sarah Jackson, Julia Jordan, Louise Joy, Eric Langley, David McAllister, Bran Nicol and my other fantastic colleagues at Surrey, Claire Sargent, Oli Seares, Jane Vlitos, John Vlitos, and Katy Vlitos.

Collette would like to thank Janette, Douglas and Martyn Lyons, Jacqui Kavanagh and Joel Kitzmiller, Rachel Lauder, Alice Wignall, Clare Ferguson, Amy Little, Kate Apostolov, Mark Smith, Sagar Shah, Eleanor O'Carroll, Tanya Petsa, Beverley Churchill, Jo Lee, and Shelley Landale-Down.

For ensuring we actually had the time to write, thank you to Karen, Linda, Claire, Anwara, Soraya, Stacey, and Mel.

Sam McGuire and Amelie Crabb, keep writing your amazing stories—we can't wait to buy your books one day.

We would both like to thank our agents, Emma Finn (thank you, Susan Armstrong, for sending us in her direction—we can't imagine a pair of hands more capable, a sounding board more wise, and we feel extremely lucky) and Hillary Jacobson (whose cheerleading for the book was exceptional). Luke Speed and Jake Smith-Bosanquet and the brilliant C&W rights team, Laurie MacDonald for getting us excited about seeing Emmy and Dan on screen one day, Dr. Rebecca Martin for her medical knowledge, Alicia Clarke for her wonderful photographs, and Trevor Dolby for his time and encouragement.

Also, of course, our wonderful editors, Sam Humphreys and Sarah Stein, everyone at Mantle (Samantha, Alice, and Rosie especially) and at HarperCollins (Alicia, thank you!), and our amazingly supportive and encouraging early reviewers on NetGalley.

Very special thanks go to our daughter, Buffy.

ELLERY LLOYD is the pseudonym for husband-and-wife writing team Collette Lyons and Paul Vlitos. Collette is a journalist and editor, the former content director of *Elle* (UK), features editor of *Stylist*, and editorial director at Soho House. She has written for the *Guardian*, the *Telegraph*, and the *Sunday Times*, among others. Paul is the author of two previous novels, *Welcome to the Working Week* and *Every Day Is Like Sunday*. He is the program director for English Literature with Creative Writing at the University of Surrey. They live in London with their baby daughter.